Everything that is Beautiful

Louise Nealon is a writer from County Kildare, Ireland. Her debut novel, *Snowflake*, was the winner of Newcomer of the Year at the An Post Irish Book Awards and was chosen for the One Dublin One Book campaign in 2024.

Everything that is Beautiful

Louise Nealon

MANILLA PRESS

First published in the UK in 2026 by
MANILLA PRESS
An imprint of Bonnier Books UK
5th Floor, HYLO, 105 Bunhill Row,
London, EC1Y 8LZ

Copyright © Louise Nealon, 2026

All rights reserved.
No part of this publication may be reproduced,
stored or transmitted in any form or by any means, electronic,
mechanical, photocopying or otherwise, without the
prior written permission of the publisher.

The right of Louise Nealon to be identified as Author of this
work has been asserted by her in accordance with the
Copyright, Designs and Patents Act, 1988.

This is a work of fiction. Names, places, events and
incidents are either the products of the author's
imagination or used fictitiously. Any resemblance to
actual persons, living or dead, or actual
events is purely coincidental.

A CIP catalogue record for this book is
available from the British Library.

Hardback ISBN: 978-1-78658-136-5
Trade paperback ISBN: 978-1-78658-171-6

Also available as an ebook and an audiobook

Line from 'Käthe Kollwitz' from *The Collected Poems of Muriel Rukeyser*,
Muriel Rukeyser (University of Pittsburgh Press, 2006), reproduced by
permission of the Estate of Muriel Rukeyser.

1 3 5 7 9 10 8 6 4 2

Typeset by IDSUK (Data Connection) Ltd
Printed and bound in Great Britain by CPI (UK) Ltd, Croydon CR0 4YY

The authorised representative in the EEA is Bonnier Books
UK (Ireland) Limited.
Registered office address: Block B, The Crescent Building
Northwood, Santry
Dublin 9, D09 C6X8, Ireland
compliance@bonnierbooks.ie
www.bonnierbooks.co.uk

What would happen if one woman told the truth about her life?
The world would split open.

                        Muriel Rukeyser, 'Käthe Kollwitz'

– Part I

Chapter 1

The Hurley

Niamh

IT HAPPENED, ALONG WITH the rest of her childhood, on the Foleys' farm. Ten years old, trying to impress Peter, who had two years and four inches on her. They were both running for a ball and Niamh knew that they were going to swing at the same time, the way she saw the men do on the telly. She heard her father's voice in her head telling her not to hold back. As her feet left the ground, it felt like flying, even as her temple collided with Peter's shoulder and everything went black.

It was the kiss of Tayto, the border collie, that brought her back to life. She batted the dog away and got up from the ground, cradling her hand and moaning in pain. Peter shushed her. They weren't supposed to be pucking around together. Peter's mother, Helen, tended to turn a blind eye to their antics as long as they were careful, but they'd sent a sliotar through the window of her downstairs toilet the week before and she was still raging with them.

Niamh got up from the ground and reached for her hurley. It seemed a lot lighter until she realised the stick had snapped in two during the clash. She turned around to see where the bottom half had landed on the other side of the lawn, then took a wild swing at Peter. 'You b-broke my good hurley!'

She dropped to her knees and started crying. He looked over his shoulder to see if one of his sisters was around. Maria was studying in her room and the other two, Kate and Bláithín, were where they were supposed to be, doing their homework at the kitchen table.

'It was going to break eventually,' he offered. He wiped bits of muck off his runners in the grass while he waited for her to get over it.

'D-do you think your dad could fix it?' she asked.

They were able to hear Liam before they saw him – the gnaw of the bandsaw against the wood got louder when they opened the door of the workshop. Niamh watched as Peter made tentative attempts to approach his father. Liam Foley was a kind and charismatic man who sometimes seemed to forget that he had children. He was cutting the outline of a hurley from a plank of timber. It was a long couple of minutes before he eventually looked up from his work and turned off the bandsaw.

'Dad, Niamh broke her hurley,' Peter said.

'P-p-p-peter broke my hurley,' Niamh corrected him.

Liam straightened himself and put his hands on his hips. 'You're in the market for a new one so?'

'M-maybe you could fix it?'

'Let me have a look at it, Niamh.'

She liked the way Liam pronounced her name – *nee-av* – as opposed to the nasally, monosyllabic *neev* that most people used, including her. One syllable was less risky than the two: *nuh-nuh-nuh-nuh-neev*.

The hurley had snapped in the middle where she had written her name in black marker. She presented the stick to him in two pieces.

Liam shook his head and let out a low whistle. 'I'm afraid there's nothing I can do with that now, pet.'

She concentrated on the wood shavings on the floor as her eyes filled up. Liam hunkered down beside her, his hand leaning on the new hurley he was working on. 'It's hard to let go of a good one, isn't it?'

The tears tripped out of her eyes as she nodded.

'I can glue it together all right, but you won't be able to play with it. How about we stick it up there?' He pointed up at the slanted roof of the shed and the display of hurleys nailed to it – hurleys that Liam and her dad had won county championships with.

'Hey!' Peter cried. 'That's not fair! She didn't even win anything!'

Liam winked at her and spoke so quietly that Niamh had to lean in to hear him. 'How about you promise me that the next time you come to me with a broken hurley, it's one that belongs to that lad over there. We could do with putting some manners on him.'

Niamh beamed at him.

Liam turned to his son. 'Well, are you going to help me make a new hurley for Niamh or are you too busy sulking? You might even get a new one of your own out of it.'

Peter's face brightened. Liam Foley was famous for making hurleys. Only a select few were invited into the inner sanctum of the workshop. Part of the reason why Peter and Niamh played in the back garden was for a chance to run into their heroes – men who played on the county team walked through on their way to pick up hurleys from Liam and sometimes joined in on their puck arounds. When no one else was there, the two of them spent hours sneaking into the workshop and sifting through hurleys, trying to find the right weight and balance to suit their game. They scarpered whenever they heard anyone coming, only taking one hurley at a time so that it wouldn't be missed.

One of the nicknames Liam picked up throughout his years on the hurling pitch was Father Foley because everyone thought he would make a good priest. There was something monastic about the way he moved through the world. The workshop was his sanctuary, so even the thought of sneaking in to rob hurleys was sacrilegious. It felt like stealing from God.

Niamh was sure Liam knew what they were doing, but it was more fun to pretend to be thieves – the rush of adrenaline they got as they made their getaway fired them up for another round of tearing into each other on the lawn with their new weapons.

'You're about to have your first lesson in where hurleys come from,' Liam said, rolling out the base of tree he used for when the television people came to film him for a documentary.

'This,' he said, leaning it into the crook of his arm, 'is the bottom of an ash tree. Not all ash trees are made equal, and so not all of them are suitable for making hurleys. Only the chosen few that have a bit about them make the cut: they have to have these lovely toes.' He twirled the stump around to display the knobbly bits protruding from the trunk. 'These fellas are what give you the natural curve of the hurley when we saw into them . . .'

Niamh and Peter knew that they had to suffer through the sermon in order to get to the action. 'It's important to keep track of the mammy and daddy trees,' Liam continued. 'You can even take the shoots of an ash tree from Tipperary and breed it with one from Clare, like an arranged marriage. And from those good roots, you can make even better ones.'

Niamh felt her finger throbbing. She tried to bend it and she flinched.

'Show us your broken hurley there Niamh, like a good girl,' Liam called to her, and she gave him the two pieces of wood. 'Now the reason I can't fix this is because of where the break is, in the very centre – it's for the graveyard. But if you broke it down the bottom here at the bas, we could work with that. You see, the grain goes all the way up the stick – straight the whole way up the handle, but when you get to the bottom of the hurley, it curves. That's what gives the hurl its strength – the bend in it.'

Niamh followed Liam's finger as he traced the wood grain.

'Nothing and nobody can exist on the straight and narrow,' he said, smoothing his hand on the hurl like he was petting an animal. 'Try to live a straightforward life and watch as it splinters into smithereens.'

Peter kicked the sawdust at his feet and waited until Liam clapped his hands together to signal that it was time to work. Liam brought them to the back of the workshop where stacks of planks were drying like giant towers of Jenga.

Peter was quick to obey Liam's commands, handing him the requested tools with the reverence of an altar server at mass. He wasn't often allowed to help Liam in the workshop. His older brother John was sixteen and had done four years of woodwork in secondary school before he started to learn the trade.

The outside world felt far away. All that mattered was the grind of the machines and the scratching of the tools they used to bring their sticks to life. The metal was still warm from Liam's hands when he passed Niamh the spokeshave. She hesitated, conscious that Liam was watching her.

'Always go with the grain,' he said, eventually, clasping his hands over hers and pushing down on the handle of the hurley in one swooping motion. A long strip of timber fell to the ground in a gentle curl. 'Never against it.'

He let go of her hands. Niamh was surprised that she could keep going on her own, shaving strips of wood away. She was about to give the hurley back to Liam when he caught a hold of her finger. A dart of pain flew up her arm. He examined her swollen knuckle, and turned the palm of her hand over in his. The back of her finger was mottled purple and black.

'Where does it hurt?' he asked.

She shrugged. He asked her to bend it. She took a sharp inhale of breath and found that she couldn't move it at all.

Liam left the workshop with them, leading them up to the house. He ushered them into the kitchen to wait for Helen to assess the situation. Peter handed her a bag of frozen peas wrapped in a tea towel.

'Thanks,' she said.

Niamh felt a pang of panic as she realised that she was going to have to explain what happened to her mother. Mary didn't like hurling, or the Foleys for that matter. Niamh didn't stutter as much when she was around the Foleys. She only felt her throat tighten when her mother came to collect her. She had developed a habit of smiling instead of talking, which Mary encouraged. 'You don't have to speak if you don't want to,' she said. 'And you don't have to tell them every last thing that you're thinking, either. Sometimes, it's best to say nothing at all.'

Niamh heard Helen's footsteps coming downstairs. She came into the kitchen with a basket of laundry on her hip, blowing her fringe out of her eyes.

'What is it now?' she asked Liam, before spotting Niamh sitting down on the chair. 'Oh Niamh, lovey,' she said, crouching down on her hunkers. 'That'll need an X-ray.'

She sighed and went to get her car keys. 'Liam, will you let Mary know where we've gone? It's probably a fracture.'

Niamh skipped into the car with Peter, relieved that she wouldn't be there when her mother heard the news.

They waited for hours in A&E. Peter sat beside her in the waiting room and gave her one of his earphones so that they could listen to Eminem together.

After watching *8 Mile*, they had learned the lines to 'Lose Yourself' and had rap battles during puck arounds, using their hurleys as microphones. Niamh was as surprised as Peter when she turned out to be good at rapping – better than him. The rhythm of it allowed her to break through the invisible forcefield that stopped her every time she went to speak. It helped that it was someone else's words that she was saying. Learning lines off by heart was a revelation. She didn't have to worry about what was or wasn't happening inside her head.

Her finger was broken. The nurse gave Niamh a splint and spoke to Helen like she was her mother. They stopped in McDonald's Drive Thru on the way home. As she tucked into her chips in the back seat of the car, all that Niamh could think about was seeing her hurley on display in Liam's workshop alongside past legends of the game.

Liam forgot all about the promise he made. Weeks passed and her finger healed without mention of the broken hurley. Niamh tried to ask her dad to remind Liam, but that turned out to be a mistake. Her stutter was always worse when she tried to talk to him. Vincent couldn't ignore his one and only child's stammer the way his wife did. He was so intent on focusing on what she was trying to say, he had forgotten the beginning of the sentence by the time she got to the end.

'I'm sorry love, can you start again?'

Niamh felt the tears coming.

'Hey, hey, hey!' Vincent said, pulling her in for a hug.

She told him that it didn't matter.

He placed his hands on her shoulders and looked her in the eye. 'Of course it matters. Everything that goes on inside that curly head of yours matters.'

She ended up having to write the words down. She listened to her dad read them out – he wasn't good at reading. He had left school when he was fourteen to work on the Foleys' farm. His voice was slow and robotic as he made out her handwriting. 'Peter broke my good hurley – the one you made for me. Liam promised he would put it up in the workshop, but I think he forgot.'

'D-d-do you think he'll d-d-d-do it?' she asked.

Vincent squinted like he was able to see into the future. 'I'll say it to him, but he's a busy man, and that workshop has a habit of swallowing things.' He shook his head. 'It's better to forget all about it, pet,' he said, patting her leg.

But Niamh couldn't forget about it. She began to follow Liam around the farm like a shadow, though she didn't dare to ask him herself. Her arms weren't strong enough to be able to hold the units of the milking machine, so he gave her the job of spraying the cows' udders with disinfectant. Peter hung around for a while, but got bored and went back into the house to watch telly.

Her father seemed embarrassed, at first, when he saw the way Niamh was hanging out of Liam but after a while, his eyes lit up when he spotted her coming into the parlour with her hurley.

Her mother hit the roof when she found out where she was spending her evenings. Niamh could hear them arguing through the walls – her dad's muffled voice trying to justify what her mother called child labour. 'You should hear her chatting away out there, Mary. It's the noise of the milking machine. Maybe it makes her less self-conscious or whatever, but I swear to Christ, she's like any other child out there.'

Once her finger had healed, Liam began to show her how to grip the hurley properly. He showed her how to practice doing figures of eight with it to strengthen her wrists.

'The hurley isn't a weapon,' he said, spinning the stick around like a baton. 'It's a wand. There's only one way to get to the magic – it's all in the wrists.'

She watched as he cast his own spells, his eyes fixated on the ball that seemed stuck to the end of a hurley that was defying gravity. The whites of his eyes were so much cleaner than her dad's, which looked like dirty snooker balls. This was another thing that her parents argued over. When her mother wanted to get to her father, she'd say that his eyes were jaundiced from the drink. Enjoying a pint at the end of a working day wasn't an illness, he told her. Liam went for pints too but he always went home early. There were cows to be milked, hurleys to be made, teams to train.

'What's the difference between hurling and camogie?' Niamh asked Liam one evening as she helped him feed the calves. Liam was teaching her how to feed the newborns by sticking a long tube down their throats, pouring milk directly into their stomachs.

'Hurling is played by men and camogie is played by women,' he said, struggling to hold a calf still to get the tube into its mouth. 'The Irish word for a hurley is a camán and when women first started playing, they used a shorter stick called a camóg.'

'It's good to use a shorter stick, though,' Niamh said, watching the calf's eyes bulge as she pushed the plastic past its butty teeth and sandpaper tongue.

'You're right. The shorter the better,' Liam said, turning the bottle of milk upside down. They both watched the level of the milk go down as the calf continued to squirm underneath Liam's firm grip.

'But hurling is better than camogie.'

'Well, I wouldn't say that now,' Liam said.

Niamh made a face at him.

He scratched his chin. 'Would you ever think about playing with the boys?'

Not long after Niamh joined the hurling team, Liam made her captain. Helen collected Niamh and Peter after training while Vincent and Liam stayed on for a meeting in the clubhouse. They sat in the back of the car, neither of them saying a word. It was Peter's last year playing under-thirteen. He was the best player on the team, and was devastated that his dad gave Niamh the nod for the captaincy over him.

'Well, what happened?' Helen asked, her eyes darting between the two in the rear-view mirror.

'Niamh got the call-up,' Peter said.

'Oh wow, Niamh, good woman yourself.' Helen took one hand off the steering wheel to reach around and squeeze her hand. 'Captain of all the men! That's the way to do it.'

'Captains have to give speeches!' Peter said, kicking the back of his mother's seat. 'Why would you give the talking job to the girl with the stutter?'

'Peter Foley, that's enough!' Helen snapped. 'Apologise to Niamh.'

'For what?'

They pulled up outside Niamh's house. She opened the door of the car. 'Th-thank you Helen.'

'You're welcome love, and don't mind this jealous scut of a yoke.'

Her first few matches as captain didn't go well. The huddle of teenage boys looked at their feet while Niamh felt her face burn and her chin tighten. She blinked hard. Her dad was there beside Liam. There were a couple of times when she could see that he wanted to step in and speak for her, but Liam put his hand out to stop him.

During the first round of the league, Liam motioned for Niamh to talk to the lads during the half-time break while he and Vincent chatted. Peter stuck an orange slice in his mouth and leered at the others who started to laugh.

Niamh tore into him, calling him out on being a selfish glory-hunter, taking stupid shots instead of passing the ball to someone in a better position. She went through what was going wrong, explaining that the breakdown in communication around midfield was causing them to lose their own puckouts, and once their heads were down, none of them were willing to get stuck in and win a dirty ball. By the time she was finished her hands were shaking and the boys were all staring at her. She had said it all without stuttering.

Liam was the only one who didn't seem surprised. He'd been telling them the same thing from the beginning of the year, but it sounded different when it came from the girl who didn't speak.

Niamh played with the boys right up until minor. They were like brothers. Things turned nasty on the pitch whenever someone from another team tried to come for her. She was used to the name-calling – bitch, man, whore, heifer. Once, her marker didn't do anything except call for a ball, but it was too late to explain this to Peter who got sent off for trying to headbutt him.

She felt a strange tenderness towards the boys when they put on a show, talking about the girls they fancied. They sometimes forgot that she was right there, behind enemy lines ready to report back. She got used to acting as a mediator. The lads appreciated her putting in a good word for them. She was surprised by their vulnerability – how intimidated they were by some of the more popular girls.

She once heard them talking about her in the dressing room before a match. They were about sixteen at the time. She was standing in the corridor after getting changed in the toilet, waiting for Liam and Vincent to bring her in for the team talk when she heard Barry say, 'You do forget sometimes that Niamh's a girl.' He had the voice of a construction worker who smoked forty a day which was both impressive and comical coming from a gangly fifteen-year-old. Barry always talked a big game – he got with a lot of girls from other schools, or so he said.

'She does have a pretty face, you know.'

Niamh felt her cheeks grow hot. It was Chris, the goal keeper, the only one of them who fancied her. She could hear them all jeering and throwing things at him.

'She's well-fed, though!'

They all cracked up at that. She could hear Peter laughing along with the rest of them.

Niamh never thought about how much she ate before that. As a child, it was a good thing to finish everything on her plate. She basked under the glow of Helen's praise at the Foleys' dinner table. The rest of the family rolled their eyes, calling Niamh the favourite child. The older she got, the more she craved Helen's approval, especially when her dad began spending more time in the pub.

Helen had been a primary school teacher before giving up work to stay at home. Before she even started school, four-year-old Niamh decided that she wanted to be a teacher too. She christened all of her Barbie dolls Helen and played with them in the Foleys' kitchen.

Her own parents had stayed together for too long. Niamh was fifteen when her mother finally kicked her dad out of the house for good. There were rumours going around that he'd been having an affair with Maggie Purcell, a married woman with five young kids who sometimes worked behind the bar. The rumours were nothing new.

Niamh had seen the way her dad and Liam glanced at each other when different women came up in conversation.

Her dad stayed with the Foleys for a few weeks before moving to a bedsit above a pub in town. Soon, he was drinking so much that he started turning up to work drunk. That's when Helen finally convinced him to go to his first AA meeting. He spent the next ten years falling off the wagon while the town watched on.

Niamh was twenty-five when her dad got sick. The cancer had spread from his liver to his lymph nodes by the time Helen cajoled him into going to the doctor. Niamh had never lost her appetite before, but she couldn't stomach the meals that Helen was giving her in batches of plastic containers every time she saw her.

'Put those in the freezer and promise me you'll eat them,' she said, thrusting the Tupperware into her hands. 'You can't afford to lose any more weight.'

Niamh usually took everything Helen said as gospel, but those words rankled her. She threw the lunchbox dinners in the bin and began to crave the feeling of emptiness. Even looking at food began to turn her stomach – the congealed grease in a slice of pizza, the mush of a banana, the sadness in a slice of toast that gave her a lump in her throat. She would never admit it, even to herself, but it was exciting when the weight began to fall off. It made her feel powerful.

The hospice was close to a shopping centre. She stole time out of her visits to sneak into changing rooms and try on clothes that were meant for other people, spending her teacher's wage in Boots on fake tan and makeup, skincare and beauty products she'd never even heard of, all the time hearing Helen's voice in her head saying she couldn't afford any of it, that it was only a matter of time before she would go back to being fat again.

The morning of her father's funeral she got a ladder in her tights and had to borrow a pair of Helen's. It was a surprise when she was able to pull the nylon over her stomach. If she sat up straight and sucked in her belly, it was almost flat. This was what she thought about in the car, following the hearse on the way to the church.

Peter's sister Maria had done her makeup, covering the dark circles under her eyes and layering on the waterproof mascara. Peter slipped her a Valium before the mass and she floated through it, right up until the eulogy when fear sobered her up and spat her out, her shoes click-clacking on the tiles on the way to the altar where her stutters echoed around the silence of the church. She couldn't stop imagining her dad looking at her as she struggled to get the words out. It was a relief when she saw Liam coming to her rescue. He put his hand around her shoulders and took over reading the rest of the speech they had prepared together.

Niamh could see the surprise in people's faces as they were lining up to sympathise with her. Nobody seemed to notice that she couldn't speak. An old woman nipped at her waist and called her a little slip of a thing. Someone else said she was the image of her mother.

Mary wasn't at the funeral. There were whispers about how poor Vincent couldn't be laid out in his own home because the bitch of an ex-wife wouldn't even allow his dead body across the threshold. The wake was held in the Foleys' house which made sense considering how much time he spent in the place.

The week after the funeral, Niamh captained St Brigid's camogie team to win their first-ever senior county title. In his final days, all Vincent ever wanted to talk about was tactics for the match, clasping Liam's and Niamh's hands, making them promise that they would go and win the thing.

The day of the match, Niamh had the game of her life, scoring 2-7 from play. They were in the pub afterwards when it all began to hit her. Liam had put money behind the bar. The girls were going to the nightclub in town. She watched as Peter got onto the minibus with the rest of the team – she wanted him to go home with her, but she didn't want to ruin his night either.

A minute later, she was throwing up outside the pub. Liam held her hair back from her face and rubbed her back in circles. 'That's it, get it all out.'

Her vision was blurred by whiskey and tears. If she threw up quick enough, she could still get on the bus and go with them.

'That's it,' Liam said, as she got the last of it up.

She looked around her, feeling the sting in the back of her throat. The bus had gone. She sat on the window ledge beside Liam and waited for Helen to pick them up.

Helen stuck on the kettle when they got in the door. When Liam suggested a nightcap, Helen told them that she was going to bed. She gave Niamh a kiss on the cheek and told her that she'd made up the spare bed for her.

She held up a hot water bottle and said, 'I'll pop this under the duvet to warm it up for you.'

They were a quarter of the way through the bottle of whiskey when Niamh reminded Liam of the promise that he made to her when she was ten years old. It had been fifteen years since he agreed to put her hurley on display. He got her on her feet and they went down the garden to the workshop. She remembered feeling like she was swimming through hurleys, searching for the lost one that Peter had broken on her all those years ago, when Liam caught a hold of her hand.

It was his tongue that hurt the most – the wet meat of it on hers insisting on what he wanted. She didn't pull away. She didn't say anything.

Niamh had kept the hurley that Liam made for her when she was ten years old. She never used it for fear that it would break. Fifteen years later, the hurley remained intact, a relic of the past propped up at the end of the bed that she still slept in in her childhood home.

Chapter 2

Sports Day

Helen

THE DISHWASHER STOPPED WORKING on the morning of Liam's third anniversary mass. It was a newer version of the old one and Helen had never trusted it. It was all turbo this and eco that. Whenever it finished, it let out a low-frequency beep that made her question her sanity until she remembered that it was only a machine crying out for attention. Liam was the one who fixed things. She had thought that in the three years since he'd died, she would have gotten angry with him for not being there when she needed him. Her blood pressure still shot through the roof every time something went wrong in the house and he wasn't around to put it right again. Her daughter Maria tried to work her magic. Helen knew that they were in trouble when Maria's partner Kevin got involved. They let him fiddle around with the buttons for a while before declaring it a lost cause.

There was talk of using her son John's who lived next door until they remembered he didn't have a dishwasher. His wife Nadine didn't believe in them. Those were the words she used at Sunday dinner, waving a dismissive hand like they were talking about a conspiracy theory. Helen had learned the hard way that it was easier to allow Nadine to exist in her own version of reality. There was no point trying to explain to the woman that a dishwasher was far more reliable than her husband would ever be. Helen should know – she raised him.

Helen had so much hope for Nadine when her son had introduced them. A solicitor, she imagined, would be good for John. Looking back, she had underestimated how much the woman loved yoga. She was forever either going to or coming from a class, her little bum poured into pants so tight that she'd be mesmerised, watching to see which arse cheek's turn it was to move. Liam didn't know where to look. He learned to disappear when he saw her coming.

The yoga was the first warning sign. The recycling was the second. Helen caught her once when she was helping to clear the table after Sunday dinner, rooting through her bin like a little racoon, clutching an armful of reusable plastic containers. At least she had the cop on to be embarrassed about it. And then, there were the nappies. She refused to use the disposable ones. They were bad for the environment, apparently. There was no talking to her, no point trying to explain that nappies were beneficial for generations of women, just like dishwashers. Helen could only watch on as the cloth nappies hung on the washing line, dishes stacked up in the sink, and Nadine's bum became even more magnetic as it grew bigger in the yoga pants that she still wore, despite having to give up yoga altogether.

Nadine extended her maternity leave before she left her job, or, as she put it, 'switched professions' to concentrate on the most important job of all. She invited everyone around to the house to announce her big news.

'To family management,' she said, raising a glass of champagne and nodding at Helen, who found an excuse to leave the room.

*

Helen was stressed in the lead-up to Liam's anniversary. There was no need to invite people back to the house after the mass. They would descend on the place anyway.

'There's no point working yourself into such a state, Mammy,' Maria insisted, while tucking into her mother's roast dinner. 'It's not like anyone is asking you to do anything.'

'Maybe I won't do anything,' Helen said, getting up from her chair to cut more meat for the table. She could almost feel Maria rolling her eyes as soon as she turned her back.

'I'm just saying,' Maria said. 'It really isn't worth it. You're tying yourself in knots over it already. I have most things sorted. And Kevin will help, won't you Kev?'

'Wait, next weekend?' Kevin looked up from his dinner. 'Aren't we going to visit my parents on Saturday?'

'Is that this Saturday?' Maria asked, mashing carrot into her daughter's potatoes. Three-year-old Aoife was just after having her latest meltdown and was watching *Peppa Pig* on her mother's phone.

'Mum has been complaining that she hasn't seen Aoife in ages,' Kevin said.

'All right. You take Aoife to your mum's and I'll stay at home. See? Don't be worrying Mam. I'll sort everything. And Bláithín will help, won't you Bláith?' Maria shouted over at her little sister. It was easier for her to believe that her sister was deaf and not ignoring her.

It was Liam who wanted to call their second daughter Bláithín – an Irish name that meant 'little flower.' Helen wasn't sure about it. They had already agreed on Emma if it was a girl, and she saw no reason to change it because the baby had Down syndrome. She had tried the name Emma in her mouth, whispering it into her little ears when it was just the two of them, but Liam had his heart set on Bláithín. *Blaw-heen! Blaw!* Helen could always tell where Maria was in the house by the direction from which she heard her call her sister by name.

'Bláith works in the café on Saturdays,' Helen said.

'Surely she can take one day off.'

'Bláith, would you like to help your sister or go to work?' Helen asked.

'Work,' Bláithín said, without looking up from her phone.

The following Friday evening, Maria came in and collapsed onto the couch beside Helen. Every September, Helen braced herself for the gossip from the staff room as the school year started back. Maria was midway through a story about the crackpot of a music teacher who was covering maternity leave when she asked how the preparations for Sunday were going.

'I thought you had it all under control,' Helen said, without looking away from the television.

'I know, I just mean the food side of things.'

'Nobody asked me to do anything.'

Maria shot up from the couch and went out to the kitchen. 'You didn't do the food shop?'

Helen pretended not to notice the panic in her daughter's voice.

'No worries,' Maria said, calling her mother's bluff and sitting back down on the couch beside her. 'I'll do it in the morning.'

The next day, Kevin took Aoife to visit his parents and Helen was left with the house to herself. She sat through the entire omnibus of *Fair City*, even though she had already seen the episodes during the week. On second viewing, the characters' interactions were even more stilted. She'd gotten sucked into watching the soaps on the telly. The Sky box had broken on her a while back, and she hadn't gotten around to fixing it, so she was stuck with limited options: *Home and Away*, *Neighbours*, *Emmerdale*, *EastEnders* and *Fair City*, or *Fair Shitty*, as the kids called it. She was starving, but avoided the kitchen, savouring the last few sweets from the packet of Werther's Original she found down the side of the couch, twirling the ends of the wrapper to open each caramel, sucking until they formed sharp little discs on her tongue.

Maria burst into the room to inform her that there was a crash on the motorway. It had taken her two hours to get to the shop, and another hour and a half sitting in traffic on the way home. She had put the groceries away and had changed into her pyjamas before she remembered that she'd forgotten to stop at the butchers.

She paused, waiting for her mother to say something. 'Mammy?'

'Yes love?' Helen said, looking up from the sudoku that she was pretending to do.

'Could you please go to the butchers for me?'

'I'm sorry, love, I'm busy,' Helen said, scribbling the number eight into a box at random.

It was after midnight when Helen found Maria struggling to open a first aid box in the kitchen. She was after cutting the fingers off herself trying to grate a carrot. The plastic clasp broke and the box sprung open, sending the contents flying across the table. Helen fished a bit of gauze out of a bowl of mayonnaise and sat down beside her.

'Why didn't you just buy coleslaw, love?' she asked, taking a plaster from her daughter's hand and wrapping it around her finger.

When Maria looked up at her, Helen saw the face of a five-year-old. 'You always make coleslaw,' she said, wiping her nose with the sleeve of her pyjamas.

Helen took up the knife and started shredding the white cabbage.

Maria leaned against her mother and closed her eyes. A moment later, she groaned. 'I need to get bags for the sack race,' she said, sliding her head off her mother's shoulder and abandoning her to the coleslaw.

'Where are you going to get them in the middle of the night?' Helen called after her.

'John will have some in the calf shed,' Maria said, putting on her shoes at the back door.

'Can it not wait until the morning?'

'No, Mammy, it can't,' Maria snapped, slamming the door behind her.

The sports day at Liam's anniversary had begun as a small thing for the kids. What had started as a few races quickly morphed into several events which even included heats, all culminating in a medal ceremony at the end of the day.

Maria had tried her best to get Bláithín involved. 'Come on, Bláith. We'll set up the goals for the football. You like football.'

Bláith pretended to like football. She liked watching boys in shorts run around so she could admire their good bone structure and fresh haircuts. Bláith prided herself on her excellent taste in men. She was mainly interested in them for aesthetic reasons and closely monitored their lives online. She hated their wives and girlfriends, but Helen reasoned that she could be at worse.

It took more coaxing than ever to pull Bláith away from her phone. Maria got upset about it, no matter how much Helen tried to explain to her that her sister was happy in her own little world. She had hoped that Maria would understand once she became a mother herself, but if anything, she'd gotten worse.

On the morning of her grandad's anniversary mass, Aoife was buzzing around the kitchen dressed in her Sunday best, wielding her favourite pink fly swat. Helen lifted her up so that her little feet touched the top of the radiator and put her hand over her chubby fingers. They slapped the swat against a bluebottle that was frantically bumping into the window. Aoife shrieked with delight.

'We got him!' Helen exclaimed.

'Nudder one Gwanny!' Aoife pointed at her next victim. She had a good eye for spotting them.

Maria was trying to wrestle a tartan bow into her daughter's cloud of red curls while Helen distracted her with fly extermination.

'I could ring Niamh?' Maria asked. 'We could use her dishwasher?'

'Niamh Ryan?' Helen raised her eyebrows. 'You want to cart our dirty dishes up the hill and knock on Mary Ryan's door? Well now, wouldn't that be a sight for sore eyes?'

'I'm trying to think, Mammy.'

Aoife picked up the carcass of a fly and dropped it into her mother's cleavage.

'Ah for Christ's sake, Aoife!' Maria tried to retrieve the body from between her boobs.

'For Christ's sake,' Aoife parroted back.

Helen started to laugh.

'Mammy!'

Maria was looking at her like she was the one to blame.

Helen had never actually agreed to mind Aoife when Maria went back to work as a secondary school teacher. She was only supposed to be helping out, but Kevin didn't have hands to bless himself. It was like having a teenager in the house. He was starting a business, apparently, which involved taking over Helen's sitting room and eating her out of house and home.

It wasn't the most ideal situation for him either. She knew that he was a bit afraid of her. Helen didn't think much of him. He was handsome, at least. They had met in a nightclub in Dublin a few years ago. It wouldn't have lasted if he hadn't gotten her pregnant. Aoife was three and a half now, and Maria was still waiting for him to get down on one knee.

They were only supposed to be living with Helen temporarily. A few years back, Liam had talked her into building an extension onto the house to give Bláithín a sense of independence. Bláith's enthusiasm for her new place had lasted a few weeks before she was back in the main house where the internet connection was more reliable, leaving an entire ensuite bedroom and kitchenette free at the gable end. It was an ideal space for Maria and Kevin to use while they tried to get planning permission on a site beside the homeplace.

Their planning applications had been rejected twice. Mary Ryan had objected both times. Sometimes, it was hard to believe that she was the same Mary Crowley who was her best friend in primary school. Mary had married Vincent and Helen had married Liam. They had had a double wedding. They had even gone on honeymoon together. Vincent and Liam had died within a month of each other, and still, Mary wanted nothing more than to be a thorn in Helen's side. The woman had no good reason to throw her toys out of the pram and object to

Maria and Kevin building beside her. It had made things awkward between Maria and Niamh, especially because Niamh was still living at home with her Mam. It was Bláith who brought them back together again, Bláith who didn't know or care about the drama and insisted on keeping up her weekly visits to Niamh's house to watch *The Great British Bake Off* and eat homemade scones.

'We could get disposable plates and cups?' Maria's voice snapped Helen back to the land of the broken dishwasher. 'I know it's bad for the environment. Nadine will have a conniption.'

'It's a good job we're not in Nadine's house then,' Helen said.

Kevin was sent to the shop with a list. He nodded along to Maria's instructions, trying to hide his delight that he was getting out of going to mass.

Helen got excited when she saw Father Angelo's little red Peugeot outside the church. Liam's mother, Nan, claimed that she couldn't understand what Father Angelo was saying, though Helen didn't think his accent was that strong. He was from somewhere in South America – she kept forgetting which country – and had lovely brown eyes.

It was hard to believe that he'd been curate in the parish for more than ten years now. Helen still remembered the speech he'd made from the altar at the end of his first mass. He said that he hoped that he could learn some Irish, and teach them some of his language. Nobody seemed to notice when she hung around outside the sacristy after mass like a schoolgirl waiting backstage at a concert.

'Céad míle fáilte,' she had greeted him when he reappeared, still dressed in his vestments. 'It means a hundred thousand welcomes.'

He smiled and bowed his head. 'How do I say thank you in your language?'

'Go raibh maith agat,' Helen said.

It took him a few goes to get the pronunciation right. Helen told him that the direct translation of the phrase was, 'May you have goodness.'

'How wonderful,' he said, his eyes shining.

'Hello is "Dia dhuit", which means "God be with you,"' Helen rambled on. 'And the response is, "Dia is Muire dhuit" – God and Mary be with you. It's like a competition to see how many holy people you can bring into the conversation.'

'I think I am going to be very fond of your language,' he said.

'Well, it's not *my* language,' she replied. 'I haven't spoken it since my school days. I used to be a teacher.'

Father Angelo looked at her with a steady gaze. 'You are still a teacher. You are my teacher.'

They turned up to the church in plenty of time to get a seat. Helen sat in a pew with Bláith on one side of her and Maria on the other. Aoife bounced on her knee with a *Peppa Pig* book in one hand and her fly swat in the other. She had won the fight to bring it to mass and had so far kept her promise not to hit anyone with it.

Helen kept an eye on her granddaughter as she bent down on the kneeler with her hands clasped. She was going through a phase of feeling the material on other people's clothes, crawling under the seats and becoming mesmerised by a pair of tights that an elderly neighbour was wearing. There was only so much apologising Maria could do.

Two of Helen's children were missing. Peter was in Australia, and Kate was in Belfast. She had sent a message into the family group to say that she couldn't get the time off work. It was the third time in a row that she hadn't made her own father's anniversary mass. There was nothing Helen could do about it. It wasn't like she could go up and drag her back across the border. Helen wished that she had a job in Belfast she could hide behind, instead of having to sit in a church full of Foleys. At least she didn't have to deal with having Kate's beady eyes on her. It was enough to try and make it through the day.

John and Nadine were late. They finally walked in with their two as everyone was muttering the Act of Contrition. Nadine always made an effort for mass. Helen wished she wouldn't. She was one of those people who looked worse whenever they tried to look better. The fake tan made her look like she had a skin condition. Their little fella was making his communion later in the year. It was seven years since he was born, and even now, Helen struggled to say his name. She could still remember the shock on Liam's face. Their first-born grandchild – the pair of them floating on cloud nine when John sent the text through: *Welcome to the world Elmo John Foley.*

They thought it must have been a joke. The next message was a link to a baby name website that gave several arguments in support of Elmo as a reasonable name for a child. It was a derivative of Erasmus, a great philosopher. There was a St. Elmo, who was the patron saint of sailors. 'What better name to give your baby as it sets off on this great voyage of life?' the website claimed.

'You wouldn't name a dog that,' Liam said.

'Don't you dare say anything,' Helen warned him.

When Nadine announced her second pregnancy, Peter sent a photo of Big Bird into the family group and said, *Good luck with the labour Nadine!*

They called their second little one Arwin. He was five now and was mad about the farm.

Helen looked at the two boys messing at the back of the church. She would have liked the firstborn to be called Liam after his grandad, and the second John after his daddy who, as a little boy, loved the farm too.

She wasn't really concentrating on what Father Angelo was saying. He had already said Liam's name at the start of mass, and she expected that he would mention him again.

The President of Ireland was at Liam's funeral. On the worst day of her life, the President shook her hand and gave his condolences. He said that Liam was the finest hurling player that he had ever seen, and an even better man.

The first anniversary mass was well attended, but it was nothing like the funeral. The second anniversary felt like just another Sunday. This year, the place was packed. A documentary about Liam had aired a few weeks back. Helen couldn't bring herself to sit down and watch it, but lots of people got in touch with her about it. It felt like he had died all over again.

She did a quick head count of the Foley faces in the congregation – relations, mostly cousins of Liam that she knew to expect back at the house after mass. They all had that same, distinctive Foley nose that she could spot a mile away. Every time she gave birth, she'd inspected their little noses to see if the tip was inclined to droop a bit. Helen came from a long line of good noses, which she had passed down to only one of her children, Kate, who took it for granted. If Helen had the choice, she would have given it to Maria. She needed it more.

As soon as she saw Father Angelo come out of the sacristy, Liam's mother Nan had a face on her like a slapped arse. At eighty years old, Nan still milked cows in the parlour with her grandchildren. She'd been up with John that morning just so she could boast about it for the rest of the day. To the rest of the parish, Nan Foley was a living legend, but to Helen, she was a mother-in-law. The woman took every opportunity to make sly digs at her, turning people against her in the subtlest of ways. A lady of leisure, she called her, when Helen gave up teaching. She didn't want to give up her job, but she wasn't Wonder Woman. She couldn't do it all.

Nan couldn't understand why Helen refused to set foot on the farm. She wouldn't listen to the excuses that there were nappies to be changed, because she had done both.

Liam's father had died from a heart attack when Liam was six months old, and Nan took over the farm herself, milking cows and feeding calves while breastfeeding and changing nappies.

The farm was still in Nan's name. Liam said it was for tax reasons. Helen had asked him about it when they first got married, and she'd noticed all of the post that was addressed to Annette (Nan's birth name) and Liam Foley. A few weeks after Liam's funeral, Nan had summoned John over to her kitchen to talk business. John reported back to Helen, of course, panicking about what he should do. Helen had told him to talk to Nadine about it. There was no point in having a lawyer in the family if they couldn't use her. The next thing Helen knew, the postman was delivering envelopes addressed to Annette and John Foley. It was lucky that Liam's life insurance policy had paid out, given the circumstances. Herself and Liam used to joke all the time about what they'd do with the money if either of them died before sixty. She considered giving a few bob to the kids before she stopped herself. She didn't want Nan catching wind of it.

'She's a tough act to follow,' Helen would say whenever people asked her about Nan. They wouldn't have believed her if she told them otherwise – she wouldn't even know where to begin unravelling the bitch, she was that good at twisting everything. The woman had her finger in every pie in town, from the choir to the drama society to the local council. Whatever Nan Foley said was the gospel truth.

It didn't bother Helen, at first, the way Nan thought that the truth belonged to her. Every day when she came in for dinner, the conversation would always go the same way. It was a small world, and it was getting smaller, and did they know that so-and-so was married to so-and-so's sister who was a neighbour of your man who lives in the back of beyond? Liam would interrupt her to say she'd gotten the wrong end of the stick, and that would be it – a fight would break out over who was right.

Helen was used to blocking out the noise, rising above it all until the day Nan insisted that Anne-Marie Hinchy was in her late sixties.

'She's not,' Helen interrupted her. 'I went to school with her.'

'Are you sure that it wasn't her sister Martha?' Nan said, spearing some turnip with her fork.

'I'm sure.'

'I don't know about that, now, I think you're thinking of Martha.'

'I sat beside Anne-Marie for three years in primary school,' Helen insisted, feeling her jaw tighten. 'I am one hundred per cent sure.'

Nan gave it a second's thought before shaking her head. 'I think it might be Martha you're thinking of.'

Helen watched Nan on the other side of the church, frowning at Father Angelo, annoyed that her choice of priest had let her down. Father Angelo invited the kids up to the altar and started talking to them about Zacchaeus. It was only then that it dawned on Helen that it was a First Confession mass. She looked over at Maria and recognised the panic in her face. Maria had been counting on a quick sermon. She would either have to slip out early to take the meat out of the oven, or risk giving instructions to Kevin and hope for the best.

Helen remembered her teaching years and all the time she spent preparing the First Communion classes for their First Confession. Father John had stifled a laugh on the altar during one child's admission. After the mass, he had pulled Helen aside and said, 'God forgive me, I know I shouldn't, but it's too good not to share: he told me that he coveted his neighbour's wife.'

Times changed but kids stayed the same. All of the children made up their sins. Helen had done the same when she was their age. The nuns dragged them across the street to confession every week. Her heart pounded as they filed into the pew, her bony bum on the hard bench, having to scoot up every time the next girl disappeared into the confession box. Helen was an only child, which wasn't helpful when it came to sinning. She didn't have a sister's hair to pull, or a brother to insult, so she made up stories about a bold brat who did and said awful things. She grew to love that girl. Sometimes, she wished that she was brave enough to be her.

Helen was desperate to be God's favourite. On the morning of her First Communion mass, she knelt down by her bed to say the rosary before changing into her dress. She had been chosen to do the First Reading. She knew all the words to the Second Reading, and all the Prayers of the Faithful. She had even learned the Gospel off by heart. In the end, it wasn't enough. Mary Crowley stole the show by singing the psalm. Helen wanted to run away and cry in the graveyard after the mass, far away from her classmates who were celebrating on the other side of the wall. That was the story she told the priest a week later in confession, embellishing the lie by saying that she kicked the headstone of a grave with her new shoes. It felt like she was telling the truth.

The nuns kept a strict eye on them while they waited in the pew every week. The afternoon sun streamed in through the stained-glass windows onto their faces and they'd whisper to each other whenever the colours landed on them – blue, red, green. Helen looked up at the window. Angels were crowning the Virgin Mary who was holding the baby Jesus. Two women were on either side of them, looking on. Helen remembered asking who they were but the nuns shushed her – that meant that they didn't know either. One woman was offering a bowl of grapes to the baby Jesus who was too young to eat them. Helen preferred the woman on the other side with the sword.

At first, Helen thought that she was imagining the sound of birds chirping as she sat there looking up at the women in the glass, but Mary Crowley heard them too. Helen asked her father about them, but he wasn't sure what kind of birds they were. When they disappeared, he said that they must have migrated for the winter. Helen used to imagine their shadows dancing behind the glass. She liked to think she was keeping the place warm for them by remembering that they belonged there.

Eventually, the time came for her to go into the darkness of the confessional booth. She breathed in the smell of polished mahogany. Her knees were forever in danger of slipping off the kneeler, no matter how hard she tried to position them on the leather beam. When the priest pulled back the shutter of the grille, she concentrated on the tobacco-stained fingernails of the hands that were clasped in his lap. 'Bless me Father for I have sinned, it has been a week since my last confession ...' she began, spilling out the lines she rehearsed as she watched the birds soar behind the stained glass.

Helen watched now as the children went up onto the altar to mutter their lies to the priest. The confession box had been done away with and everything was out in the open now. She supposed it was a sign of the times – nothing could be private anymore.

It was confession that killed Liam, in the end. It wasn't her idea or Liam's. Kate had barged in on her while she was watching *Fair City* in the sitting room. Liam was ashen-faced, trailing behind her. Helen thought someone had died, but no, Kate said that Liam had something to tell her. Liam couldn't get a word out. She didn't want to hear it anyway. It was like *Fair City* had burst out of the telly and the action was unfolding live in front of her, complete with a bad script and worse acting.

She couldn't even make out what Kate was trying to say. Something about Liam and Niamh? *Niamh?* Kate was shouting at her now like it was her fault. The slap came out of nowhere. Helen had only wanted her to calm down. She wanted it all to be over so she could go back to putting her feet up and watching people scream at each other on the TV.

'Apologise to your father,' Helen said.

Kate put her hand to her cheek. 'You want *me* to apologise to *him?*'

'Yes,' Helen said. 'He's told you that you've gotten the wrong end of the stick.'

Kate raced out of the room and Liam followed her. Helen closed the door and left them to sort it out between themselves.

She wasn't worried when Liam didn't come to bed that night. He was a bad sleeper at the best of times. He used to sleep in the spare room so as not to wake her when he came in late from the yard and slipped out at the crack of dawn to milk the cows.

That was what she imagined had happened the night before, when she padded down the stairs in her slippers the following morning. The fridge door seemed heavier than usual. She lost her balance as she pulled the handle and stumbled into its light.

Her hand automatically reached for the sausages, pudding and rashers. She peeled the slimy pink strips of bacon away from each other and laid them out top to tail on the tinfoil, before placing them under the grill. John and Peter liked their bacon cremated but Liam hated the edges burned, so she took his share out early while the fat was still translucent and towelled the grease off them in kitchen paper.

It was Liam's sixtieth birthday and the fry was a treat. The boys usually had to make do with porridge and scones.

Helen was supposed to say her prayers in the morning after she laid out the table for breakfast, but she had found herself reaching for the iPad before she had time to think. She got stressed if she couldn't find it, as though it needed her too.

That morning, the iPad was exactly where it should have been – hidden in the basket of kindling and old newspapers behind the television. She brought it onto her lap and slid her finger across the screen to unlock it. She went to Google and typed 'Liam Farmer Foley,' into the search engine. With a tap of her finger, endless incarnations of her husband were summoned to the screen.

Helen could recite the introduction to Liam's Wikipedia entry as though she was saying the rosary:

Liam 'Farmer' Foley is an Irish hurling legend, widely regarded as one of the greatest players in the history of the sport. After his retirement from the game, Foley went on to become a popular pundit and media personality. Foley is a dairy farmer and lives with his wife and five children. He turned down several offers to manage senior hurling teams at inter-county level to coach St Brigid's camogie team, on which two of his daughters play . . .

There was a time when Helen felt a surge of pride seeing Liam floating around in cyberspace. She took it upon herself to stand guard over her husband's online presence. Every morning, she googled his name three times. It was a stupid superstition. She knew it wouldn't change anything, but it felt like she was keeping him safe.

Kate was fixing the internet connection on the tablet for her when she stumbled across her search history. Helen hadn't realised that the bloody thing was tracking her.

'Why wouldn't I be interested in what people are saying about your father?' Helen said.

'Oh, I'm sorry Mam, I didn't mean to laugh. It's cute!' Kate gushed. 'It's really cute.'

Helen was annoyed at herself. She knew that Kate would tell the whole world and their mothers, and everyone would have a great laugh behind her back.

That morning, she was nervous opening the browser in case the internet's antennae had somehow reached into her sitting room the night before. She searched for him once, twice, three times. Nothing. She allowed herself to breathe again and got on with her scrolling, surrendering her thoughts to the whims of whatever caught her fancy.

She heard the back door open and presumed it was the lads coming in from the yard. She got up to put on the kettle for them, but it was Kate who threw open the door. She was in hysterics. John rushed in behind her. By the look on his face, Helen knew that it was serious.

She couldn't take any of it in. Even when the ambulance arrived and they tried to explain what had happened, all she could think about was the breakfast that she'd laid out on plates in the kitchen, going cold.

*

There were piles of paper plates on the kitchen counter when they arrived home from the church with *60th birthday!*

splashed across them. Stacks of paper cups proclaimed *Let's party!*

'Ah Kevin, for God's sake,' Maria snapped. 'We can't use them!'

'I went to three different shops and they had no plain ones. It was between these and Peppa Pig,' Kevin said, popping a nut in his mouth and scanning the table for more snacks.

'Peppa would have been fine?'

'I thought they might be inappropriate.'

Most of Kevin's attention was taken up with trying to open the shell of a stubborn pistachio.

'Inappropriate,' Maria said, unwrapping the bowls of salads and trays of sandwiches that were covered with cling film.

'Yeah.'

'And you thought a sixtieth birthday theme for the anniversary mass of a man who died on his sixtieth birthday would be more appropriate?'

A cascade of pistachios fell from Kevin's hand.

'It's fine,' Maria said.

'Oh God—'

'I said it's fine. We'll just use normal plates.'

There were so many people. Helen didn't recognise half of the women who were milling around the place, carrying teapots like gardeners with watering cans. The delph that she usually kept hidden was in the hands of men who could break bones with an enthusiastic handshake.

A complete stranger took Helen by the hand and led her into the utility room.

'How are you now, Helen, really?' she asked, her piggy eyes wide, hungry for some second-hand grief.

Helen could have hit her. Instead, she pushed past her as though she'd said nothing at all – went back into the kitchen and concentrated on cutting slices of brown bread, smiled as people introduced themselves, nodded every time someone said they couldn't believe it had been three years now. Whenever she felt like it was all getting too much, she looked out the window at her grandchildren who were delighted with their bouncy castle. It was hard to find them though in the swarm of other children who had no business being in her back garden.

An hour later, the sports day was in full swing. Maria was trying her best to orchestrate the chaos. Bláithín was nowhere to be seen. The only thing that would bring her out of hiding would be the members of One Direction showing up for the sack race. Helen scanned the crowd, trying to find someone she could tolerate a conversation with. That was when she saw her – Niamh's mother, Mary, sneaking into her utility room, unloading a stack of clean plates from a plastic crate and filling it up with dirty ones.

Helen marched out to the garden, pushing past people until she found Maria arm-deep in a sack of spuds, preparing for the potato-and-spoon race.

'What is Mary Ryan doing in my utility room?' she asked.

Maria sighed. 'I asked Niamh for help. She must have sent Mary down.'

'Well, you can ring Niamh now and tell her we don't need her help.'

'Why don't you ring her, Mam?'

A man appeared in front of Helen. He introduced himself and his grandson, a young boy who was bouncing a sliotar on his hurley. She wondered aloud if they had met before. The man shook his head and said no, but he was a huge fan of her husband. He gripped the hurley in his hand and said that it was one of Liam's. He had gotten it as a gift.

Helen smiled. It wasn't unusual for people to be overfamiliar, but she was rarely in the mood for them.

The man explained that he had watched the documentary the week before.

'I haven't been able to watch it yet,' Helen said.

He nodded sympathetically. 'You must be questioning why there are so many people in your back garden, so.'

'That's exactly what I'm wondering, to be honest with you.'

He told her that it was Liam's mother who had advertised the time and date of the anniversary mass, and extended an open invitation to anyone who could make it back to the house for the sports day.

Helen looked over at the old woman sitting on her throne on the patio, delighted at the spectacle unfolding before her. Easily knowing she had nothing to do with the preparations. She hadn't even the good sense to give Maria a heads-up.

The man gave her a sheepish look. 'I was just wondering, Helen, would you mind if I showed the workshop to my grandson?'

'No,' Helen said. 'I'm sorry, I can't . . .'

'That's fine!'

'I'm sorry.'

'Not at all! I was only chancing my arm,' he said, staring off over her shoulder towards the workshop at the bottom of the garden.

Helen made her excuses and found her way back into the house, trying her best to hold it together. Her heart was hammering away in her chest as she set foot in the kitchen again. She peered into the utility room. It was empty. Mary Ryan was gone.

The conservatory was the only room in the house that wasn't thronged with people. Bláith was sitting on the couch scrolling through her phone. Aoife was lying on her tummy playing with her older cousins' farm set. Kevin, who was supposed to be looking after his daughter, was doing a better job at keeping an eye on his beer.

Aoife often gravitated towards her Auntie Bee, despite Bláith having limited interest in her. If Kate was there, Aoife would be hanging out of her, dragging her here and there, but even at three and a half, Aoife knew she wouldn't get that much energy out of Bláith. Neither of them were watching the One Direction concert playing on the television. Bláith was absorbed in the spectre of her great love who lit up the tiny screen in her hand.

Helen sat down beside her. 'How are you doing, love?'

Bláith ignored her. Helen looked at the young man in the palm of her hand. She knew more about Harry Styles than any respectable woman in her late fifties should. Bláith was smitten from his very first X Factor audition.

She was sceptical about the formation of a boy band. It took her a while to warm to the rest of them, but the dimples and haircuts eventually won her over.

Bláith wriggled away when Helen tried to stroke her hair. 'Go away, Mam.'

Maria appeared at the door. 'Bláith? The soccer match is about to start.'

'I don't think she wants to play,' Helen said.

'She told me she wanted to earlier.'

'You made her promise she would,' Helen corrected her.

Maria got distracted trying to wrestle the fly swat that Aoife had been licking out of her screaming child's hands.

Bláith remained unfazed by the chaos. She murmured to herself, smiling at her own private jokes. Helen envied Bláithín's ability to disengage from whatever was going on around her.

Helen stayed in the conservatory for the rest of the evening. People peered in the windows at herself and Bláith on the couch. She closed her eyes to block it out. Her eyelashes fluttered. A muscle in her forehead kept twitching. There was a fly somewhere in the room. She could hear it whining, even through the sound of a stadium of One Direction fans screaming . . .

Helen woke up to silence. The television had been switched off. Bláith had disappeared, along with everyone else. She went out to the kitchen to stick on the kettle. There were dirty dishes all over the place. The flies were having a field day in the leftover coleslaw.

She pulled on a pair of yellow rubber gloves that had been left in the sink and were wet on the inside. She started by washing the pots, emptying out the basin of greasy black water down the drain and refilling it. She got to the dishes, scraping leftovers into a wobbly pile on a dinner plate that she gave to the dog. She stacked the dishes with the pink willow pattern separately and put them in the crate in the utility room, ready to be transported back up the hill to Mary Ryan.

Helen was scrubbing hardened lasagne from the corner of an enamel casserole dish when Maria and Kevin landed at the door. She knew by the sing-song tone of Maria's voice that something was wrong.

'Hi Mammy!'

Helen looked up from the sink. Maria's face was flushed. She pulled Kevin across the kitchen. It was unusual for them to be holding hands.

'Where is Bláith?' Helen asked.

'She's in with Nan,' Maria said.

'And Aoife?'

'She's asleep.'

'Who is looking after her?'

'We put the monitor in the conservatory while you were sleeping. We didn't want to wake you.'

'So, I have been looking after Aoife while you two were off gallivanting,' Helen said.

Maria dropped Kevin's hand and rushed out of the kitchen. Kevin followed her, less out of concern, Helen thought, and more out of a fear of being alone in the same room as her.

Helen filled the kettle for something to do while she waited for the pair of them to reappear.

'Sit down there,' she said, when they came back in. 'The kettle's about to boil, I'll make a pot.'

'I'm sorry for leaving you to look after Aoife without asking you,' Maria said, taking a seat at the table.

'That's OK.'

'After everyone left, we decided to visit the grave.'

The kettle shook before it clicked off, sending water out of its snout. Helen didn't see Maria's face when she told her that Kevin had asked her to marry him.

There were no teabags in the canister. Helen bent down to check if there was a box in the press.

Maria was babbling now – something about Kevin wanting to ask Liam for his blessing.

Helen turned around to face her daughter. There was silence in the kitchen. Maria's face was pleading with her now. Out of all of her children, Maria was the one who craved her approval the most. It broke her heart.

When the kids were younger, Helen made a barmbrack every Halloween and put two rings in it – one for Bláithín and one for Maria. The idea was born out of necessity. Holy war broke out over who got the ring in the shop-bought loaf. If anyone else found the ring in the brack, they would quickly pass it to Bláith who got most of the things she wanted. Maria was especially good to her little sister. The only time she got upset was when she was the one who found the ring in the cake.

Helen remembered one particular Halloween night when the kids were still in primary school: Bláith was in hysterics in the corner while Peter pinned Maria's hand to the wall, prying her fingers apart in order to retrieve the flimsy bit of metal from her closed fist. After that, Helen had started making her own loaf. There was no need to put more than two rings in the mixture – Kate had no interest. She spaced them out so that there would be one either end. Bláith lost her ring within hours. Maria wore hers until the cheap material snapped, leaving a green stain that served as a replacement ring until it faded away.

Helen went looking for a diamond on Maria's finger, but Kevin said that they were going to pick one out together. She slipped her own engagement ring off and passed it to Maria.

'Try that on for size.'

She remembered the day Liam had taken her ring shopping in Dublin. She knew as soon as she saw it that it was the one – a simple solitaire with a plain gold band. The salesman told them that it was vintage and tried to sway them towards the new section, but she liked the thought of wearing the mystery of another woman's marriage as well as her own. It made her feel less alone.

The ring would only fit Maria's little finger, but Helen was glad to make a fuss over her.

'I've Daddy's sausage fingers.' She sniffed, happy tears rolling down her face.

'Does Bláith know yet?' Helen asked.

Maria shook her head. 'We're going to tell her tomorrow.'

Helen nodded and listened as Maria retold the story of going to visit the grave at sunset, Kevin going all quiet on her and thinking he was bending down to tie his shoelaces.

'Dad would be thrilled, wouldn't he?' Maria asked her mother.

'He would, of course,' Helen agreed.

As she got into bed that night, she imagined her husband lying beside her. She knew exactly what Liam would say. What sort of gobshite proposes in a graveyard?

Chapter 3

The Tree

Kate

THERE WAS A TREE near the border that reminded Kate of home. It sat on a hill in the middle of a field that seemed a world away from the motorway that blasted through it. She knew that it was a fairy tree by the way the farmer took care to plough around it. It wasn't a hawthorn or an ash like most fairy trees, but a majestic oak with strong branches that were made for climbing. It looked like it belonged inside a children's book. Kate felt an urge to point it out to Ellius as it came into view in the windscreen.

'Look at that tree,' she said, her heart thumping in her chest.

He barely took his eyes off the road. 'What about it?'

'I don't know.' She wavered. 'There's something about it.'

He laughed. 'Yeah, it's a tree.'

Her stomach gurgled. Her insides had been at her all day. She'd gotten ready for Maria's engagement party in the staff toilet after her shift in the café and had already sweated most of her makeup off.

'Is Niamh coming tonight?' Ellius asked.

'I'm not sure,' Kate said. 'I would put money on it that Maria is going to have her as a bridesmaid. That'll be fun.'

'You could try talking to her,' Ellius said.

'Are you serious?' Kate glanced over at him. 'Ellius, I'm the one who sent messages, letters, texts – I spent years reaching out, begging her to talk to me.'

He turned on the radio. All of the preset stations sank into static once they crossed the border. The radio came up for air, making a brave reach for a local station while the static still hissed in the background, threatening to drown the host who was introducing a segment. 'Time to talk all things menopause. Angela in Dundalk says she's fit to throw herself down the stairs – don't be doing that now Angela . . .'

Dolores, Ellius' mini dachshund, was dozing in the back seat. Her small snout rested on top of her two front legs. The vibrations of the car hurtling down the motorway shook her tiny body. Dolores was the most recent candidate in Ellius' mission to foster every dog in Belfast. She was a welcome relief from the other eejits he usually went for who were desperate for attention and made bits of the furniture. Dolores was above all that. She had the air of an aristocrat about her.

'She looks like a Protestant,' Kate had said, when Ellius brought her home from the shelter. In another life, Dolores could have been a widow from the Lisburn Road who got her hair blow-dried twice a week and was involved in church fundraisers.

'Shit,' Kate said. 'I forgot to say to Maria that we're bringing Dolores.'

'She won't mind, will she?' Ellius asked.

'I don't know. She's a bit funny about dogs.'

Maria was messaging her now, panicking about last-minute practicalities. Kate felt bad that she wasn't there to help. She didn't know what the etiquette was, but she was pretty sure that it wasn't usually left to the bride-to-be to organise her own engagement party.

Is it ok to bring the dog? She snuck the request in between Maria's anxieties about there being enough finger food to feed the camogie team. *She's only small, and, believe it or not, extremely well bred. Think Lady Diana with an extra pair of legs.*

Maria messaged back. *Just make sure it doesn't shit on the carpet. Btw how are your guts?*

Kate regretted telling her about them. It was Maria who persuaded her to get a colonoscopy. She tried to convince her to get it done down south, but Kate went with the NHS who put her on a waiting list. She secretly hoped that would be the end of it, but they sent her a letter soon after, giving her a date with a gastroenterologist. In the end, they found nothing. Irritable bowel syndrome made it sound like some crabby old bitch had set up camp in her intestines.

'What do you work at?' the consultant had asked.

'I'm a barista.'

'Do you drink a lot of coffee?'

'I used to. I cut caffeine out of my diet for the last six months. I've been doing all the right things and it hasn't gotten better.'

She didn't tell him that she wasn't eating much. She found that she could survive on rice cakes for days at a time, especially when Ellius was working late shifts in the bar and she could get away with it. There were nights she was so hungry that she snuck downstairs and raided the kitchen cupboard on her hands and knees, almost choking on the shards of cornflakes that she shovelled down her throat.

'What's wrong?' Ellius asked, slowing the car down as they queued up for the toll.

'Maria is asking about my bowels.'

'I hope she told Kevin about them. It will be the first thing he'll ask when we get there. "Have you tried sitting backwards on the toilet, Kate? That's what I do when I have difficulty."'

'Stop it,' Kate said.

'I hope he brings up his plans for a United Ireland again.'

Kevin's eyes lit up every time he saw Ellius. All he wanted to do was talk about the North and Ellius loved winding him up.

It wasn't just Kevin who asked stupid questions. When Kate came home, everyone acted like she had come back through the wardrobe from Narnia and not straight down the motorway. She didn't mind it so much when people in Belfast asked her how she ended up there. A taxi man had once told her you were more likely to hear a Spanish accent than one from the Free State.

'And you like it here, aye?' he'd asked, eyebrows raised, catching her eye in the rear-view mirror.

'I do.' Kate had given him the usual reason – the rent was a lot cheaper than Dublin, and she loved a good traybake. 'You can't get carmelitas or fifteens down south.'

'Ach, now,' he'd scoffed. 'They'd want to catch themselves on down there.'

When she first moved up, she was charmed by the redbrick buildings and funny street names, the pink buses and taxis that you had to order online instead of getting off the side of the road. There were unwritten rules to getting a taxi in Belfast. Ellius always hopped into the passenger seat.

'You're a psychopath,' she told him. 'They don't want you to sit in the front.'

'How do you know?' he asked.

'Look, here,' she said, passing him her phone.

'You asked what people do in Belfast?' he asked. 'What the fuck would Google know about it?'

'How else am I supposed to know? You won't answer me whenever I ask questions about the way things work up here.'

'What do you mean, "up here"?'

'In Northern Ireland.'

'Northern Ireland?' He raised his eyebrows. 'Never heard of it. I grew up in Ireland, Kate – the same island as you.'

Kate thought that moving to Belfast would be good for them. When they were at university in Edinburgh, they worked as a pair but Ellius was different in his home city. He went back to wearing the same baggy clothes he wore before university.

In their first year of studying in Scotland, he bought a sewing machine and began to tailor charity shop clothes. They laughed at his first few attempts, but he enjoyed putting outfits together for both of them. He was good at it. There was never a coming-out – not really – just brightly coloured socks and sweater vests. She loved him. That was all that mattered.

She was nervous when they flew home for the summer and Liam picked them up from the airport. Ellius shook his hand and Kate watched as her father took in the skirt and paisley-print blouse on her boyfriend's narrow frame.

'You poor craytur,' Maria said a week later, when she was tipsy at a cousin's wedding.

'What do you mean?' Kate asked.

'Well, we all wondered what was happening between you two, until, well, you know.' She pursed her lips.

'What?' Kate asked.

'Well, he's obviously *gay*.' Maria whispered it.

'He's bisexual,' Kate said.

'Oh well he's that anyway,' Maria quipped, taking a sip of her wine. 'He'd be fond of a pair of dungarees.'

'We still have sex sometimes,' Kate said.

'*What?*' Maria grabbed her by the wrist. 'No, Kate, that's not OK.'

'Why not?'

'Because!' Maria said. 'It's not fair! Kate, listen to me. You deserve more than the occasional fuck, especially when that person is interested in the opposite *sex*.'

Kate laughed and put her hand on top of her sister's. 'Honestly, the occasional fuck is underrated. I'm living the dream.'

Sex was never a problem. Ellius had a way of making her feel comfortable in her body. She didn't have to suck in her stomach or act like a porn star. Whenever she thought about sex with Ellius, she remembered the time he picked her nose in bed. It was a lazy Edinburgh morning. They'd been out the night before and were both hungover and horny. The sun was shining in through the blinds, lighting up the dust motes that were dancing around them as he pushed himself inside her. She could see herself reflected in his eyes, her hair spread out in a fan across the pillow, her mouth open. It all felt so glorious until he took his finger and stuck it in her nostril, scooping out a blob of snot.

'EW!' She shoved him off her.

He raised his finger and popped it in his mouth.

'You minger!' She squirmed around the bed.

'Why are you acting like you've never picked your nose,' he said, laughing at her.

'Yes, my *own* nose – not someone else's.'

'Well, you're OK with exchanging other bodily fluids.'

'Hang on,' she said, propping herself up on an elbow. 'Does this mean you'll let me pop your spots?'

'Nope,' he said, wrapping the duvet around his shoulders as a shield.

'*Please*,' she begged, trying to burrow her fingers down his back.

'No, fuck off Kate,' he said, slapping her hand away. 'I mean it.'

It wasn't just his spots that he wouldn't let her touch. There were other parts of his life that he didn't know how to share. Ellius barely spoke about his family or his upbringing. He never spoke about his parents. He was raised by a single mother, a nurse who sometimes came up as a suggested friend on Facebook: Bernadette Walsh. Kate had met her a handful of times. The more she tried to make an effort with Bernie, the less patience the woman seemed to have for her. Kate learned to keep quiet at family events, knowing that the best she could hope for was to be considered harmless, a benign presence in Ellius' life.

Ellius was an only child, but he had cousins and aunts and uncles around every street corner. The first time they went for a drink together in the city centre, Ellius bumped into a fella at the bar. They broke into a conversation in Irish while Kate stood there, waiting for an introduction which never came.

When they parted ways, Ellius wouldn't tell her how he knew him until a couple of drinks in, when he mumbled something about how the man blew up half of Belfast back in the day.

Kate stood up from her seat and craned her neck to get a better look at him. Ellius pulled her back down into the snug.

'Don't,' he said.

'I'm just getting another round. Relax.'
'Don't,' he repeated, looking her dead in the eye.
'Don't what?'
'Right, go ahead,' he said, letting go of her hand.
'Stop being so dramatic.' She took her empty glass with her to the bar.

The man introduced himself as Mick. Kate found a way into the conversation by chatting about the GAA match that was on the television. He was trying to convince her to join the local camogie team when Ellius finally came over.

'She hasn't told you who her da is yet, has she?' Ellius asked, leaning over her shoulder. 'You're talking to the daughter of Farmer Foley.'

'Is that right?' Mick's voice went up an octave.

For a man of few words, Liam Foley was well able to take over a conversation.

As they were leaving, Mick gave her his phone number to pass on to her dad. 'We'd love him to present a few medals at the dinner dance this year.'

'Are you going to pass the message on to your da?' Ellius asked her on the walk home.

'I doubt he'll do it. He doesn't have the time.'

'Fuck's sake,' Ellius said. 'Mick will be like a dog with a bone about that.'

'You're the one who brought him up.'

'Only so you wouldn't say something stupid.'

'Like what?'

'Kate, we both know that you're liable to say anything.'

Kate stopped in her tracks. 'I didn't say a word!'

Ellius kept walking. 'Are you telling me that if we stayed for another drink, you wouldn't have started asking questions? I was sweating back there waiting for you to . . .'

'What? Blow up the conversation?' Kate asked, quickening her step to catch up with him. 'Maybe that's why Mick enjoyed my company.'

That was back when she used to laugh about asking questions, demanding explanations for things she knew nothing about.

It was getting more difficult to go home. Kate's stomach was in knots as they crossed the border. She stared out of the passenger seat window at the road signs that had changed from green to blue. Irish italics hung like ornaments over English words, lending a poetic slant to placenames and cautions. They drove past a sign that read *Maraíonn Tuirse* / Tiredness Kills. It reminded her of the time her Dad drove her up to Belfast to help her move into her old flat with Ellius. She'd pointed out how existential the words on the sign were. Liam had ruffled her hair and smiled at her.

'I need a toilet soon,' she warned Ellius.

'There's a service station up ahead.'

'How far away are we?'

'Ten minutes. Less.' He took one hand off the steering wheel to squeeze her shoulder.

'I don't think I can wait.'

'You can. Take deep breaths,' he said.

'I can't wait.'

'You can.'

'Pull over,' she said.

'Really?'

'Pull over!'

Ellius swerved the Micra onto the hard shoulder. Kate opened the passenger door as it was still rolling to a stop. He climbed over the gear stick to get out on her side of the car, took off his jacket and opened it out to shield her while she squatted in the grass.

A steady stream of traffic whooshed past, shaking the car and sending tremors through her. He handed her down a tissue without looking.

'I can't just leave it here, can I?' she asked. 'Do we have a bag?'

Ellius produced a plastic bag from the inside pocket of his jacket.

'Thank you,' she whispered.

'You can thank Dolores, they're hers.'

Dolores had woken up from her nap and was looking down her snout at her through the crack in the door. Ellius pressed his lips together, trying to hide a smile.

'Stop it,' Kate said.

They got back into the car. Kate placed the plastic bag at her feet. Ellius turned on the ignition and whispered a motivational speech to the Micra, looking in his rear-view mirror, trying to find the perfect moment to make a break for it. His eyes widened as he spotted a gap in the stream of cars. He let the handbrake down and slammed on the accelerator.

They drove in silence to the service station with the windows down. When they pulled up at the petrol pump, Ellius reached across and picked up the bag at her feet. He got out of the car and ran away with it, disappearing around the back of the building. A moment later, he re-emerged, dusting off his hands.

'Job done,' he said, jumping back into the driver's seat.

'I would have done it myself,' Kate said, wiping her eyes with the sleeve of her cardigan.

'You OK, Blue?' he asked.

She nodded. It was her dad who started calling her Blue. Kate was an anxious child. While other kids were off having fun, Kate would often be crying in a corner. Helen was impatient with her, but Liam would pull her up on his knee and point out how much bluer her eyes turned when there were tears in them. 'You're as deep as the ocean, Blue,' he told her. He started calling her Blue around the house, and everyone joined in. By her late teens, she had leaned into the nickname by dying her hair turquoise. Her niece Aoife loved her hair, so Kate made sure to dye it the night before she went home. The dye would fade within a few washes and she'd go back to looking like a My Little Pony who'd seen better days.

She went to the bathroom in the service station. Notifications from her siblings' group chat were piling up on her home screen. She tapped into them. Bláithín had sent in a Harry Styles music video. Everyone liked it, even John. Maria was worried about Helen again.

Maria: *Mam's gone AWOL.*

Peter: *G'wan Mam.*

Maria: *She's been gone since yesterday. It looks like she'll be missing the engagement party.*

Kate messaged Peter privately: *Cop on.*

Peter: *What?*

Kate: *Send Maria a nice message saying how much you wish you could be here for the party.*

She waited, sitting on the toilet seat in the cubicle while Peter typed into the group. Finally, he sent in a selfie. He was on the beach. The sun was setting behind him.

Sending love from Bondi. Wish I could be there. Have a great time!

Maria replied with a heart emoji.
Kate messaged Peter: *Thank you.*
She cleaned herself up and fixed her makeup in the bathroom mirror. She finished cleaning up the wing of her eyeliner and messaged Maria: *I'm in the shop. Will pick up a few more bags of crisps.*

Ellius laughed at the amount of Tayto she tried to bundle into the front seat of the car. 'Do you have enough there?' he asked.

'I panicked,' she said.

He started the car up again. 'We'll be there in an hour. Do you want to text Helen to let her know?'

'She's not at home.'

'What?'

'Yeah, she's gone missing. She's been doing it for a while now. Ups and vanishes for days at a time and comes back like she's just nipped to the shop.'

'That's not like Helen,' Ellius said.

Kate decided to let the comment slide. Ellius thought he knew her mother better than she did. The first time he visited the farm, it was like he had been called in to revamp a failing sitcom. She watched as every member of her family turned into a caricature of themselves, flinging witty quips back and forth for his entertainment. Helen played her part so well that she became his favourite.

'Do you think she'll make it back for the party?' he asked.

'I doubt it. Listen, don't mention anything. Maria is cut up about it,' Kate said. 'Are you ready for Bláith?'

'I don't know,' he said.

Every time she saw Ellius, Bláith acted like he was a celebrity who had just climbed out of her phone. She talked about him incessantly when he wasn't there, but as soon as he entered the room, she avoided him.

Over the years, Bláith had invented a story about how Ellius used to be her boyfriend before Kate stole him away from her. Any time Kate visited home, she expected the same speech from Bláith about how difficult it was for her to see her and Ellius together. She would hug Bláith and apologise, breathing in her big sister's little-girl smell and Bláith would forgive her all over again.

*

Kate had met Ellius in the Gaeltacht when she was fifteen. Helen had sent her off on a bus to Connemara for three weeks of the summer with Niamh on the pretence of learning Irish. They were under the supervision of Peter who was a veteran, having gone the year before. When the girls tried to ask questions about it, he acted like they were stupid for not knowing that they were going to have to live in someone else's house. On the west coast of Ireland, legions of women given the title of Bean an Tí, or 'woman of the house', were waiting to squeeze as many teenagers as they could into bunk beds for the summer.

There were twelve girls in Kate's house. Four of them were from a posh boarding school in Dublin. They called dibs on the best room which had six beds. Niamh and Kate were last to arrive, so they ended up having to bunk in with them.

Kate watched as Niamh's jaw tensed up when one of the girls from Dublin asked her name.

'Emmmmmmm . . .' Niamh tried.

'My name is Emma too!' the girl gushed.

'Her name's Niamh,' Kate jumped in. 'She has a bit of a stammer. It's usually fine, it just gets worse whenever she has to say her name.'

Niamh smiled and nodded, putting her stuff on the bottom bunk to claim the bed. The girls from Dublin all looked at each other as if trying to decide what to make of them.

The only time they spoke Irish was when the Bean an Tí was within earshot. She was an elderly woman who smelled of soup and tucked each one of them into bed at night, folding their thin blankets underneath the mattress and into the metal frame like she was closing envelopes.

'Oíche mhaith cailíní,' she said, every time she turned out the lights in the bedroom. *Good night, girls.* 'Oíche mhaith,' she repeated in a menacing whisper, before closing the door, shutting out the slice of light coming from the hallway.

The first night, Kate burst out laughing as soon as the door was closed. She heard Niamh chuckle from across the room, and for a moment, it felt like it was just the two of them having a sleepover at home until the girls from Dublin began to join in. Kate imagined Niamh's face in the dark as they listened to them bitch and moan about their lives like they were on an American reality television show. One of them swore that her friend had slept with the Bean an Tí's son the year before and had to go to England to get an abortion. Another one of them climbed down from her bunk and went rummaging through her bag for a razor. She'd already shaved her arms that morning but could feel the stubble growing back. This prompted a debate on whether it was better to wax or shave arm hair. Kate rubbed the soft down on her arms while murmuring in agreement that waxing was best.

Helen had taken Kate shopping before the Gaeltacht and had lost patience with her in the dressing room of River Island when she started crying over trying on new jeans. In the end, Helen had bought an ugly pair that were too big, insisting that she would grow into them. Kate had packed the new jeans at the bottom of her suitcase and wore her old ones every day.

Before she left, she promised her mother that she would eat her dinner while she was away. It was a relief when the Bean an Tí turned out to be a terrible cook. Nobody ate the boiled vegetables and grey slabs of suspicious-looking meat that she served at dinner time. Kate watched as the other girls tucked into the supplies they got in the local Co-op – cookies slathered with chocolate spread. The smell of the sweetness was enough to satisfy her. She could imagine the taste which was better, she thought, than the messy reality of things.

Kate wasn't interested in the idea of making friends. It was easier for her to sit by herself rather than waste energy pretending to enjoy the company of others. The teachers would come up to her and try to get her involved in a game, but she'd point to Niamh and Peter who were nearby, having a puck around. She made sure to sit near enough to them so that people knew that they were hanging out together, but far enough away that she wouldn't get hit with the ball. Then, she took a book out of her bag and pretended to read. The words on the page seemed to wander off, along with her concentration. It was the pose that mattered. Peter hated her reading in public. Kate didn't mind people laughing at her, as long as no one tried to talk to her. Some of the boys had begun to mock the way that she walked with her feet turned out and her nose up in the air.

She could still remember the shock of Ellius sitting down on the grass beside her. When he asked what she was reading, she could feel her face grow hot and her heartbeat in her eardrums. She closed the book to show him the cover. It was an autobiography of a Russian ballet dancer. Her dad had found it in a second-hand bookshop and had given it to her for her birthday.

He asked why she hadn't brought an Irish book to read while she was here. It was difficult to understand his dialect of Irish, and harder still to answer him.

'Why don't you speak English like everyone else?' She asked the question in English, but he answered in Irish. She couldn't understand what he was saying, but she liked the sound of his voice.

The next day, while she was lining up to go into a classroom, Ellius slipped her a battered paperback. The book was called *An Béal Bocht* by Myles na gCopaleen. When she flicked through the yellowed pages, she was intimidated by all the words she didn't understand. She brought it to bed with her, along with a dictionary, and woke up early to read it the next morning.

The girls from Dublin interviewed her about her interactions with the boy from Belfast who they decided was hot in a nerdy way. It was Niamh who Ellius asked to dance at the céilí. Kate overheard the girls bitching, convinced that he chose Niamh as the safe option.

'She *has* to be a lesbian,' Emma said, mocking the way that Niamh carried her hurley around with her everywhere like she was one of the lads.

When Niamh rejected him, Ellius was stoic about it. He still pucked around with her, before making his way over to sit down beside Kate on the grass. She made more of an effort to speak Irish whenever he was around.

She told him that she hadn't wanted to go to the Gaeltacht. There was an intensive ballet summer camp that she had wanted to enrol in instead, but her mother thought she was too young to take dancing so seriously. That didn't stop her from waking up at six o'clock every morning and sneaking out to the back garden to practice on her own. She was able to squeeze in an hour before the Bean an Tí got up at half seven. She used the wooden fence as a barre and played the syllabus music on her MP3 player while she did her exercises. The donkeys in the neighbouring field had come sniffing around the first couple of mornings, but they had gotten used to her. She liked the feeling of getting back into bed after her secret workout with the cold morning air still in her lungs. When the Bean an Tí called them for breakfast, she pretended to be as sleepy as everyone else. None of the other girls noticed, not even Niamh.

Ellius had looked at her differently after she told him that. He began to look at her the way that she looked at him. She wasn't mad about kissing, at first. She much preferred holding hands in front of everyone and seeing the looks on the faces of the girls from Dublin. When they hugged goodbye at the end of the month, she realised that she would miss the smell of him.

She made him promise to write to her. Every couple of weeks, a letter with a Royal Mail stamp addressed to Kate would arrive, and everyone would tease her about her Nordie boyfriend. He got a typewriter for his sixteenth birthday, and stamped out the poetry of Heaney, Kavanagh and Yeats. Kate sent back Plath, Rich and Bishop in frantic scribbles, along with embarrassing sentences of her own.

When she went into hospital, the only thing that mattered was making it out in time to sit the Leaving Cert. Ellius had sat his A-levels the year before and had deferred his course for a year. They were going to study English in Edinburgh together.

In her nightmares, the hospital staff locked her in a room an hour before her exam and she had to scramble to find a way out, climbing over the furniture to squeeze through the skylight onto the roof, breaking out of a prison of her own making to go and sit in another one, putting her hand up for more paper, feeling the weight of the entire room staring at the mad anorexic bitch in a baggy jumper, pulling out whatever was left of her hair.

They let her out of hospital in the end. Her mother was tight-lipped and tired when she arrived to collect her. Her dad had tears in his eyes as he pulled her in for a hug. He held the back of her head like he was holding a baby.

'Come on Blue,' he whispered into her ear. 'Let's get you home.'

*

Ellius had just indicated to take the exit off the motorway when Maria sent a photo into the family group. The camogie team had arrived at the house. Kate scanned the photo for Niamh. She wasn't there.

Her heart began to beat faster as they reached the turn-off for the village. The last time she was home, she'd gotten into an argument with her brother John about the way he scalped the heads off the hedges in the fields instead of allowing them to grow, which was what their dad had always done. John had said that he was all for conservation, but not when it endangered lives on the road. Nadine had chimed in then, as if nobody could tell that she was the driving force behind her husband's sudden development of a social conscience, giving statistics of local accidents which could have been avoided if drivers had a clearer view of the road.

The valley unfurled in front of them as they rounded the bend for home and there, around the back of the workshop, stood the fairy tree. She imagined its roots clinging to the earth the way her dad gripped her hand tight in a crowd. He had left a mark on the branch he chose to tie the rope around. She wondered if the tree got a shock when he fell – if it was able to feel the weight of him.

Chapter 4

First Touch

Niamh

SHE DIDN'T MISS THE BRUISES – that was what Niamh told people who asked if she would consider picking up a hurley again. Most people had the good sense to change the subject, but there were always men down the pub – friends and former teammates of her dad and Liam – who would beckon her over after a few drinks to bestow their wisdom.

'Life is short.' Bob Healy's bloodshot, watery eyes fixed on hers. 'And a hurler's life is shorter. And I tell you something for nothing, your best hurling years are ahead of you, young lady,' he said, prodding her shoulder.

Bob was a full-back in a previous life with hands like digger buckets. He was a mechanic who broke just about every car he was meant to fix, but people still went to him because they couldn't be seen to pass his garage. He used to be a selector on the hurling team but left a few years back. Dessie McCarthy was telling the lads on the team about the time he had to pull Bob's Ford Ranger out of the ditch after he slipped on a patch of black ice. Bob was blaming the bad weather and Dessie said, 'Bob, if I rode my girlfriend like you ride that jeep, I wouldn't have a girlfriend anymore.'

That opened the floodgates to more stories of Bob making all kinds of mistakes, both on and off the pitch. He couldn't take a slagging, Peter said. He stepped down from management and became St Brigid's biggest sideline critic – the man who people made a beeline towards in the pub when the team was having a bad run to bitch and moan about what they were doing wrong.

'What age are you now?' he asked Niamh.

'Twenty-eight.'

'You have a legendary few years left in you yet, Niamh Ryan – legendary! Your father would want it for you, not to mention the Farmer. Foley wanted great things for you. You know that.'

Niamh felt her face grow hot. She knew what Bob was getting at. Liam had changed the game for women in the GAA. The year that her dad got sick, Liam persuaded her to go on *The Late Late Show* with him to help to launch a foundation that aimed to support and celebrate girls and women in the GAA.

Helen, Maria, Kate and Bláithín made a day out of going shopping in Dublin to help her to pick out an outfit to wear on television. Niamh regretted the length of the dress. They'd chosen it because it was the same shade of blue as St Brigid's club colours, but it was far too short. She didn't know how to position her legs when she sat down on the couch. Backstage, Liam had tried his best to calm her down. Niamh had learned to manage her stammer by then, but it came back whenever she was in stressful situations. That day, it was so bad that she couldn't even attempt to make small talk with the women who did her hair and makeup.

The host introduced them onto the set underneath the hot studio lights. He'd come into the green room before the show to introduce himself. The sound of his voice made her feel like she was already inside the television. As she sat down beside Liam in front of the cameras, she recognised Peter's wolf-whistle coming from the audience – it made her smile.

She'd learned off her lines, memorising answers to the questions like she was sitting an exam. She'd even practised where to take breaths so that she wouldn't freeze or stumble over the words.

It was Liam who brought the charm, sitting back on the couch like he was in his own front room. 'When I first saw Niamh puck a ball, she was tiny – knee-high to a grasshopper,' he said. 'And I immediately thought, "'Tis a pity she's not a boy."'

The audience laughed.

'We could have done with her on my son's underage hurling team. But then, I copped myself on and put her on the team anyway.'

The host clasped his long fingers together and leaned forward. 'You were saying earlier that it was your daughter, Kate, who challenged you to really change your attitude when it came to women in sport.'

'Yeah, listen, I've learned more from my kids than I've ever been able to teach them,' Liam said. 'I suppose the irony is that Kate wouldn't be mad into hurling herself. Ballet is her game – she was into it in a massive way in her teenage years, especially . . .' he paused. Niamh could tell that he was thinking about Kate growing thinner and thinner until she had to give up the thing she loved doing the most.

'Christ,' Liam continued, 'when I saw the discipline involved in dancing at a high level. Have you ever seen the shoes they wear – the pointe yokes? What ballerinas put themselves through – it's more intense than any training regime I've ever done. But yeah, I suppose Kate started going at me a small bit around the dinner table, and to my shame, I didn't pay her much heed. Then she started posting things online about gender inequality in the GAA, and the backlash she got for it was horrendous. It was mostly men in the comments – young fellas, but also a lot of men around my own age. I don't know which is worse, to be honest.'

'What kind of things were they saying?' the host asked.

'Awful stuff.' Liam shook his head. 'Not worth repeating.'

Niamh had seen some of it. Kate was wearing a nose ring in her profile photo. An anonymous account had taken her face and had photoshopped it onto the face of a cow with the caption *One of Farmer Foley's heifers has gone rogue.* It had gone viral, as had the comments underneath the post. Niamh worried that Kate would relapse. She was home for the summer from Edinburgh and was three years into her recovery. Anyone else would have deactivated their social media, but Kate had doubled down. She reposted the worst comments, printed them off and gave them to Liam to read.

Liam got quiet when he was angry. He was silent for a long time, rifling through the pages that Kate had given him. When he finally spoke, it was to call Vincent to ask him to record an episode of the podcast they did together. He asked Niamh and Kate to join them to talk about their experience as women in the GAA. That was how the idea for the foundation came about. Liam used his connections to wrangle a slot on the biggest chat show in the country to launch it.

'I wouldn't be here if it wasn't for my daughter,' Liam said, looking out at the studio audience. 'Sometimes, the things that are closest to you are the hardest to see. Every father just wants to protect their children, and Kate opened my eyes to things I hadn't noticed before. I know I'll get a bit of backlash for doing this as well – a man helping to launch a foundation for women in sport. I know that I'm no saint in all of this. I have been as complicit in gender inequality as any other man – and some women – working within the GAA. Somehow, there are funds for men's inter-county teams to go on training camps abroad, while the women's team in the same county don't have access to proper changing room facilities. And I suppose, going back to the first time I saw Niamh play – a grown man watching a young star on the rise and wishing she was a different gender? It says a lot about the world we live in.'

The clap from the audience seemed to embarrass Liam who grimaced and shifted in his seat.

'And what was it about Niamh that told you, this girl is going to be a star?' the host asked.

'She had a magic first touch,' Liam said and Niamh blushed, feeling the eyes of the nation on her. 'The best first touch of any young person I'd ever seen.'

'Is that what you would say to any young girl or boy looking to improve their game: focus on their first touch?'

'Oh yeah, first touch is everything: the relationship between yourself, your hurley and the sliotar – that's where the power lies. That's your practice. That's your game.'

*

Liam had never touched her before that night. She wasn't a child, either, but a twenty-five-year-old adult woman. She could have said no. She could have pushed him away. Looking back, Niamh should have realised earlier. At her dad's wake, she remembered introducing Liam to a distant relative as her second father. He gave a pained smile and squeezed her hand.

It was Peter who everyone presumed was Niamh's boyfriend – Peter who stayed up with her that night to keep vigil over the coffin before Liam took over, telling them to get some sleep before the funeral; Peter who Liam began making sly digs at, scolding him for drinking so much during the wake as if Vincent wouldn't have wanted a party; Peter who Liam sent out to the yard at any given moment to feed calves or fix fences or milk cows when

Niamh wanted him there beside her; Peter who was finally looking at her the way she wanted him to – it had always been Peter.

He would have to come home from Australia for Maria's wedding. That was the first thought that Niamh had when Maria told her the news. She was on her way to work in the local primary school when Maria's name flashed up on her home screen. She tapped into the message – it was a photo of Maria and Kevin smiling at Liam's graveside. Kevin was down on one knee. The photo was accompanied by an emoji of a diamond ring and a message underneath: *So this happened! x*

Peter would have to come home for the wedding. That's all she thought about in work while her Junior Infants class were trying to spell new words:

'C-A-T.'

She was going to have to see Peter again.

'H-A-T.'

And Helen.

'R-A-T.'

And Kate.

Later that day, when she got home from school, Niamh ate her dinner quickly and went up to her room to log onto a video call with a new therapist. The serene face of a handsome older woman appeared on screen. It was difficult to put an age on Beth. Her blonde hair always looked professionally done, and she had a good skincare regime. In their first session together, Beth mentioned that she had been a nurse for years before retraining in psychology. Niamh liked Beth – she reminded her a little of Helen.

'One of my close friends, Maria, has just gotten engaged,' she said, as soon as Beth asked how she was. 'I don't know how to feel about it.'

Beth tilted her head to the side. 'Why do you think that is?'

'I don't know . . . I suppose . . . I feel a bit self-conscious at the moment. I've put on a bit of weight and the thought of trying to fit into a dress . . .'

It wasn't a lie, exactly. Niamh knew that all her nervous energy would go into trying to look her best for the wedding.

When Beth asked about her relationship with food, Niamh found herself talking about Kate.

'I wouldn't say I've ever had a problem with food. My friend Kate – that's Maria's younger sister – she had an eating disorder when we were teenagers. It was horrific. It started when we were about twelve. Kate just stopped eating altogether . . .'

Niamh still remembered the tension around the dinner table. Everyone pretending not to notice the way Kate took forever to peel her potatoes. She spent the whole meal pushing vegetables around the plate until Helen lost patience with her.

Niamh couldn't understand how Kate refused to eat anything at all, even when Helen shouted at her and threw her out to the back hall to eat by herself. There was part of Niamh that admired Kate's determination.

She came to see her eating disorder as another one of Kate's childhood games – a universe full of rules that she couldn't explain.

The therapist left some space for Niamh to come back to herself before she said, 'I notice that every time I ask you a question about yourself, we end up talking about the Foleys.'

Niamh stared into her laptop screen. They were only a few weeks into their sessions together and Niamh wanted Beth to like her. She wanted to be good at therapy, and that sometimes meant slipping into a character who was better equipped to deal with life. Beth kept telling her how self-aware she was, and how well she was doing in such a short space of time. Niamh had to remind herself that the woman didn't actually know anything about her. She had yet to explain why she was hiding from her mother in her childhood bedroom trying to talk about her life through a computer screen.

It didn't help that the therapist kept forgetting who the Foleys were. They weren't just neighbours; they were a language. They were the only way she could talk about herself.

As they scheduled in a session for next week, Niamh was already thinking about the break-up text that she'd sent the other therapists. There was always a moment, two or three sessions in, when she realised that she was leading them down the same old cul-de-sac, away from the reason she tried to reach out in the first place.

*

After it was over, Liam had gotten a cushion for her head. She was lying on the floor of the workshop with her eyes closed, pretending to be asleep, when she felt his warm, calloused hand lift up her head and place the cushion underneath her. He got his coat and put it over both of them, folding his arm around her waist and nuzzling into her hair.

She waited until she was sure he was asleep before she slid out from underneath him and felt around in the darkness for her clothes.

The sun was rising as she made her way back up the hill to her mother's house. The dawn chorus was breaking around her – she was always able to pick out the robin's song. Liam taught her how to spot it when she was younger. The robin's voice followed her – nesting in her head, even when she got into her car and turned the radio on.

She drove to a town forty minutes away to make sure she wouldn't run into anyone she knew. She was sitting in the car, waiting for the pharmacy to open, when she checked her phone and saw a message from Peter: *Where are you?* She imagined him getting home from the nightclub and sneaking into the spare room where he expected to find her.

The pharmacist brought her into a room to ask questions. He looked like the type of man who took his kids swimming and volunteered at parkruns. She came in armed with a story about a boyfriend and a split condom, but the first question he asked was when she had her last period.

After a few failed attempts of trying to get the words out, he handed her a clipboard and pen. 'I'll tell you what we'll do. You can write your answers on the form for me. Take your time and don't be worrying,' he said, smiling at her. 'You're not in any trouble. These things happen all the time.'

The following day, Niamh had gone to school as normal. It was the Monday after the big championship win and the kids were out in the yard wearing their club jerseys to celebrate their teacher bringing home the title, waving blue and white flags and banners, chanting her name as she got out of the car. 'Múinteoir Niamh! Múinteoir Niamh! Múinteoir Niamh! Múinteoir Niamh!' The crowd parted and Liam was in the middle of them, walking towards her with the cup. She took it from him and raised it into the air so the kids could cheer, feeling his hand on the small of her back.

They brought the cup around to all the classrooms. He came into the staff room at breaktime. She made an excuse to go to the bathroom to make sure they wouldn't be in there alone. When he was leaving, he looked at her with a helplessness in his eyes. She put on a smile and waved goodbye.

*

Kate was the only one who didn't ask any questions when Niamh stopped going down to training. She had moved home when she heard that Vincent was sick. She acted like it was the most natural thing in the world for her to uproot her life in Belfast to be there for her best friend. She even went as far as going back to camogie to spend more time with her. It was a novelty to see her togged out in a pair of old football boots, her blue ponytail poking out the back of an ancient helmet. There wasn't a hope of her making it onto the team, but she joined in the sessions and made sure that there were treats after training – ice creams during the cool-downs and tea and biscuits in the clubhouse after everyone had showered and changed.

Niamh had practically moved into the Foleys' house when her father was ill. Her mother had decided to drink herself through the whole thing and was becoming more and more insufferable to be around. After years of never mentioning Vincent in conversation, Mary suddenly wanted to talk about nothing else, drunkenly blaming him for destroying himself with drink. Helen had kept offering Niamh the spare room until she eventually gave in.

One night, when they had gotten back from the hospice, Helen had sent Peter up to ask if she wanted a hot water bottle.

'No, I'm all right,' Niamh said.

He feigned offence. 'That's me out of a job so.'

'I didn't think a human hot water bottle was an option,' she replied.

Peter yawned and stretched on his way out of the door. 'It's always an option. Hypothetically speaking.'

The night after they won the first round of championship, she texted him: *I think I'll need a hot water bottle tonight.*

He replied straightaway. *I've the kettle boiled.*

She came back to a hot water bottle in her bed and had to text him to clarify: *I meant the human kind.*

She heard the particular creak of his bedroom door and his footsteps across the landing. He knocked gently before he came in and got into the bed to spoon her, wrapping his arms around her waist.

They had kissed only once before when they were kids, behind the workshop in the garden. Peter was ten and she was eight. He called it a movie kiss. It didn't count because they were only pretending, he said. It was long and wet and serious, and never happened again.

Now, she found his mouth in the dark and it was happening – she couldn't believe that it was happening. She could feel him get hard. She took his hand and pulled it down between her legs.

'Are you sure?' he whispered, when she pulled down his boxer shorts and asked if he had a condom.

'Peter, please.'

He kissed her harder then, bit her bottom lip, pulled her towards him, inside, deeper until she felt the release of everything she'd ever wanted.

'Fucking hell,' he said, after it was over. 'How have we never done that before?'

He slipped out early the next morning and she woke up alone. Niamh went to work and training, visited her dad and dodged Helen's attempts to get her to eat a proper meal. She wasn't ready to sabotage her chance to be in bed every night with Peter, talking in whispers, laughing and crying into his chest. They spent every night together, right up until the night of the county final.

*

A week had passed since she had snuck out of Liam's workshop in the early hours of the morning. Peter thought that she was angry with him for not going home with her and going to the nightclub instead. When she didn't respond to his messages, he tried to call her but she didn't answer in case it was Liam ringing her again. She didn't want to talk to either of them.

Kate had invited Niamh to a housewarming party. She was moving back to Belfast. After everything her friend had done for her, the least Niamh could do was to help her move into her new home. She was half-expecting Peter to be in the passenger seat when Kate arrived outside her house to collect her. She was relieved when it was empty.

'So, what's going on with you and Peter?' Kate asked, once they hit the motorway.

'What do you mean?'

'You've gone all flirty with each other.'

Niamh pretended to be horrified. 'We're like brother and sister.'

'See, that's what I told Maria. I thought she was losing her mind when she said it to me, but she told me to watch you two together.'

'She's seeing things that aren't there,' Niamh insisted.

Kate sighed. 'Well, we've decided to give you both our blessing. We haven't told Bláith yet but she'll be happy for you too. You have three bridesmaids and sisters-in-law in waiting.'

Niamh turned her head to look out the window. If she didn't bring her hands to her face, there was a chance that Kate wouldn't be able to see the tears.

'Niamh? Oh no, it was a joke, I'm sorry. Fuck, I've done this all wrong.' She started indicating towards the hard shoulder.

'Don't pull in!' Niamh said, putting her hand on the steering wheel. 'I'm fine.'

'I'm not fine! This is not fine.'

Kate put on her hazard lights and veered off the road into a layby. The car came to a stop. She switched off the engine and turned to look at Niamh, who was wiping tears from her face now with the bottom of her T-shirt.

'You love him,' Kate said. 'You love Peter.'

Her head was about to burst. Kate was monologuing about it being a good thing.

'He's always had the worst taste in women. You'd be the first girlfriend we'd actually like. Niamh! What the fuck? How have you never told us this before?'

'This isn't about Peter.'

When Kate started to protest, she cut her off. 'I'm serious. I don't want to be in a relationship with Peter. We would kill each other.'

'That's not true,' Kate said. 'You'd be so good for him. You would be good together. And if you're worried about an awkward break-up, you know we'd choose you over him every day of the week. You're Helen Foley's favourite child, remember?'

That set her off again. She flinched when Kate tried to hug her.

'I swear to God Kate, if you repeat this conversation to anyone, I'll never speak to you again.'

'I just think—'

'Kate.'

'OK,' Kate said.

An hour later, they parked up on a curb outside a narrow, redbrick terraced house on Sunnyside Street. The door was open when they arrived, framing Ellius who was sitting on the front step of the house smoking a cigarette.

Niamh pulled down the visor and fixed her makeup in the small rectangular mirror.

'We're going to have fun tonight,' Kate told her. 'We're going to have a few drinks and forget about everything.'

Niamh often joked that Ellius asking her to dance at the céilí in the Gaeltacht remained the greatest accomplishment of her teenage years. It was like something out of an American high-school film. Every girl was dying for him to choose them, and he'd gone and made her feel like Hilary Duff. She was still weirdly grateful to him for boosting her confidence at such an awkward age. She knew that Kate was mad about him, so she turned him down. There were still times when they were drinking together that she would see something in his eyes and she'd have to tell herself to cop on. The man was a huge flirt. He was like that with everyone.

Ellius had become something of a celebrity since Niamh had last spoken to him. His music had begun to take off which hadn't come as a surprise to anyone. Hot Press described it as 'psychedelic traditional music infused with a queer sensibility.' He was busy playing gigs and festivals while still holding down a job behind the bar of a pub on the Ormeau Road.

It took a few moments for Ellius to open the garden gate by the clasp. Kate sunk into his chest and sniffed his fleece.
'Did you make the Focaccia?' she asked.
'I did,' he said. 'And there's pasta bake in the oven.'
She closed a fist in triumph.
Niamh waved awkwardly at him. The last time she'd seen him was at her father's funeral. Even then, she could see the girls from the camogie team trying to play it cool that he was there.
Ellius gave Kate a kiss on the top of her head. Niamh looked away to give them a bit of privacy. A ginger cat was sunning itself on the other side of the window.
'That's Sharon,' Ellius said. 'I named her after the local GP receptionist because she has no fucks left to give. She belongs on a sun lounger in Benidorm.'
He pulled up the sleeves of his jumper to show them the scratches Sharon had inflicted when he tried to move her from the window.
'It's my own fault. I should have known better. We're living like a divorced couple now. I have my bit of the house – she has hers.'

The cat's golden eyes were staring out at Niamh. She blinked slowly, yawned and stretched out on her back again, exposing her soft white belly to the sun.

They went to help Kate in with her bags. Niamh was lifting a box of books out of the boot of the car when her phone vibrated in her pocket again. She asked where the bathroom was and Ellius directed her upstairs. She sat on the lid of the toilet seat and looked at her phone. Messages from Liam piled up on her home screen. She couldn't bring herself to click into them.

Downstairs, Kate was stumbling over the bags that were clogging up the hall.

'What do youse want to drink?' Ellius called out from the kitchen. 'We've beer, wine, cider . . .'

'I'm grand for now,' Niamh said. 'Kate, do you need a hand up the stairs with those?'

Kate looked up at her gratefully.

'Leave the stuff there for now,' Ellius said, appearing in the doorway.

Niamh knew that Kate wanted to get her things out of the hall – she wanted to see the upstairs of their new house, to open the door to their bedroom and look out of the windows . . .

Ellius started walking towards the kitchen. Kate dropped everything and followed him.

*

The Foleys were shook the summer that Ellius showed up to the farm wearing a skirt. Helen had presumed that Kate would come home when the term finished after her final year at university in Edinburgh, but she explained that there were still a few months left on the lease of the room she rented with Ellius. Liam made half-jokes about them taking the soup and rang her every few weeks to remind her to let him know the date that he could pick them up from the airport.

Niamh arrived at the house early on a Saturday morning to welcome them home. She helped Helen set the table for breakfast. Peter came in from the yard and washed his hands at the sink. Helen got a towel off the radiator and brought it over so he could dry them. It was one of the automatic things that Helen did for everyone who set foot in her kitchen. The Foleys took it for granted, but Niamh enjoyed seeing visitors' eyes light up the first time they were handed a towel, presuming that they were getting special treatment on their trip to the farm.

They sat down for a cup of tea while they waited. Helen slid scones off the cooling rack into the wicker basket and brought them over to the table. Bláithín showed Niamh the Welcome Home poster she made. It was decorated with love hearts and glitter. It originally read WELCOME HOME ELLIUS. Helen had to ask Bláith to add her sister's name.

When Niamh reached for a scone, Helen jumped out of her seat and went to get a jar of Nutella out of the press. The Foleys had Niamh to thank for getting their mother to add it to the list of her weekly shop, a habit she kept up long after they'd grown out of their obsession with chocolate spread. Niamh still got a childhood thrill out of piercing the golden foil with the knife. The scone was still warm, crunchy on the outside and tender in the middle where the chocolate melted.

Liam beeped the horn when they came down the driveway. The pair of them looked sheepish getting out of the car. Ellius had planned on getting the bus to Belfast from the airport, but Liam met them at arrivals and talked him into staying the night on the farm. Ellius looked hungover as he got out of the car. It was only when everyone began to hug him that he seemed to wake up and remember where he was and what he was wearing – a blouse and skirt, with the remnants of makeup from the night before still on his face.

Peter was quiet at the breakfast table. Niamh helped Helen to clean up after everyone finished eating and went to find him.

He was outside whacking a sliotar against the gable end of the house. She got an old hurley out of the shed and joined him. Every time the sliotar hit the wall, it felt like it was landing inside her head.

'Did you know?' he asked.

'Know what?'

He caught the sliotar and turned to face her.

'He's bisexual,' Niamh said.

Peter went back to walloping the sliotar against the wall.

'And they're still together?'

'They're in an open relationship.'

He was putting more power into the strikes now, hitting the sliotar harder and harder so that it rebounded quicker. 'So, he goes and rides the hole off some fellas and then comes home to Kate?'

'Stop!'

'It sounds like he's getting a pretty good deal to me.'

'It's not like that. You *know* Ellius,' Niamh said.

Peter wouldn't admit it, but Ellius was one of his closest friends. He was the only man Peter could talk to without having to rely on sport as a scaffolding to hold up the conversation.

The Foleys really did believe that Ellius was the best thing that had ever happened to Kate. He was the one who saved Kate from herself. Helen credited him with looking after her in Edinburgh. Every time they came home, Niamh could see the relief on everyone's face that Kate wasn't skin and bone. She looked healthy. She was in love.

There was a tension between Liam and Ellius from the very beginning as the two men sized each other up. Ellius didn't bow to the great Farmer Foley the way most people did. If anything, he looked at the things Liam said and did with quiet suspicion. The pair of them seemed to bond over music. Liam played the accordion, and enjoyed joining in on the occasional trad session in the local pub. He got excited when he saw that Ellius had brought his fiddle back with him from Edinburgh and invited him down to the pub that evening to play a session with the lads.

Later on, Ellius changed into a black T-shirt and jeans. Liam drove the four of them – Peter, Niamh, Ellius and Kate – into town. Ellius played a few tunes with the aul lads before leaving the session early to play a game of pool with Peter.

'Where do you think you're off to?' Liam asked when Ellius stood up to put his fiddle back in its case. 'We're just getting started.'

'Ah now, Dad,' Kate said, giving Ellius a pat on the back. 'You have him worn out.'

'I do not,' Liam insisted. 'He has plenty more left in the tank.'

'It's been a pleasure playing with you, lads,' Ellius said, tipping his imaginary hat to Liam's posse of friends who were baffled that the young lad Liam had brought with him had been allowed to escape so easily.

'He's figuring out his sexuality and I need to give him space to let him do that,' Kate told Niamh, as they watched Peter and Ellius play pool on the other side of the bar. 'I just can't imagine not having him in my life. And the sex is great. It really is,' she said, looking to Niamh like she was some sort of sex umpire.

Niamh couldn't think of anyone less suited to being in an open relationship. Back in primary school, Kate got jealous whenever she caught Niamh playing with the other kids without her. Kate was a Foley though – she couldn't help but be competitive about everything, even if that meant being the best at adapting to someone else's version of reality.

Years later, Niamh could see the lengths Kate had gone to in order to live within the boundaries of Ellius' life, from the food that was in their fridge to the small talk they made with each other, using a shorthand that pushed the rest of the world away from them. Niamh noticed the way they bounced off each other as they sat down for dinner. They were halfway through the meal, going from one in-joke to another when Ellius realised that Niamh hadn't found a way into the conversation.

'How's the hamstring Niamh?' he asked as he topped up her glass of wine.

Kate shot him a look across the table.

'What?'

'She's sick of answering that question.'

'Sorry,' Ellius said, holding up a hand. 'I didn't realise—'

'It's OK,' Niamh replied. 'It'll take a few weeks to mend, but by then, the season will probably be over. I can't see us getting through to the next round.'

'We won't win the next match without Niamh, which is why everyone is obsessed with the hamstring,' Kate said.

After the county final, Niamh had sent a message into the group, reporting a fake injury. Her phone exploded with messages from people panicking. She knew that she was still expected to go down and stand on the sideline, but she couldn't do it. She couldn't even bring herself to listen to the voicemails or open any of the messages that Liam sent.

'I think it's healthy for you to take a step back,' Kate said. 'Everyone expects too much from you.'

Niamh's phone vibrated on the table. She tried to reach it but Kate got there before her.

'Why is Dad ringing you?' she asked, looking at the screen. She swiped to answer the phone and got up from the table. 'Hello, Dad? It's me. Hello?' She frowned and sat back down. 'He hung up. Why do you have seven missed calls from him? He's never called me that much in his life.'

'He's probably asking about my hamstring.'

Her phone was still unlocked in Kate's hand. She watched as Kate clicked into the messages. She watched her frown.

'What's wrong?' Ellius asked.

Niamh dived across the table but Kate wouldn't give the phone back to her. She was hunched over, staring at the screen, trying to hold Niamh off for as long as she could. It was like being at training and fighting over a sliotar. Niamh always underestimated Kate's strength. She had a tiny frame but sharp elbows and was more than able to stand her ground. Niamh ended up having to throw her on the ground and pin her down to wrestle the phone out of her hand.

'What is going on?' Ellius asked as Kate ran out of the room.

He followed her outside into the garden. Niamh watched as they argued on the other side of the window. He was trying to calm her down, but she was already walking towards the car.

Niamh paced the length of their living room. The cat jumped down from its seat at the window and started winding its way around her legs. She unlocked her phone again and scrolled through the messages on the screen.

Niamh, can we talk?

Can you please answer your phone?

Niamh, I'm sorry. I'm sorry for what happened. It was a mistake.

We can't pretend it didn't happen.

I can't stop thinking about you.

I don't know what to do.

I love you.

When Niamh was a child, a bird flew into the house and she hid in her bedroom until it was gone. Her mother was outside in the garden and didn't notice the bird going berserk inside. Niamh couldn't move from her bed, even though she wasn't the one whose sky had turned into walls. She didn't know how long she spent underneath the tent she made from her duvet, waiting for her mother to come in from the garden to open the windows and let the bird back into its own world. When she went to sleep that night, she felt its frightened wings flapping inside her head.

Chapter 5

Maiden Names

Helen

MARIA WASN'T HAPPY when Helen told her that she was going away for the weekend.

'You know our engagement party is tomorrow?' she asked, taking her frustration out on a saucepan that she was trying to shove back into the drawer. Helen had tried showing her the right way to sort the pots that would allow the drawer to close, but Maria insisted on doing things arseways.

'Parties are for young people,' Helen said. 'You wouldn't want your old relic of a mammy there anyway.'

'Well, I'm inviting the other relics. It would be nice for them to have company.'

The thought of trying to make small talk with Nan Foley made Helen want to scream.

'Where are you going?' Maria asked.

'I've booked into a B&B in Donegal.'

'What's the name of it?'

'I forget,' Helen lied.

'Well, will you keep your phone on you? We were worried about you the last time when you weren't answering. And listen, I don't mind you going away Mam, but it's just nice to have a bit of notice so I can arrange for someone to look after Aoife.'

'Bláith and Kevin managed for a few days the last time,' Helen said.

'Kevin has a job, Mam. He works from home.'

'I didn't realise that minding Aoife was such a big deal,' Helen said. 'Maybe I'll have to start charging for my services.'

Helen knew when to play her trump card. She was saving them a fortune on childcare. Kevin could somehow find it within himself to plonk his own daughter in front of the television for a couple of days and feed and water her.

She waited until Maria and Kevin had gone to bed before she started getting ready for the next day. Over the years, Helen had come to accept that living with her adult children meant sneaking around her own home. She padded downstairs in her slippers and grabbed one of Liam's old winter coats out of the press in the utility room where they kept the farm clothes.

John still used the room to change in, leaving his filthy rags for her to wash and changing into fresher clothes before going back to his own house. Maria used to tease him about letting his mammy do his laundry, but she shut up fairly quickly when Helen pointed out that she washed her clothes as well.

She opened the back door gently. The dog was curled up on the mat. His sad eyes looked up at her. She gave him a scratch behind the ears before she stepped over him and made her way to the workshop at the bottom of the garden.

It was as good a hiding place as any. Nobody went near it after Liam died. She unbolted the door and stepped inside, turning on the light. There were piles of boxes stacked on top of each other. It took some manoeuvring to work her way towards the other end of the workshop. She opened the cardboard box marked M.R. and checked that it had everything she needed. She lifted the box with both hands and made her way back towards the house to get ready for the next day.

A few months after Liam's funeral, Maria had become fixated on trying to get Helen to do things outside of the house.

'Would you not go back to the choir Mammy?' she had asked, as though it was as easy as singing a few hymns and not a cesspit of jealous bitches fighting over solos.

Maria brought home a flier for evening classes in the local secondary school and pressed it into her hands. Helen glanced through the options to humour her – Bridge for Beginners, Flower Arranging, Ballroom Dancing.

'Next stop the nursing home,' she said.

'Stop it, Mam. It will be good for you to get out and about.'

All Helen wanted to do was sit in front of the television and disappear into her phone. She'd gotten into the habit of looking up the profiles of women she'd gone to school with. She zoned out of whatever Maria was saying to scroll through Paula Nugent's photos of hiking in Glendalough.

'You could even go away for a few days,' Maria was saying. 'Treat yourself. You never really go on holidays.'

Later that night, Helen had looked up accommodation in Glendalough. It was rare for her and Liam to spend a night away. If they did, it was usually for a wedding of some young lad he used to train down the country where she knew nobody and sat like a gobdaw at some table in the far corner.

They had always booked into accommodation under Liam's name. The first time she typed *Helen Foley* into the spaces on the online booking form, it felt wrong. She tried using her maiden name, *Helen Lawlor*, and it still wasn't right. Then she tried *Paula Nugent*. It sent a thrill through her body that she couldn't explain. Playing the part of another woman – that would be the real holiday.

Helen could still remember where everyone sat in Sister Imelda's classroom. After casting Helen as Dorothy in a school production of *The Wizard of Oz,* the nun told Helen's mother that she belonged on stage. She even suggested that Helen audition for the local dramatic society, but June Lawlor sniped that her daughter was far too young to be treading the boards.

Her mother wasn't the only one who was suspicious of Sister Imelda. Most of the parents were wary of her. The other nuns could wither her with a look. She had gotten the nickname Maria von Trapp after she started making outfits for the school play.

There was a globe in the classroom on a golden stand behind her desk. When the others went out to play in the yard at break time, Helen stayed behind and asked if she could spin the globe. The nun indulged her and over time, the two of them ate their lunch together.

It felt miraculous to watch her teacher take little nibbles of a brown bread sandwich with cheese, wiping the corners of her mouth with a tissue she kept up the sleeve of her habit.

Sister Imelda always gave half of her sandwich to Helen. The bread was claggy and stuck to the roof of her mouth – it hurt when she swallowed, like she was trying to eat a sod of turf.

Helen spun the globe around and stopped it with her finger, calling out the names of the places she landed on. Sister Imelda told her about the great explorer Tom Crean's adventures in Antarctica, and Amelia Earhart who flew across the Atlantic Ocean.

'How do I get into the world?' Helen asked one day.

She could still remember the look on the nun's face.

'You're already in the world, Helen,' Sister Imelda said. 'We all are.'

Helen blinked at her, disappointed with the answer. 'It doesn't feel that way.'

Sister Imelda left at the end of the school year to go to America. That summer, a cardboard box addressed to Helen was delivered to her house. Inside, wrapped in old newspaper, was the world.

*

It was Maria who had introduced her to online shopping. Helen used to give out about the number of parcels that were being delivered to the house. The first thing she ordered was a notebook that looked like the roll book Sister Imelda kept on her desk. It was satisfying to rip open the cellophane wrapping and run her fingers over the rough surface of it. It felt like she would open it to find her old classroom inside.

There were twenty-one girls in the class. It took Helen a few days to remember them all. A name would come to her as she made a cup of tea or took a load out of the washing machine and she'd do a shuffle in her slippers to celebrate. She filled in the names of her former classmates in Irish on the left and English on the right, placing the notebook in the middle of *The Irish Times* so that if anyone came into the room, she could hide it in a flurry of pages.

She stole snatches of time away from her day sitting at the kitchen table trying to glean as much information as she could about her old classmates. Some of them settled down locally and became neighbours that she'd run into in a shop, and either pretend not to notice or exchange a few pleasantries with. Even when they did get to chatting, they spoke about the weather, their children and grandchildren – hardly anything about themselves.

There were the girls who left town that she knew very little about, so she filled in the blanks. She gave them nice husbands. She had a soft spot for Fred, the owner of an antique shop in Tipperary – he was entirely imaginary, but Michael, the sheep farmer who climbed Mount Everest for Down Syndrome Ireland, was based on an actual husband.

She wanted the women to be happy. It was fun to browse clothes she would never dream of wearing and better still to add them to her basket. She went from looking over her shoulder while entering the three little numbers on the back of her credit card to allowing the tablet to automatically fill in her details for her without even blinking an eye. The orders were placed in Maria's name so that when the delivery man arrived with the packages, she could shake her head and throw out the same line about her daughter spoiling herself again.

Sister Imelda's roll book was filled with ideas for trips away – menus that she'd printed from the internet for fancy restaurants where she would dine alone. She imagined ordering things she'd never dream of eating – oysters! Steak! – while doing a crossword in *The Irish Times*, because that's the kind of thing Monica McManus who she'd sat beside in sixth class would do, looking over her reading glasses at couples and families in the restaurant as they wondered, who *was* this mysterious woman who dared to take up a table for two, who didn't feel a stab of loneliness every time the waiter took the extra setting away.

The evening she sat down to meditate, Helen wasn't sure what to expect. She was curious to see what Anne-Marie Hinchy got out of it. Anne-Marie was a bit of a whinger in school, always giving out about things not being fair.

No one would ever have guessed that she'd end up having a successful career as a psychotherapist.

Helen listened to an interview that she did on a podcast. It was only when Anne-Marie's husband died that she discovered therapy and trained in psychology while raising two small children.

When the interviewer asked her how she did it all, she said, 'I do nothing. Some people call it meditation. I call it doing nothing. For ten minutes, every day, I sit down, close my eyes, and do nothing at all.'

Helen propped up the pillows on her bed and scrolled past videos of pretty girls in their twenties sitting cross-legged on cushions until she found an Indian man with a baritone voice and a beautiful smile.

Before he began the meditation, he told her that it was normal for her mind to wander.

'Keep coming back to the breath,' he said.

She thought she made a good stab at it for the first minute or so, but soon her mind shot off in all different directions. Her tooth was killing her. The last time she went to the dentist, he told her she needed a root canal. It didn't seem fair that she had to fork out an arm and a leg when she brushed her teeth every morning and night. Liam's teeth were awful. He had a plate of false teeth he used to flick in and out at the dinner table which always made her stomach turn. He thought he was being funny, but it scared the wits out of the grandchildren. The bins needed to be put out – she was the only one who ever remembered to do them – and she needed to take beef out of the freezer for the stew she promised Nan and she hated meditation. She hated herself, hated the kind of rubbish that came to mind when she could be thinking about something nice – something else . . .

She paused the video and went to find a silk scarf that seemed like something Anne-Marie might wear. She draped the scarf around her shoulders before coming back to the man who was frozen on the screen. She pressed play. This time, she closed her eyes and tried to imagine what it was like to be Anne-Marie.

It was an exercise in empathy. That was what she told herself. She still went to confession, but never told Father Angelo anything about her trips away. Instead, she admitted that she didn't visit her mother as much as she should, and the priest nodded his head in sympathy.

The last time Helen took her mother out of the nursing home was for her birthday. It didn't get any easier seeing her sitting lopsided in the wheelchair, a blanket taut across her knees. The nurse gave Helen a plastic bag with nappies and wipes and gave instructions on what to do if Mrs Lawlor became agitated.

June Lawlor hadn't spoken in years, but Helen thought she might get a smile out of her if she made her favourite roast dinner. The gravy ran down her chin and Helen wasn't quick enough to catch it with the serviette before it stained her blouse. June stared off into space as Maria and John tried to introduce her to their kids, while Helen wiped spittle away from her mother's mouth.

Maria came with her to drop her back to the nursing home in time for supper.

'Lord have mercy,' June said, as they lifted her into the passenger seat of the car.

The receptionist asked them to sign her back in. A laminated sheet of paper in the elevator advised them to seek a member of staff if a resident was in the lift unattended.

'Promise me I'll never end up like that,' Helen said, reaching over to grab the sleeve of Maria's coat on the way home in the car.

'Of course you won't,' Maria said, as if she could do anything about it.

June had stopped leaving the house after her husband died. Whenever Helen tried to suggest doing something, she would shake her head and say, 'That wouldn't be for me now.' Helen noticed the way that her mother spoke about herself, batting away compliments as though they disgusted her. She didn't have friends. Helen didn't have friends either, but she was an only child. She was used to playing by herself.

Chapter 6

The Scribbeen

Niamh

ON THE TUESDAY EVENING before Maria's engagement party, Maria and Bláithín were in Niamh's sitting room watching *The Great British Bake Off*. They were tucking into homemade scones when Maria asked, 'You're coming on Saturday, aren't you?'

Niamh pressed her lips together.

'We're not going through this again, are we? Everyone will be buzzing to see you.' By everyone, Maria meant the camogie team that Niamh had left without much of an explanation three years ago.

'They're well within their rights to hate me,' Niamh said. 'I would hate me.'

'The way you're carrying on you'd swear you killed someone. Niamh, we don't care if you don't pick up a hurley again in your life – I mean, that's a lie, we do care, but we just want you to be happy.'

It was nearly impossible for Niamh to leave the house without seeing one of her old teammates. They always waved hello. She taught some of their kids and had to sit through parent-teacher meetings like nothing had changed.

Maria turned to face her on the couch. 'I just know that Mam is going to make up some excuse not to be there. John is busy with cows calving and Nadine is as odd as two left feet. Peter's on the other side of the world and Bláith might as well be,' she said, nodding to her sister who was sitting on the other side of Niamh, lost in the algorithm of her phone. 'Kate's coming down for it and I *know* she's a pain in the hole, but she's our pain in the hole. You can't ignore each other forever.'

It was obvious that Niamh and Kate had fallen out, but no one knew exactly what had happened. Niamh maintained a stoic silence whenever Kate was brought up in conversation. The more time that passed, the less patience Maria had for the situation.

'I'll think about it,' Niamh said.

'Great.' Maria reached across to squeeze her hand. 'Thank you.'

On Saturday morning, Niamh had gotten a phone call from Maria. The teenager who had agreed to babysit Aoife had gotten a last-minute ticket to a festival and had cancelled on her.

That afternoon, Maria arrived on Niamh's doorstep with her daughter in tow, launching into an impromptu re-enactment of something Aoife had said with the manic energy of a comedian trying out new material.

'Mammy and Daddy are not getting married,' she said, dropping the overnight bag on the floor and looking down at Aoife who had wrapped herself around her leg. 'Aoife is getting married, isn't she?'

Niamh squatted down on her hunkers, but Aoife turned her face away.

'I don't know why she's gone all shy now. She has been telling everyone she's going to play with her Auntie Ni-Ni. Are you going to tell Auntie Ni-Ni who you're marrying?'

Aoife held tighter onto Maria's leg.

'Jesus,' Maria said. 'She's going to marry Jesus, Auntie Ni-Ni.'

'At least he's single,' Niamh reasoned.

'Do you think he'll come down off the cross for it?'

'Stop laughing at me!' Aoife shouted, squeezing her eyes shut.

'I might have a surprise for Aoife,' Niamh said.

The little redhead opened one eye. 'You have a prize for me?'

'Only if you're a good girl, isn't that right, Auntie Ni-Ni?' Maria said.

Niamh bent down and whispered, 'It's that way,' pointing to the direction of the sitting room. Aoife sped off in the direction of her surprise.

'You're coming down later?' Maria asked.

It wasn't so much a question as it was a threat. The plan was for Niamh to ask Mary to keep an eye on Aoife so that she could go down to the party for a while.

Maria sighed. 'I was going to wait until tonight but I suppose now is as good a time as any.'

She reached into her handbag and pulled out a white shoebox with Niamh's name written on the outside in gold. Inside was a mini bottle of prosecco, a scented candle and photos of them together through the years. *Will you be my bridesmaid?* was written in gold letters on the inside.

Niamh knew the reaction Maria wanted and tried her best to give it to her.

'Mammy!' Aoife burst into the kitchen, crashing a glittery pink wheelbarrow into the fridge. 'Look what Auntie Ni-Ni got me!'

Niamh spent the evening zooming Aoife around in the wheelbarrow in the back yard, bending over to nurse a stitch while her little drill sergeant shouted at her to go again.

Her mother came out of hiding to call them in for supper. She made Bird's Eye waffles and fish fingers with baked beans, the Friday night dinner Niamh used to love as a kid.

'Thanks Mam, you shouldn't have,' Niamh said, somehow annoyed at the show of kindness.

Aoife was sitting on Mary's lap, telling her all about playschool and giving her gardening tips while shovelling waffles and beans into her mouth.

'What's wrong with the fish fingers?' Mary asked. 'You haven't touched them.'

'Fish don't have fingers, you silly goose!' Aoife replied.

Mary started to tickle her. 'Who – are – you – calling – a – silly – goose?!'

'YOU!' Aoife squealed in between peals of laughter.

It was all going so well until Mary kept insisting that Aoife have just one bite of a fish finger. Once Aoife realised that it wasn't a game anymore, she started to cry.

'I'm too old for this,' Mary said, passing the screaming child over to Niamh. Aoife wriggled so much that it was impossible to hold her in her arms.

The moment her feet touched the ground, she ran towards the back door like it was a hostage situation, roaring for her mammy. Her little lungs worked as hard as they could as she tried her best to beat the door down.

'You're better off leaving her out there,' Mary called from the kitchen.

Niamh helped her mother clean off the table. Every few seconds, Mary tutted at the ear-piercing screams that were coming from the back hall.

Niamh remembered all the times her mother left her in the hall when she couldn't stop crying – how once, in the middle of the night, she had walked down the hill to the Foleys' house, the grass of the verges wet against her bare feet and the night air rushing through her pyjamas. She remembered the happy sound of the doorbell. Helen's face when she answered the door. The smell of her hair when she hugged her.

Eventually, Aoife began to hiccup. Tears ran down her ruddy cheeks, a deluge of snot streaming from her nose to her top lip. Niamh scooped the child up in her arms and made her way upstairs to her bedroom.

Her mother disappeared into the sitting room. Niamh imagined her heading straight to the cupboard where she kept the wine. Mary would deny that she hid the bottles. She chose not to chill the white wine in the fridge, even though whenever she had a glass with dinner, she always remarked that it was nice and cold.

Sometimes she drank a bottle a night, and two or three bottles at the weekend. There were the weeks when it seemed like she didn't drink at all, but it was hard to know. They were never the type of family to keep drink in the house, not like the Foleys who seemed to have a never-ending supply of the stuff. Helen was the only non-drinker in the family. It always seemed like there was a story behind her abstinence, but Niamh knew better than to ask.

A bowl of chocolate ice cream and a few episodes of *Peppa Pig* later, Aoife was feeling like herself again. They were sitting on Niamh's bed. She was beginning to get a cramp in her arm from holding the phone.

It was coming up to bedtime and Aoife wanted to go outside again. When Niamh suggested changing into her pyjamas, she began to roar the house down.

'Look who I have!' Niamh said, taking the teddy out of the overnight bag and waving it in front of her.

'Gwandad!' Aoife reached for the teddy. 'Auntie Ni-Ni! This is my Gwandad Liam. Would you like to say hello to Gwandad?' she asked, holding the bear out to her.

Niamh made the most of the moment of stillness to put the pyjama top over her head, before Aoife wriggled away to play with the soul of her dead grandad.

The overnight bag Maria had packed for Aoife smelled of childhood. There was a part of Niamh that wanted to crawl inside and fall asleep in it. The Foleys smelled like hurling. They smelled of sweat and wet grass and muck and long evenings down the pitch.

She loved them all. John and Maria were older and treated Niamh like the rest of their siblings. When Maria was in a good mood, she had let Niamh, Kate and Bláithín try on the clothes in her wardrobe and the heels she kept under her bed.

The best person to play with was Peter. They built their own den using things they found in the scrapheap in the yard, and spied on everyone including the cows, who they pretended were aliens biding their time, planning a hostile takeover of humankind.

They once made up a game called roller-ball, a cross between rollerblading and basketball, and got caught in the rhythm of gliding around each other wearing a rollerblade each, one foot on wheels, the other ready to brake and take a shot.

They played until it got dark and Helen called them in for their dinner. Niamh watched Peter gulp down a pint of water in the kitchen, his chest heaving, sweat dripping down his forehead. Helen asked Niamh if she wanted beans with her dinner and caught her eye just as the thought of kissing Peter was all that was there. She saw it and smiled at her.

*

'Would you not go down for an hour?' her mother asked once she put Aoife to bed.

Niamh said that she had nothing to wear.

Mary made a face. 'And you're happy to be used as a babysitting service?'

'I offered,' Niamh said.

They were in the sitting room watching the nine o'clock news. Mary stood up and pulled the curtain to stop the glare of the sun on the television screen. Her glass of wine was strategically placed out of sight on the floor beside the couch. She hadn't taken a sip from it since Niamh came into the room and set up the baby monitor on the mantelpiece.

'I just think it would be good for you to get out of the house,' Mary said.

'I'll go for a walk tomorrow,' Niamh replied.

Her phone vibrated in her pocket. It was a message from someone she'd matched with on a dating app a few weeks ago. *Stephen has sent you a new message.* She clicked into the conversation thread: *Yet another one I have to unmatch because she's lost the ability to speak.*

She tapped into his profile. He played hurling and liked her profile picture – a photo of her and Liam in the pub after the county final holding the cup. Niamh hated that photograph. She hated that she was too competitive not to catfish men with the thinnest version of herself.

Is that Farmer Foley?

What a legend.

Did you know him?

She got off the couch and put her ear to the baby monitor to listen to Aoife's little snores. Peter Foley's sandy head popped up on her screen. He was on a beach. There was a crowd behind him, three men and two blonde women in bikinis. She liked the photo and tried to forget about it.

The weatherman was smoothing the palm of his hand over a map of Ireland like it was the rump of a horse.

Peter replied straightaway with a photo of a building site. *Back to the grind. Hope you're having a great night.*

'I might go down for an hour,' Niamh said. 'Would you mind keeping an eye on the monitor?'

'Of course,' Mary said. 'Are you OK?'

'Yeah.' Niamh sighed, getting up off the couch. 'Why wouldn't I be?'

*

When she was in primary school, Niamh used to pretend to be sick so that she could go to the Foleys' house and have Helen all to herself. Within minutes of her mother dropping her off, Helen would set her up on the couch with the Looney Tunes sleeping bag, a pink frilly pillow behind her head and a hot water bottle tucked under her arm.

Helen never turned on the television during the day, even when someone was really sick, so there was nothing to do except lie there. On the other side of the sitting room was an out-of-tune piano – a casualty of a local pub. Most of the keys were broken. The owner was throwing it out and Liam brought it home with the intention of fixing it up. When Niamh lifted the lid, it smiled out at her like a pensioner hanging onto the last of their teeth.

Next to the piano was an antique globe that seemed so out of place it might as well have been beamed down from outer space. Helen used to give out to the others for messing with it, but turned a blind eye when Niamh was there on her own.

Niamh spun it around faster and faster and faster – the colours flying past her eyes. She used the tip of her fingernail to lightly touch the paper to slow it down. It always got sucked into the golden circle that held the world in place. She tried pulling away before it bit her, but she was never quick enough. She wondered if Helen ever spun the world around like she did – if it ever bit the fingers off her.

Niamh loved the way time moved through the house. Morning came wrapped in the smell of freshly baked brown bread and scones. Helen set the breakfast table for the men coming in from the milking parlour. Once Niamh heard the muffled sounds of Vincent and Liam's voices in the kitchen, she rushed to the radiator to try and warm her face before Helen came in with the thermometer to check on her.

They used to play a game called Our News. Helen hung a felt poster on the wall. It was Niamh's job to fill in the blanks by choosing from the words in the pouch and sticking them onto the poster by their Velcro backs: TODAY IS <u>MONDAY.</u> IT IS A <u>CLOUDY</u> DAY . . .

Niamh played the same game in school, but everyone had to take it in turns to stick the words on the poster. The teacher wouldn't move on with the class until Niamh said the words out loud. Helen never made her say or do anything.

'You're a topper,' Helen would say whenever Niamh did anything to help around the house. The others made fun of her for sucking up to their mother. It was because of Helen that the Foleys were able to say that they loved each other in such a casual way. They all hugged hello and goodbye like it was normal for love to be easy.

*

It had been three years since Niamh had last stepped inside the Foleys' house. As she walked down the hill to Maria's engagement party, she had an aerial view of the garden. There were people out the back, sitting on the patio. She caught sight of a figure at the side of the house, smoking. She wasn't close enough to tell for sure, but she was nearly certain it was Ellius.

It was Ellius who told her about Liam. She had woken up on his couch in Belfast to the sound of him on the phone to Kate. She'd stayed up most of the night imagining Kate driving back down the motorway, arriving home and ... what? She knew that Kate would confront Liam. She imagined her screaming in the kitchen in front of Helen, and Peter, Maria, John, and even Bláithín – she saw the disbelief in their eyes, their confusion settling into disgust. She checked her phone again. Nothing. Not even another message from Liam, but she could tell by the panic in Ellius' voice that something was wrong.

'I'll drive Niamh home,' he was saying. 'I'll drive Niamh home. I'll wake her now. We'll see you soon.'

Niamh climbed the stairs and saw him pacing back and forth on the landing, running his hands through his hair.

'What happened?' she asked.

She could see the panic in his face.

'I think . . . I just need to drive you home.'

'Ellius, tell me what happened.'

She couldn't remember much after that, apart from begging him not to make her go into the house. He placated her like he was talking to a toddler. 'I won't make you do anything. I'll bring you home, OK?'

He didn't understand that her mother's house had never been home.

The back door of the Foleys' house still creaked when Niamh opened it. In all the time she'd spent running in and out of the farmhouse, she hadn't noticed the way Jesus stared down at her. She squinted up at the writing in the top right-hand corner:

I will bless the home in which the image of my Sacred Heart shall be exposed and honoured.

The Sacred Heart was oblivious to the craic that was thumping against the pane of glass in the door that separated them, or the way her own heart was punching its way out of her chest.

The door was flung open and the flood of noise spilled out into the hall. Kate was carrying a small dog and stopped in her tracks when she saw her.

They looked at each other for a split second before Maria appeared behind her sister.

'You made it!' Maria pushed past Kate to give her a hug.

'You look beautiful,' Niamh said, making sure to admire the outfit Maria had tormented herself for weeks over, finally landing on a white corseted top and tulle skirt.

'I'm overdressed,' she said.

'You can't be overdressed at your own engagement party,' Niamh told her.

She looked over her shoulder, but Kate and the dog had gone.

'Come with me.' Maria took her by the hand. 'Guess who's here?' she announced to the room.

Niamh didn't know what she expected to happen when she walked in. She didn't have time to process seeing all her former teammates together before they flew towards her, hoisted her up on their shoulders and started parading her around the place.

The chaos carried her through the house. They passed Jesus showing off his wounds in the back hall – he looked, now, like he'd been injured during a Junior B hurling match and was disappointed at being taken off.

Niamh ducked her head under the doorframe. Josie and Lynn, who she'd hurled with since Junior Infants, led the charge out into the back garden, where Kevin and his friends were sitting eating burgers and drinking beer, looking on in amusement, phones raised to record the commotion as they kept going past the workshop, through the gap in the hedges and out into the open fields.

The girls let her back down onto the ground once they got to the shed, where they'd stashed their gear bags. They all scattered and started changing into training gear. Niamh stood there watching them until Maria handed her a hurley and an old helmet, along with a bag with everything she needed.

'If Muhammad won't go to the mountain, then the mountain must come to Muhammad,' Maria said, bending down on one knee and holding the stick out to her.

Niamh took the hurley and sat down on a bench.

About a decade ago, Liam had refurbished an old cattle shed so that it looked like the inside of a changing room, with wooden benches and hook rails all along the walls. Niamh felt like she'd arrived back into her teenage years. Mags sat beside her and gave her shoulder a reassuring squeeze. They were used to sharing a quiet corner of the dressing room while the rest of the girls blasted the tunes on the speaker, and gave each other piggybacks, shouting over each other.

Niamh ran her fingers down the ash in her hand. Maria knew the kind of hurley she liked – thirty-two inches with a bit of a spring in it and a groove halfway down the handle where the grip ended. The groove in the hurley was an old superstition. The best hurley she'd ever played with had a chip in it. She'd asked Liam to put a hollow in every stick that came after it. During a tough training session or match, she'd rub her thumb over the groove – it helped her focus. She wondered how Maria got her hands on this one – if she got John down to the workshop to shave it down to her specifications. She wouldn't have put it past her.

It was a pre-match ritual to go down the Scribbeen and have a puck around the night before a big game. Liam turned the field into a training pitch. The Scribbeen sessions began at dusk where they established a rhythm, repeating a combination of passes that continued as the light faded and they got used to finding each other in the dark.

The night before the county final, they sat on the grass listening to Liam who was leaning on a hurley like it was a walking stick.

'This field is called the Scribbeen,' he said. 'Scribbeen is an old Irish word for a small strip of bad farming land. Generations of hard work have transformed this little field. Lots of hands had to get dirty before we ever set foot in the place and the same can be said about hurling. A swing of a hurley can cut through time. It's one of the few tangible connections we have to our past, present and future, one that you can feel with every puck of the ball.'

Niamh looked around the dressing room and realised that Maria had choreographed her engagement party around getting a hurley back into her hands. She felt sick at the thought of letting them down again even though she was there now, in the middle of them all.

Maria led them out of the dressing room into the deepening blue of the evening. Kate and Ellius stood on the sidelines with a few other spectators who had come to watch. Nan Foley was directing one of Kevin's friends as to where to set up the picnic chairs she'd brought with her.

'Speeeeeech,' the girls prompted and Maria waved her hands to quieten them.

'I was trying to think of a way to celebrate my engagement to Kevin—' she paused and waited for the cheers and the wolf-whistles to die down. 'I knew I wanted to have a party at home. These last few years have been tough and we need each other to get through the bad times as well as celebrate the good. There are two men missing today. I can actually hear Dad and Vincent in my head every time we come down here to have a puck around. I can't think of a better way of honouring two legends of the game.'

The team formed a circle and put their hurleys in, one on top of each other, ready to do the same chant that they'd been doing since they were seven years old, slapping their hurleys together. 'Three, two, one, Brigid's!' they shouted, raising the hurleys into the air and breaking away to take their places in the field.

Niamh looked down at the hurley in her hand like it was a phantom limb. She tried a few swings on the grass, feeling the weight of the helmet on her head. The bars on the face guard were making her cross-eyed. A wave of panic rose in her chest as she looked over to the sideline and saw Kate and Ellius huddled together watching her. She couldn't do it. It was time to stop pretending that she could.

She was about to take off her helmet when Maria sent a high ball into the air. Niamh's hand flew up, reaching to remember what it was like to pick a sliotar out of the sky. Her fingers closed around the feeling that she brought down to her chest. Josie called for the sliotar across the field. Niamh swung the hurley and connected with a power that ricocheted through her body and back into her life again.

Chapter 7

Love Me Tender Guesthouse

Helen

It was late by the time Helen arrived at the Love Me Tender Guesthouse. She parked on the gravel and turned off the ignition, interrupting the automated voice that was congratulating her on reaching her destination. She glanced at the notifications in the family WhatsApp group. Maria's engagement party was in full swing. She zoomed in on one photo – Kate with a dog in her arms *inside* the house, in Helen's good room. She took a deep breath and put her phone on airplane mode.

She dragged her suitcase across the gravel towards the conservatory at the front of the house and searched for a doorbell. After a couple of minutes of knocking, she tried the door which slid open with a shush.

'Hello?' she called out, stepping into the hall.

A life-sized cutout of Elvis in a Hawaiian shirt was holding a sign that read *Aloha*. She wheeled her suitcase past him into a living room where a black and white film was playing on the television.

On the screen, a man smoking a cigarette walked into a cabaret club and handed his hat to a girl in a cloakroom. A piano was introducing a song, and the camera panned to Elvis on stage dressed as a busboy with a brass band playing behind him.

Just as Elvis opened his mouth to sing, a man wearing a tricolour conquistador jumpsuit sprang up from behind a couch.

'Jesus Christ!' Helen exclaimed, her hand flying to her chest.

The man seemed to mistake this for swooning, and tried his best to maintain eye contact as he channelled Elvis from the television into his sitting room. Helen didn't know where to look. He was singing about being trouble when a shout came from upstairs.

'Shut up Dennis!'

'You'll have to excuse Priscilla,' the man said in a dodgy drawl, swinging his hips towards her. 'She don't like me talkin' to other girls.'

As he thrusted in her direction, the brass band kicked in and he took her by the hand to dance. He was twirling her around when the music came to a stop.

'Dennis! What the fuck are you at?' A woman in a dressing gown stood beside the television with her hands on her hips.

'I'm welcoming the guest,' he said.

The woman looked at Helen with the same panic in her eyes as Liam had when he saw that cattle had broken out of a field. 'I am so sorry about him,' she said, dragging him away. 'We didn't think you were coming so I went to bed. I didn't count on this eejit staying up and scaring you half to death.'

Elvis threw his hands in the air in exasperation. 'It's called the Love Me Tender Guesthouse. People are expecting to be entertained!'

Helen gave them a tight smile.

'You must be tired,' the woman said, coming over to take her suitcase. 'I'll show you to your room.'

Helen followed the woman upstairs, leaving Elvis alone in the dark.

The bedroom was smaller than it looked from the photos on the website.

'Sorry about that,' the woman said, leaving her suitcase down at the end of the four-poster bed. 'I'm Judy, by the way.'

'Mary,' Helen said.

'Nice to meet you Mary. I'll leave you to get settled in. If you hear any commotion in the morning it's only the peacocks. They aren't usually this noisy but it's mating season.'

Helen found herself nodding along like they were talking about a spell of bad weather.

It was only when Judy left that she was able to take in the rest of the room. A vase of oxeye daisies sat on a bedside table and a portrait painting of Elvis hung over the bed. He was in full performance mode, swinging his hips, tilting the microphone away from him. When she looked closer, she realised it wasn't Elvis at all, but the man downstairs.

The peacocks did wake her in the morning. Their honks made her feel like she was somewhere more exotic than Donegal. Helen hadn't slept much during the night. She stayed up watching Meryl Streep interviews, videos she'd seen so many times before that she could recite the answers along with her.

She spent a long time getting ready in the ensuite bathroom, fixing herself in front of the mirror.

'Hello,' she said to her reflection in a voice she'd been practicing for weeks. 'Mary. Mary Ryan.'

It took her a while to realise it was the energy behind the words that she needed to change. Mary wasn't like most women. She didn't have the involuntary urge to placate whoever happened to be around her. It didn't matter if she was talking to a bank manager or a child – her voice stayed the same.

The smell of bacon wafted through the house as Helen made her way downstairs. The place was messier in the daylight. She tiptoed her way around cardboard boxes full of Elvis trinkets and piles of books into the living room.

Judy came out of saloon doors with a spatula in her hand. 'Breakfast is ready when you are.'

Helen followed her through the swinging doors into a kitchen that looked like the inside of an American diner.

'This looks great,' Helen said, sitting down to admire the spread on the vinyl gingham tablecloth. She didn't know why she thought the fry would be soaked in grease.

'Have you come far?' Judy asked.

There was a pause when Helen mentioned the town.

'I grew up there,' Judy said. 'Did you go to the convent?'

Helen felt her stomach drop to the floor. 'I did.'

'What's your maiden name?'

'Crowley,' Helen said.

'Mary Crowley, Mary Crowley . . . Jesus, the amount of Marys in there, you'd hardly move for them. That place was a loony bin.'

'I loved school,' Helen admitted.

'You must have been one of the good ones,' Judy said. 'I haven't met anyone from home in a long time.'

She walked over to the ironing board to where layers of Elvis lay crumpled in a laundry basket, waiting to be straightened out.

'How did you end up in Donegal?' Helen asked, desperate to change the subject.

'I met Dennis in London,' Judy said, running the iron along the seam of a pair of pink suit pants. 'Don't worry, he's not going to jump out at you this morning. He's away down at the nursing home to try and scare the Alzheimer's out of them. He puts on a show every Saturday. I'm not sure who's humouring who at this stage. I'm sorry about last night. He promised me he'd stop doing it. I left him to check in guests on his own before and they called the guards on him.'

'No!'

'The man accused Dennis of manhandling his wife, whatever that means. Sure, the guards knew what the craic was. They called up to the house for a cup of tea anyway.'

A bang at the window made them both jump.

'Vernon!' Judy shouted at a peacock that was rapping on the glass with his beak. The bird recoiled its long blue neck and tilted its head to the side. Judy closed the gingham curtains before Helen could get a better look at it.

'I swear to God, he sees his reflection in the window and turns into Robert De Niro. We should have named him Travis Bickle.'

'How many do you have?' Helen asked.

'Just two. Vernon and Gladys – the happy couple. Are you married yourself?'

'Separated,' Helen said.

'Any kids?' Judy asked, setting herself up behind the ironing board again.

'A girl – well, woman. All grown up now. Do you have any children?'

'Not unless you count The Colonel,' Judy said, pointing to a Persian cat curled up on a rocking chair that Helen hadn't noticed amongst the clutter. 'I'd love a daughter. I always wanted kids. It was Dennis who didn't want them, but you know yourself.' She paused, lifting up the iron to let it breathe. 'You can't have everything.'

*

Back in her room, Helen paced back and forth. Judy didn't seem to recognise her. Mary was booked in to stay another night. It would seem suspicious if she left now.

Mary Crowley was the biggest Elvis fan she knew. When they were teenagers, she told Helen that she kept the cover of his record underneath her bed so she could kiss him every night before she went to sleep.

Elvis wasn't the only older man that Mary spoke about with a reverence that Helen didn't understand. Her older brothers were on the hurling team, and fourteen-year-old Mary had her heart set on Liam Foley. Helen was sick of him before she ever laid eyes on the boy, and when she did, she wasn't that impressed.

'He's a big nose,' she said, when Mary pointed him out to her after mass.

Vincent was the handsome one. He'd a strong jawline and beautiful brown eyes. She could understand why all the girls were mad about him. It was only when Mary took her to a hurling match and she saw Liam play that she began to understand the kind of magic that settled around him.

They waited years for either Liam or Vincent to notice them. Helen was doing her teaching training when she began to feel Liam looking at her during mass. He was twenty-four and she was nineteen. The first time he asked her to dance, he took her hand in disbelief like he couldn't believe she was real.

Helen had only gone out with Liam to impress Mary. If she was being honest, she didn't know the extent to which she fell in love with Liam to spite her best friend.

Vincent and Mary got together around the same time. They ended up having a double wedding. Liam had talked her into it and then left her to fight with Mary over every last detail. Mary made sure the train of her dress was longer, and that she had an extra tier on her wedding cake.

Liam didn't tell her where they were going on honeymoon but let slip that a Franciscan friar had offered them a place to stay. She was expecting someplace in Italy, not the arsehole of Donegal in the rain. When the four of them arrived, they were shown to two small rooms, each with a pair of single beds that looked like coffins. All they could do was laugh.

Vincent and Mary spent a lot of time in their bedroom. Liam was patient with her. They hadn't done anything besides kiss and cuddle. She was still trying to get over the shock of seeing him naked. She'd never seen a penis before. She didn't know that they were able to stand up by themselves. Helen tensed up when he tried to go further and he listened to her, bringing his hands back above her waist. When it finally happened, she heard the chime of a bell in the church tower. She lay back on the pillow and imagined a man in a robe pulling a rope in celebration that there was nothing wrong with her.

It lashed rain on the second day of the honeymoon. They stayed in bed all afternoon. In the evening, they heard the news that Vincent's sister had given birth to a baby girl. The boys went down to the pub to wet the baby's head. Helen feigned a headache and Mary stayed behind with her.

Helen was under the covers with pillows plumped behind her, feeling the weight of Mary sitting at the foot of the bed.

'Well?' Mary asked. 'How did it go?'

'What?'

'The sex?'

Helen burst into tears.

'I'll be fine,' she said. 'It's just . . . I don't know what I was expecting.'

'My first time with Vincent wasn't great,' Mary said. 'It gets better.'

Helen sighed. 'Kissing is enough for me. I can't do the rest of it.'

'Just kiss then.'

'No, I know he wants to do more.'

'Listen to me,' Mary said, taking her by the hand. 'You're *Helen Lawlor*. Look at me.'

Helen looked into Mary's eyes and remembered her first-ever kiss. Mary had made the argument that they needed to practice if they were going to land a man worth having, and they couldn't practice with other boys in case they got a reputation. They spent hours in Mary's bedroom with only an Elvis poster as their witness. Those memories had remained locked away until that moment, when they came spilling onto the single bed of the monastery. She could see it in Mary's eyes, until she pulled her hand away.

'Right, I'm going to head down to the pub,' Mary said. 'Are you coming?'

'No, I'll stay put,' Helen replied.
'OK. Don't be sad, all right?'

Helen heard them coming back from the pub late that night. It was Vincent's singing that woke her. Mary tried to shush him, but Vincent insisted on saying goodnight to the whole monastery. Helen waited for Liam to come to bed. It was quiet. Then, she heard whispering. She got out of bed and opened the door. The hushed voices stopped for a moment before starting again.

Mary and Liam were arguing. She couldn't hear what they were saying, but if she crouched down, she could make out their silhouettes through the crack in the door. Mary turned to go, but Liam grabbed her by the hand and pulled her towards him. They started kissing.

Helen backed away from the door. It was relief, she decided – proof that she wasn't going crazy. She got into bed and waited for her husband to come back to her.

Whatever went on between Liam and Mary didn't last long. There was no way of knowing what exactly happened, but Helen could take a good guess that it was Liam's idea to break things off. That didn't mean that there weren't other women over the years. Helen got used to smelling them on Liam's clothes. The truth was that she didn't mind what he was doing, as long as he was careful about it. Liam knew how much she hated sex, so he outsourced the problem. He didn't make a show of her. Not like poor Vincent who couldn't keep it in his pants. Everyone knew about that. As soon as he got a drink into him, he'd throw himself at anything with a pulse down the pub. It was Niamh that Helen used to feel sorry for. Mary had made her own bed. She could lie in it.

*

When Judy asked her what her plans were for the day, Helen told her that she was going to the friary.

'That's a bit of a drive from here,' Judy said. 'Mind yourself.'

Whenever Helen went away, she tried to do at least one thing that she would never dream of doing herself. Mary Ryan didn't do very much anymore, but one thing Helen knew for sure was that Mary was a terrible driver. It was an effort, at first, to take her eyes off the road and let them wander towards the views of the mountains, the purple heather in the fields, but soon, she found herself swerving at the last minute to avoid hitting sheep.

Spending time with Mary Ryan had never been easy. Everything they did turned into a competition. They got pregnant around the same time, but Mary had a miscarriage. Helen couldn't help but feel guilty when John was born, and then Maria and Bláithín. She was so relieved when Mary's pregnancy finally stuck and Niamh came along. She offered to mind her when she went back to work in the bank and Mary took her up on it, dropping her off at the crack of dawn and leaving it until late in the evening to pick her up again.

When the girls were about six, Mary tried to convince her to go back to work again. They were in the kitchen. All four of the girls had gotten head lice from school. Helen was after spending hours dosing their scalps and combing through strands of hair to find the fuckers. Niamh was the worst because her hair was so curly.

They were having a cup of tea in the kitchen. Helen couldn't get rid of the smell of the treatment from her nostrils. Every sip of tea tasted of it. Mary was on the other side of the table telling her that the principal of the local primary school was pregnant again.

'They'll need someone to cover that maternity leave. You know that they'd have you back in a heartbeat.'

Helen frowned. 'I have a job. I'm a housewife.'

'You're a childminder,' Mary corrected her.

Helen scoffed. 'Niamh is like one of my own.'

'You won't even let me pay you.'

'Liam and Vincent have sorted it between themselves,' Helen said. It was an old argument. Vincent did enough work around the farm to pay for the childcare a million times over.

'Does he pay you a salary? Mary asked.

'Who? Liam? Jesus Christ, he's my husband, Mary. Why are you looking at me like that?'

The truth was that Helen was relieved when Mary and Vincent's marriage fell apart. They were civil towards each other over the years, right up until Mary objected to Maria's planning permission. She found that hard to forgive. Still, every time she laid eyes on Mary, she remembered the hours they spent together as teenagers in her bedroom under the gaze of Elvis staring down at them from the wall.

*

'How was it?' Judy asked when she got back to the house that evening.

'Beautiful,' Helen said.

There was a coffee shop at the friary. She ordered a cappuccino and read a leaflet that advertised spiritual retreats. It wasn't at all like how she remembered. She went for a long walk in the forest before she gave up trying to find her way back into the past.

'I'm having a glass of wine outside if you'd like to join me?' Judy asked.

'That would be lovely,' she said.

Helen didn't drink, but Mary loved wine. She followed Judy outside to a patio with deck chairs. A meadow of wildflowers stretched out in front of them. There was a shed and a path that cut through the grass and led to the rest of the garden. Judy pulled out a chair for her to sit down, apologising for the noise of the peacocks.

'I've put Vernon and Gladys into the pen for the evening,' she said. 'You'd think they'd like a bit of alone time, but they don't seem too happy about it. Is white OK? I have a bottle of red in the kitchen.'

'White is perfect,' Helen said.

'Dennis does a gig every Saturday night in the local hotel,' Judy said.

'Does he do it full time?' Helen asked.

'He was an accountant for years,' Judy said. 'A good one, but he hated it. He got more into Elvis after he retired. He gave up drinking too. He'll be ten years sober this year. I lasted a week. I love a glass of wine in the evenings. I try my best not to love it too much around him.'

'Do you go home much?' Helen asked.

Judy sighed and folded her arms. 'No. I never felt *at home* at home if you know what I mean. I have a sister who still lives there. Annie Doherty?'

'I was in the same class as Annie,' Helen said.

Annie lived in an estate on the other side of the town. Helen always saw her in the pharmacy and they pretended not to recognise each other while they browsed the shelves waiting on prescriptions. She booked into a spa in Wicklow last year under Annie's name and ended up crying during a massage. She could still remember the gentle voice of the masseuse trying to calm her down as she apologised through tears, assuring her that it happened all the time.

'You were a few years ahead of me in school then,' Judy said. 'Who else was in that class?'

'Do you remember Helen Lawlor?' Helen asked. 'She ended up marrying—'

'Liam Foley,' Judy said. 'I felt so sorry for her when he died. It's bad enough for your husband to die by suicide, but for it to be all over the news? I don't know how I would cope.'

'Liam was a gentleman. Now, between you and me, Helen was always a bit . . .' Helen stuck her nose in the air and flicked the end of it with her index finger.

'Really?' Judy's eyes widened and Helen nodded.

'We were friends for years. Our families were like *that*,' Helen said, crossing her fingers. 'My ex-husband, Vincent, worked on their farm. Helen looked after my daughter while I was working. Niamh used to cry when I picked her up from the Foleys' house. She never wanted to go home. Vincent was a divil for the drink. He'd go on benders for days on end. He could never have held down a real job. The Foleys completely enabled his alcoholism. There came a point when I just couldn't take it anymore. I knew that they would take his side but I wasn't expecting them to cut me out the way that they did. Vincent passed away from cancer, just a few weeks before Liam died. I would have liked to have visited him before he went. I wanted to go to the funeral but I couldn't face being in the same room as them.'

'God, that's tough,' Judy said.

'The GAA is a cult,' Helen said, running a finger around the rim of her wine glass. 'If you're not in with them, you're nobody. I warned my Niamh. She was – *is* – a brilliant camogie player, but she stopped playing. If Helen really cared about her, she would check in on her, but she hasn't spoken to Niamh in years.'

Judy reached for the bottle to top up her glass.

Helen focused on a butterfly which flitted across the garden, eventually disappearing behind the shed. 'I'm sorry. I wasn't expecting all of that to come out.'

'Don't be sorry,' Judy said. 'It sounds like you've had to deal with a lot.'

Helen didn't know how she got to bed that night. Dennis came home and coaxed her into the kitchen to try on his outfits. Judy put a wig on her and fake sideburns that ended up in her boobs. The last thing she remembered was pulling on a rhinestone jumpsuit over her own clothes and singing 'Suspicious Minds' into an empty bottle of wine.

The room wobbled as she got out of bed. She pulled back the curtains and looked into the garden, her brain still pickled in white wine. The mesh enclosure for the peacocks looked like it belonged in a zoo, with perches and ladders up to a wooden house. A path of stepping stones wound its way from the shed down to the far end of the garden where Helen could see the sun rising, shining its beams through the trees. She put a coat on over her pyjamas and made her way downstairs.

There was a lock on the shed door, but she found a key underneath a flowerpot and opened it. Inside was a studio space. A collage of stained glass was assembled on a large table like a jigsaw: Jesus as a drag queen on the cross, wearing makeup and a bikini; cows staging a demonstration, demanding the right to fart; a desert island made entirely out of biscuits floating on a sea of tea.

It took Helen a long time to pry her eyes away to look at the rest of the room. In the corner was an old school desk with the chair attached and an inkwell in the top right-hand corner. She lifted the lid and found scraps of paper with even more sketches of ideas for pieces. Beside the desk was a contraption that looked somewhere between a toasted sandwich maker and a time machine. Dozens of plastic containers with pieces of glass were organised according to colour. Before Helen left the shed, she did a quick scan of the drawings again. There wasn't an Elvis in sight.

She was sheepish when she came down for breakfast later that morning. Judy wasn't a conventionally attractive woman, but there was something about her – a glint in her eye that was difficult to read. Helen had seen more of it the night before when Judy put her to bed. They burst into her room in hysterics when all of a sudden, they were face to face and silent. Helen sat down on the bed. Judy knelt down and took off her shoes for her, untying the laces slowly and with such tenderness that Helen didn't know what to think. She couldn't help but wonder whether, if Mary were actually there, they might have gotten up to all sorts.

When Helen came in from the garden, she tried to find a photo of Judy when she was younger, but there wasn't even a wedding photo to go by. She wore men's plaid shirts that did nothing for her figure and let her hair go grey, making her look much older than she was.

She tried her best to hide her disappointment when Judy didn't stick around to chat during breakfast. Helen ate quickly and went up to her room to pack bits and pieces of Mary Ryan into her suitcase. When she came downstairs, she was almost too nervous to say goodbye, even before she reached into her handbag for her purse and found that it was missing. As if on cue, Judy walked out of the kitchen with the purse in her hand.

'It must have fallen out of your bag last night,' she said.

The clasp was broken and it flapped open. Helen saw her driver's licence peek out of the plastic window of a card slot.

'What am I like,' she said.

'Listen, Helen—' Judy tried.

Helen put her hand up to silence her. Her hands trembled as she took three fifty-euro notes from her purse and left them on the coffee table. Then, she pulled up the handle of her suitcase and wheeled it towards the door.

The car wheels skidded as she accelerated down the driveway. The faster Helen drove, the better she felt. A lorry rounded a corner and blared its horn at her. It thundered past, knocking the wing mirror off the side of the car.

She drove on until the sound of her heartbeat faded from her ears. Once she got to a main road, she pulled into a lay-by and turned on her hazard lights. Bits of wires were sprouting out of where her wing mirror used to be. Helen opened Google Maps on her phone and searched for home.

Chapter 8

The Mass Podcast

Kate

WHEN KATE COULDN'T SLEEP, she put on headphones in bed and played episodes of *The Mass Podcast*. She told Ellius that she was listening to white noise, even though they shared a Spotify account and he could see her search history.

The podcast began as a drunken conversation one Christmas Eve. Liam and Vincent had arrived home from the pub after Midnight Mass, rattling off prayers they had learned as kids. It was Peter who had decided to turn remembering childhood prayers into a drinking game. Maria drew up a list of the hymns off the top of her head and Vincent and Liam joined them for a few rounds of choir karaoke, stopping to take a sup of their drinks every time they sang 'Lord.' Kate was just after closing the show by bellowing out a dodgy rendition of 'Here I am, Lord' when she joked that they should start a podcast about mass.

That would have been the end of it, if it wasn't for Vincent's new girlfriend, Deirdre. Deirdre was at least fifteen years younger than Vincent and was a radio producer who he had met while working as a pundit for hurling matches. She had her heart set on convincing Liam and Vincent to start a podcast together. She brought the equipment to the Foleys' sitting room and set up the microphones on stands while Helen served tea and sandwiches.

For their very first episode, Kate and Niamh had joined them to help explain the conception of the podcast. They had gotten off to a rocky start, listening to Vincent stumble over his words before Liam interrupted him.

'Let the girls tell everyone what's happening, will you? They're the brains behind this.'

Kate leaned into her microphone and explained the premise of the podcast, finishing by opening up her line of questioning. 'How often do you go to mass?'

'Once a week for me,' Liam said. 'Sunday morning mass at St Brigid's.'

'Vincent, you're looking sheepish over there,' Kate said.

'I don't go as often as I should,' Vincent replied, scratching his beard.

'Do you feel guilty when you don't go?' Niamh asked.

'Ehhhh.' Vincent folded his arms and leaned back in the armchair. 'I try not to think about it.'

'Some podcast this is going to be,' Liam said.

Vincent laughed. 'Why do you feel the need to go every Sunday, Foley?' he asked.

Liam drummed his fingers along the armrest of the couch. 'In all honesty, I go to keep my mother happy.'

Vincent's eyes widened. 'Really?'

'Yeah. And Helen, I suppose. My wife, Helen, is a fan of a good mass.'

'I thought you liked mass, Dad,' Kate said.

'I'm not saying I don't.' He closed his eyes for a moment. 'Do you know what I like about it? I love the boredom. There's too much entertainment in the world nowadays. People talk about how the Catholic Church needs to up their game. And don't get me wrong, in many respects, I agree, but I do love a mass where you can let your mind wander. I reserve the right to be bored.'

Niamh joined the conversation, her eyes solely focused on the microphone in front of her. 'I think I should step in here to mention that Liam trains our local camogie team, and he has, on occasion, made us go to mass together.'

'Hang on now,' Liam said, putting up a hand in defence. 'I don't demand it of you – I ask. I think that going to mass as a team in the week leading up to a big game makes all the difference. Even if you have no faith at all, a church is a great place to have a bit of a think. We've done it before big games, haven't we Vinnie? It is a gift to have the whole team sitting together in silence. It gives you a chance to appreciate the opportunity to go out onto the pitch and express yourselves when the time comes.'

'Just because something feels right for you doesn't mean you should impose it on a whole group of people, though,' Kate argued.

Vincent rubbed his hands together. 'Now we're sucking diesel. What do you say to that, Foley?'

'I say that my daughter is right, but that's not what I'm doing. I make no demands of the team. I suggest things. It's up to them to follow my lead if they want to.'

'Like Jesus asking the apostles to leave their families?' Kate said. 'That worked out well.'

'Well, we're all sitting here now, talking about them,' Liam countered.

'And what about the wives and kids they abandoned?' Kate asked.

'Who's your favourite apostle?' Vincent mused.

'I feel like Judas wasn't all that bad,' Liam said.

Kate knew that her dad was only trying to annoy her, but the longer the conversation went on, the looser it became. She looked over at Niamh, and then turned to Deirdre who gave her a thumbs up. That was when she knew that they had made a mistake.

Deirdre had tried to calm her down after the recording had ended, when she voiced her reservations.

'As it stands, the podcast lacks structure. And also, you both really have to be more careful about what you say on a public platform like this.'

'Ah relax, Kate, we'll be grand!' Vincent said, slapping her leg and getting up to pour everyone a celebratory glass of wine.

The show turned out to be a hit. Every week, they invited a new guest into Helen's sitting room to have a cup of tea and a chat. Kate became the podcast's unofficial guardian, supervising from her home in Belfast. She asked Deirdre to send her the episodes before they went out so that she could edit out the jokes that might be considered offensive – Vincent slut-shaming Mary Magdalene, or the time that Liam joked about how someone could try to assassinate Pope Francis when he visited Croke Park by firing a sliotar at his head.

Ellius couldn't understand why she felt the need to keep tabs on it all.

'Is your dad paying you for the work you're doing?' he asked.

'He doesn't even know,' she replied. 'I asked Deirdre not to tell him.'

'Then, why do it?'

'Because I don't want him to get cancelled,' she muttered, writing down the time stamp of yet another conversation that needed to be cut short.

Years later, in the middle of the night, Kate held her breath when she got to the parts of an episode where those edits were made. Her whole body went rigid, and Dolores awoke from her shallow doze beside her to comfort her, whimpering and licking her face as though she knew what had happened, what was still happening.

It was almost as though somewhere, in the back of her mind, Kate held onto the hope that if she replayed those conversations enough, she could break through time and space to a moment where they were all in the same room again.

Chapter 9

Arrivals

Niamh

It was Christmas Eve at Dublin airport. A children's choir were strangling carols and playing up to the camera crew that was trying to capture the festive atmosphere. Niamh had rushed to arrivals, even though she knew before looking at the board that the flight was delayed. She was the only one who knew that Peter was coming home. He had asked her to collect him from the airport so he could surprise his family, and she was beginning to think it was a mistake.

Everywhere she looked there were Santa hats and reindeer antlers. A crowd huddled behind railings watching two sets of sliding doors open and close, as if they could transform the faces of strangers into their loved ones by sheer concentration.

Niamh sat in the back row of seats to avoid the camera crew interviewing people about who they were welcoming home. She just about fit into the pair of jeans she was wearing the last time she saw Peter. If she sucked in her stomach, she could squeeze herself back into the memory he had of her.

*

He had called to her mother's house a week after Liam died. Niamh hadn't gone to the funeral. She didn't know how much the Foleys knew about what had happened. Mary had knocked on her bedroom door before she came in and sat on the edge of the bed.

'You have a visitor, pet. It's Peter – Foley,' she added, as if there were other Peters.

Niamh's hair was wet with grease. She tied it into a bun, put on a new pair of jeans and a T-shirt and went downstairs.

He stood up when she came into the room and she searched for the truth in his face.

He didn't know. Kate hadn't told him.

His chest heaved when she hugged him. He let out a whimper and she squeezed him tighter.

'The funeral,' she said. 'I couldn't—'

'I know,' he said.

They sat down on the couch.

'I wanted to be there—'

'Niamh, you basically lost two dads in the space of a few weeks. That would wipe anyone out.'

Mary came in with a tray of tea and biscuits. It was only when Peter asked where the bathroom was that Niamh realised that he'd never been to her house before.

She turned on the television and they watched old reruns of *Friends*, unable to take anything in.

Peter moved closer to her and cleared his throat. 'My visa came through for Australia.'

She sat up, hugging a pillow into her chest. He'd talked about going to Australia earlier in the year when he tore his cruciate during a league match. She didn't think he was being serious.

'Would you ever think of going?' he asked.

'To Australia?'

'Yeah,' he said. 'I hear that it's something that teachers do. Take a career break to go travelling or work over there.'

'Are you asking me to go to Australia with you?'

'I don't know what I'm talking about, Niamh,' he said. 'I just can't stay at home.'

*

Niamh checked the flight tracker – the plane had landed, but Peter hadn't turned on his phone. The children's choir were singing Mariah Carey. A group of ten-year-old girls were doing a choreographed dance, shimmying their hips and making suggestive faces with an innocence that made everyone uncomfortable.

Niamh was scrolling back through old messages on her phone. Peter moving to the other side of the world allowed them to be close in a way they couldn't have been if he'd stayed at home. Everything had frozen in time for him – he still talked as if she was in and out of the Foleys' house every week. He didn't know that Niamh hadn't been in the same room as his mother since before he left the country.

She'd made a habit out of scrolling back through their messages – they never texted as much as they did when he was nine hours ahead of her. He used to call her when he was drunk. She was staying late at school correcting copies one evening when her phone began to vibrate. He was out having beers with the lads. She imagined him wandering off from the group by himself to call her.

'I thought it would be easier,' he said. 'Being so far away, but I can't stop thinking about home. It hurts.'

'I know.'

There was silence on the phone.

'Niamh?'

'Yeah, I'm here, sorry,' she said.

'Niamh?'

'Yeah?'

'I love you,' he said.

'Love you too. Now go get some sleep, will you?'

'No, you don't get it. I really love you.'

'Yeah, I know. I love you too.'

'Really?'

'Really. Now get some sleep.'

Then he started seeing someone. Peter was never the type to parade relationships around on social media, but she studied his photos for clues, poring over group pictures he posted trying to pick out the girl who seemed like his type. She knew when he stopped seeing her a year and a half later. The messages and drunk phone calls had started again.

He'd been so happy when she went back to camogie. He video-called her from Sydney Harbour. She kept her camera off because she didn't want him to see her double chin.

'You won me twenty quid,' he said. 'I told Maria – I *told* her you'd show up to training. I'd kill for a puck around down the pitch right now.'

'Sure, you'll be home for the wedding,' Niamh said.

'I'm after booking flights for Christmas.'

'How long will you be back for?'

He smiled into the camera. 'For good.'

She tried to talk him into telling Maria.

She can't cope with surprises.

She'll be grand.

No Peter. She's after getting worse. She won't even let us plan her hen party.

You shouldn't have told me that. Where are ye going? I'm going to order a stripper.

Niamh would have told Maria that Peter was coming home if she could have trusted her to go along with the charade, but she knew that she'd be in arrivals dressed as a Christmas tree with Aoife in her arms and Bláith by her side, ready to surprise him when he was supposed to be the one surprising them.

Beside her, a woman was telling her toddler that her daddy was only going to come home if she was a good girl. She lifted her up on her hip and tried to fix the red velvet bow in her hair, but the little girl wriggled out of her arms and ran over to play with the balloons that were next to the children's choir. The woman was panicking, looking over her shoulder at the sliding doors. Her husband's flight had landed. She wanted the moment he walked through the door to be perfect, but the child wanted a balloon.

Niamh felt a pang of urgency on the woman's behalf. She went to the shop and bought a Welcome Home balloon. Walking back to arrivals, she was imagining how to approach the woman and little girl to give them the balloon when she saw that she was too late. A man with glasses and broad shoulders had abandoned his bags to lift the woman off her feet. He ran over to his daughter and she squealed as he swung her around in the air. Niamh abandoned the balloon next to a Christmas tree and sat back down again.

It felt like a kind of miracle when Peter finally came through the doors, tired and tanned and looking around for her. She nearly wanted to hide from him so she could see more of the look on his face. When he finally caught her eye in the crowd, they were kids playing Tip the Can in the back garden again.

She hadn't expected him to make such a scene – it was more of a rugby tackle than a hug.

'Jesus Christ,' was the first thing that came out of her mouth when he drove her a few yards into the space that opened up in the crowd of people who were staring at them.

'Sorry,' he said, squeezing her tight before he let her go.

Niamh felt a tap on her shoulder. She turned around to find a microphone and camera in her face.

'Do you mind if we ask you a few questions?' asked a voice that belonged inside a television.

'That's Peter Foley!'

A middle-aged woman came over and put her arm around Peter's shoulders. It had been three years since Peter played for the county team, but people still recognised him.

'You're the spit of your father.'

'Thanks.' Peter looked at Niamh and then to the woman with the microphone. 'If you don't mind, we're actually in a bit of a rush.'

'It will only take a few moments.'

'We'd prefer not to – thanks though,' he said, putting his arm around Niamh and leading her away.

'Are you sure you're home for good?' Niamh asked, once they had broken away from the crowd. The suitcase he had with him was smaller than the hurley that was wrapped and taped to the outside.

'Sure, isn't this all I need?'

She slid the parking ticket into the machine and felt him staring at her.

'What?' she said.

'Nothing.' He'd a stupid grin on his face. 'You just look well. Healthy.'

She rolled her eyes at him and tried not to smile.

They stopped in McDonald's Drive Thru on the way home. He laughed at the way she closed her eyes and smelled the burger before taking a bite.

'Are we going to the pitch before I drop you home?' she asked.

'Better not break cover,' he said. 'I need to get back in time to play the donkey in the Nativity.'

The tradition of casting locals as figures in the Nativity for Midnight Mass was Liam's idea, fuelled by pre-mass pints in the pub. Every year, he erected a stable in the churchyard and the place would be packed to see which poor unfortunate souls Farmer Foley had bribed into throwing a tea towel on their head and a stuffed sheep under their arm. It was always the kind of people who needed a lift around Christmas that Liam asked – elderly bachelors living alone and awkward teenagers, people who were recently bereaved and needed a distraction. In later years, livestock were introduced to the stable which added a fresh layer of chaos and controversy, as in previous years, the animals were played by kids. Peter considered his performance as the donkey in the 1998 Nativity as one of his greatest achievements.

'Has Maria roped you into being an angel yet?' Peter asked.

'I'm not going to mass.'

'To fuck you aren't – if I have to throw a bedsheet and a bit of tinsel on you myself, I will.'

'I can't. I don't want to leave Mam on her own in the house,' Niamh said. 'It's Christmas, like.'

Peter looked out the passenger side window. It was late afternoon and the sun was already going down behind clouds. 'Would she not go down?'

'Mam? She hasn't been to mass in years.'

'So, you won't be coming to ours for drinks tonight?'

Niamh laughed. 'No, I'm not. Is that OK?'

'Sorry, I just . . . I presumed. Sorry.'

Every Christmas Eve, Niamh and Vincent went back to the Foleys for a drink after Midnight Mass. Inevitably, someone would bring up the story about the time Peter locked himself into the downstairs bathroom, heartbroken over the news of Santa. He was so convinced by the magic, resolute in his belief that he had to be real. Niamh had never believed. It was another thing that her parents fought about. Her mother had insisted on telling her the truth. Sometimes, Niamh pretended to go along with the charade for her dad's sake. It was Peter who nearly convinced her that there was an actual man in the North Pole, even though she could have shown him where his Santa presents were stored in the spare room of her house. Every year, Helen did her Christmas shopping early and gave the gifts to Vincent for safekeeping. Niamh was always jealous whenever she saw the glint of the wrapping paper in the wardrobe. She wished she could have been in the Foleys' house on Christmas morning when they came downstairs to see the parcels underneath the tree.

Peter was eight when he had a crisis of faith. The other kids in school were beginning to doubt, so he'd come up with a plan. He wrote his Santa letter in secret and wouldn't tell anyone what he had asked for.

On Christmas Eve, he whispered to Niamh that he had asked for the power to talk to animals. He woke up on Christmas morning to a letter underneath the tree from the man himself, explaining that the ability to grant supernatural gifts wasn't in his wheelhouse, but that he'd tried his best to guess what he would like instead. Peter landed into school after the Christmas holidays with the letter in hand and was hailed a hero.

The summer before he was due to start sixth class, Niamh was in the back garden playing with Kate and Bláithín when Helen called her into the kitchen. Peter was sitting at the table with his head in his hands.

'Niamh, we're having a chat about Santa,' Helen said. 'Peter doesn't believe me when I tell him how we knew what he wanted for Christmas.'

Peter only had to look at her face to confirm his worst suspicion. 'You lying bitch.'

'Peter!' Helen shouted.

Maria appeared in the hall. 'What's wrong?'

'Did you know?' Peter demanded.

'About what?' Maria asked.

'Santa,' Niamh said.

Maria started laughing.

'You were all in on it!' Peter shouted, running into the bathroom and slamming the door.

*

They were on the back roads when Peter began to talk tactics. 'I think you should go in first and distract them.'

'I'm not going in,' she said.

'What do you mean?'

'I'm dropping you at the door.'

'Why are you being like this?' he asked.

'Like what?'

He frowned. 'Nothing.'

They were pulling into the driveway when he started to plead with her. 'Will you not come in for five minutes?'

'Fine.'

'Yes Niamh!' he said, punching her on the arm. 'That's the spirit. It's Christmas! I'm home!'

The entire family was in the kitchen having Christmas Eve lunch. Niamh opened the door to the chaos of communal sandwich-making and everyone talking over each other. She looked around and saw Nadine trying her best to break up a fight between her two boys who were dressed as shepherds, Aoife sitting on Kate's lap playing with her hair, Bláith showing John something on her phone and Helen bending down to get something out of the fridge. Maria shouted, 'Niamh!'

Bláith turned around. 'Niamh! Sit beside me.'

'No offence taken, Bláith,' John said, getting up from the seat next to her.

'Auntie Ni-Ni!' Aoife got up from Kate's knee and raced over to hug her, stopping in her tracks as soon as she saw Peter hiding in the back hall. 'Who's that man?'

Peter popped his head around the door and everyone screamed.

Niamh bent down to comfort Aoife who had burst into tears. 'It's OK,' she said, pulling her into a hug.

'It's too loud!' Aoife cried, sticking her fingers into her ears.

Niamh picked her up and brought her into the sitting room.

'That's your Uncle Peter,' she said, sitting her down on her lap. 'He surprised everyone by coming home for Christmas.'

Aoife looked at her suspiciously. 'Uncle Peter is only in the phone.'

'He used to be in the phone because he lived in Australia, but now he's in real life.'

'Can he go back in the phone?' Aoife asked.

Niamh brushed her hair away from her face. 'It might be a bit scary when people come out of the phone, but I promise you, your Uncle Peter is so much fun. You'll love playing with him. Now, can I guess what you're dressed up as? Are you a princess?'

'No silly! I'm an angel – look at my wings,' she said, turning around.

'Oh, they're beautiful. Guess what? Your Uncle Peter wants to be a donkey.'

Aoife's eyes lit up. 'What are *you* dressing up as?'

'I don't know,' Niamh said, taking her by the hand and leading her back into the kitchen. 'Maybe I'll be a sheep.'

It only took two glasses of wine for Niamh to agree to go to mass.

'I can't believe they gave my part to a donkey,' Peter said, shaking his head.

The kids laughed at him.

'I mean, I've travelled from the other side of the world to audition!' he said, getting down on his hands and knees and braying.

By the time they were leaving for mass he was still on all fours and Aoife was hanging out of him, taking straw from the shepherds' outfits to poke up his nose and slapping him on the backside to make him go faster.

Father Angelo met them outside the church and shook Maria's hand, thanking her for her hard work in setting up the stable and assembling the cast. Maria's production of the Nativity was less spontaneous than her father's had been. She knew that she didn't hold the same sway as Liam, who could rock up to the pub half an hour before mass on Christmas Eve and come out with an entourage ready to fill an empty shed. After months of searching, a couple with a newborn who'd just moved to the area had agreed to be the Holy Family after Maria ambushed them at a parkrun. She put a notice in the parish newsletter that invited every child to dress up as an angel or a shepherd.

Niamh looked around at everyone standing in the cold listening to the kids singing 'Away in a Manger'. She wondered how many of them missed the old days – the year Liam forgot to find a baby and they had to use a doll, only for a drunk shepherd to take the Baby Born out of the crib and shout, 'The fucker's a fraud!'

She told herself that she'd go home to her mam after the mass, but Aoife came running up to ask if she wanted to help make jam sandwiches for Santa.

'Auntie Blue is going to help too,' she said, pointing to Kate who was lagging behind her niece, unsure whether to join in on the conversation.

'Merry Christmas, Auntie Blue,' said Niamh.

Kate smiled at her. 'Happy Christmas.'

'Are you best friends?' Aoife asked, looking up at both of them.

'We are best friends with *you*,' Niamh said, bending down to tickle her.

'Are you coming back for a drink?' Kate asked.

'I should go home.'

Maria came over to join them. She linked arms with Niamh and took a deep breath, puffing out her cheeks in relief. 'Was that all right?'

'I would have done more with the role of Joseph, myself,' Kate said. 'But you get what you pay for.'

'I gave them a nice restaurant voucher.'

'Is that coming out of the collection basket?'

'Absolutely.'

Maria nodded over to the crowd that surrounded Peter. 'The Messiah has returned. Niamh, I have no idea how you kept that from us.'

'Me neither, to be honest,' Niamh said.

'He knew he couldn't trust anyone else. If he'd told Kate, the whole world would have known.'

'They would not!'

'Ah now, Kate, you can't hold your own piss.'

'Here, I'm going to head home,' Niamh said.

'Woah, hold your horses.' Maria took her hand. 'You're coming back to ours for a drink, aren't you?'

*

Crossing the threshold of the Foleys' back door for the second time that day, Niamh couldn't help but feel like she was trespassing into Helen Foley's world. Everything in the house seemed like a projection of her headspace. Mostly, Niamh noticed the absence of things that were usually there around Christmas – cake tins lined with cereal box cutouts, fresh holly picked from the fields and made into wreaths to give as gifts, shortbread wrapped in brown paper parcels, the candle lit on the windowsill in the kitchen.

Niamh was very young when Helen told her why she lit a candle on Christmas Eve. 'It's to welcome anyone who is lonely into the house for Christmas.'

'But I don't want anyone else here,' Niamh said.

'That's what all the innkeepers said to Mary and Joseph that night in Bethlehem, until they found one man who was kind to them.'

'So, we can put them in the cowshed?' Niamh asked.

Helen laughed. 'No love. We'll give them sweets from the tin of Roses and a cup of tea.'

Now, when Niamh walked into a new room of the house, she was terrified that Helen would be there. Earlier that day, there had been too much going on to look Helen in the eye. She still didn't know if Helen knew what had happened, if Kate had told her. Somehow Niamh made her way to the front room without seeing her. She sat on the couch and played with the tassels of the old throw, plaiting the strands absentmindedly and thinking about the way Helen used to have her kneel down in front of her in that same spot after a bath on Friday evenings, how gentle she was brushing out the knots in her hair.

Peter was playing host, going in and out of the room to boil the kettle for hot whiskeys. He wheeled over the drinks cart that he'd made for Liam's fiftieth birthday. Peter knew that he wanted to be a carpenter since he was a teenager, but he had worried about what Liam would think. 'He thinks I'm not able for hard work. Just because I don't like milking cows doesn't mean I'm lazy. It's the same with hurling, he doesn't respect the way I play.'

'I don't think that's true,' Niamh argued.

'Then why has he never given me captaincy?'

'I think he might be afraid of how it might look, maybe.'

'Because I'm not good enough? Is that what you're saying?'

'Of course not.'

The older they got, the clearer it became to Niamh just how much Peter craved Liam's approval. He designed his life around the need to prove that he was better than the little boy his father made him out to be. When he became captain of the county minor team, he let out an angry cry of joy that scared her.

For Liam's fiftieth birthday, Peter had taken the antique globe from the sitting room and cut it open, placing bottles of whiskey and tumblers into the hollow of it. He didn't think to ask Helen if he could upcycle what must have seemed to him like a bit of old tat. Niamh didn't know if Peter even knew where the globe came from.

On days Niamh pretended to be sick from school, Helen had gotten down on her hands and knees to spin the globe with her, and had told her all about the nun who'd given it to her as a little girl. Sister Imelda had taught her for a year in school before she went to America. Niamh watched as Helen walked two fingers across the world, all the way to Boston. Helen had told her the story so many times that she knew it by heart.

Niamh didn't know if Helen had ever told Peter the story of Sister Imelda. On the evening of Liam's birthday, Peter had wheeled the trolley into the front room, a bedsheet shrouding his father's surprise. He whipped off the sheet for the big reveal – nobody else noticed the look that passed over Helen's face.

Peter handed Niamh a glass of whiskey and let his hands rest over hers for a moment too long. She took it from him and looked around to see if anyone had noticed. Kate and Maria were too busy looking at a funny video on Bláithín's phone. John and Nadine came over to join them for a drink when the kids went down. The signal of the baby monitors stretched to the window ledge of the front room so they could keep an eye on the boys who were fast asleep next door.

'What age is Elmo now?' Peter asked.

'Eight,' Nadine said.

'You better take the camera out of the room before the teenage years hit.'

Nadine didn't even crack a smile.

'Well,' John said, reaching over to slap his brother's knee. 'It's good to have you home, Pete.'

'I'm sure you all missed me.'

'Are you up for milking in the morning?'

'As long as I don't have to work sober.'

Milking cows was something Niamh missed about Christmases as a kid. There came a time on Christmas Day when Vincent decided he had endured the company of his in-laws long enough. Niamh turned it into a game in her head, trying to gauge the exact moment that her dad would clasp his hands together, stand up and announce that he'd better give Liam a hand with the cows. She always volunteered to go with him. It was her job to spray the cows with disinfectant. She went down the line squirting vaporous clouds of luminous pink onto cows' udders.

Sometimes, when a cow would do something stubborn or stupid, Liam would get a length of a Wavin pipe and whack its legs. She was shocked by the violence that came from such a quiet man, but as time went on, she took pride in hardening up to the way things were. She grew to admire his striking ability as he lay into a heifer – the hurler's stance and follow-through that made him a living legend.

She was eight years old the first time she was allowed out to the milking parlour. The best part was when it was over and she got to go inside for Helen to fuss over her. Helen sat her up on her lap in front of the fire and rubbed her hands in hers to warm them up, slipping her toffee pennies that she had saved for her from the tin of Quality Street.

'You'll have to get Niamh on the payroll at this rate,' she said to the men, rocking her back and forward on her knee as Niamh snuggled into her Christmas smell.

*

'Where's Mam?' Peter asked.

'She's gone to bed. It's probably a good time to talk about Mam actually,' Maria said. 'I'm worried about her.'

'To be fair, Maria, there's not much you don't worry about,' Peter said.

'She keeps going off by herself on mini-breaks down the country.'

'Isn't that nice?' Nadine said. 'I'd love a break.'

'She's developed a shopping addiction, hasn't she Kevin?'

Kevin nodded solemnly. 'The amount of parcels that are delivered to the house during the day is insane. They're all addressed to Maria—'

'So I opened one of them,' Maria cut in. 'And it was full of clothes that just so *aren't* Mam.'

Niamh looked down at the cloves stuck into the slice of lemon that was floating around in her hot whiskey.

'And she's drinking,' Kevin added. 'She's started to drink wine in the evenings.'

'Wait, hold on,' Kate said. 'Mam doesn't drink.'

'It's something we need to talk about,' Maria said.

Niamh looked over at Nadine who was shifting around in her seat, fixing her skirt.

'Just maybe not tonight,' Kate said, eventually.

'Wait, hold on,' Peter said, leaning forward in his chair. 'Since when is Kate the one who avoids these kinds of conversations?'

'What do you mean, "these kinds of conversations"?'

'Come on, Blue, you live for this shit,' John said, digging into a box of Quality Street. 'You love a bit of drama. Mam drinking? I'm surprised you haven't gotten her out of bed and dragged her to an AA meeting by now.'

'I'm not that bad.'

'Remember that time you told us you were an alcoholic? You were fourteen and got tipsy off one can of Bulmers.'

'I was reading a lot of Jack Kerouac.'

'Of course you were.'

The conversation turned to everyone imagining what it would be like to live in Kate's brain for a day.

'I reckon I'd be OK if I slept through it all,' Peter said. 'I couldn't hack being conscious in there. Too many opinions.'

Niamh silently agreed with him. Her own opinions had the constitution of Victorian women on their sick beds. A strong breeze could blow them over the rare time she took them out for a bit of exercise. Kate's opinions had meat on their bones, were fed on facts and figures. Her appetite for anger was insatiable. She spent years canvassing for the Repeal the Eighth campaign and had a huge fight with Liam and Helen over their anti-abortion stance.

'Kate, do you not think that life would be so much easier if you learned to let things go?' Maria asked.

'All right Oprah,' Peter said.

'I like to think I've grown up a bit,' Kate said.

They all gave her a knowing look.

'I *have*.'

'You did eat that chicken nugget Aoife offered you from her Happy Meal yesterday,' Maria said.

'That's the vegan card gone,' Peter said.

Kate made a face at her brother. 'Go fuck yourself.'

Niamh's stomach tightened. She always felt protective of Kate whenever anyone brought up food around her, especially her own family members. Even when Kate was at her worst, they still acted as though her illness was a choice – just another way for their sister to be at odds with the world around her.

'Gotta catch 'em all,' Peter muttered.

Kate collected labels the way she used to collect Pokémon cards when they were kids, putting them in plastic pockets in a special folder that she wouldn't let anyone touch.

'What's the one you're applying for now? ADHD or autism? What's trending on TikTok these days?'

'Peter, do you want a slap?' Kate asked.

'It just seems very popular. That's all I'm saying.'

'You're an arsehole.'

'It's IBS,' Maria said. 'Very different.'

Kate whacked Maria on the arm. 'Why are you telling everyone my business?'

'Sorry, but it is funny. She had an 'accident' on the motorway on the day of my engagement party.'

'Did you shit yourself?' Peter asked.

'Will you all just fuck off!' Kate shouted, as they rolled around the place laughing. 'Seriously, it's not funny!'

'Sorry Blue.'

'And Peter, neurodivergence isn't a social media trend. Women and girls with autism and ADHD have historically been underdiagnosed due to gender bias—'

'See!' Peter pointed at her. 'This is the Blue we know and love. Dragging us down into a pit of intellectual misery.'

'Dad was good at dealing with it,' Maria said. 'You got him to change his mind on the abortion referendum, and you still managed to be pissed off about it.'

'Yes, because he said – and I quote – 'If it means that much to you, love, I'll vote with you.' It wasn't about me! It was about making an informed choice by himself.'

'You were awful hard on him though,' Nadine said. 'He couldn't do right from wrong.'

Nadine chose her moments to get involved in conversations, and it was almost always to defend the men of the family. John put his hand around the back of his wife's chair and took a sip of whiskey. He was quiet whenever Liam was mentioned in conversation. Out of all of the Foley children, John was the one who knew Liam best, having worked alongside him on the farm. They didn't always see eye to eye. John didn't have as much natural talent as Peter on the hurling pitch, but he was a hard worker. He was always working, even when he was really young. They'd be in the middle of playing a game when John would be called out to the yard. He'd get angry, curse underneath his breath and slope out to the back hall to change into his work clothes. Sometimes, when the cousins were over and they were playing something good, like four-player *Crash Team Racing* on the PlayStation, he'd get really upset. He'd try to pass it off as anger, but Niamh could see that he was holding back tears.

'I think it's time to lay off Kate, now,' John said, sensing the shift in the energy of the room.

'Sorry for piling up on you, Blue,' Peter said, slapping her on the back as he got up to refill everyone's drinks. 'Anyone up for a game of Monopoly?'

Niamh was one too many hot whiskeys deep when she stood up to drive home.

'Nope!' Maria insisted. 'There is no way you're driving up that hill in that state.'

'I'll walk,' Niamh replied.

'It's pitch black and lashing rain. You can sleep on the couch.'

Maria brought down blankets and pillows and filled a hot water bottle for her. Bláith and Kate went to bed first, followed by the parents who left to do Santa, leaving Peter and Niamh alone.

'So much for giving you a lift home from the airport,' she said.

'Arrah, you love us really,' he said, sitting down beside her.

'I feel bad for leaving Mam on her own.'

'You have all day tomorrow to spend time with her.'

'Hmmm ...'

He put a hand to her cheek. She rested her head on his shoulder.

'Here,' he said, taking her fingers and putting them to his chest where she could feel his heart beating. 'It's been going like the clappers every time I looked at you today. I was fit to burst when I saw you at the airport.' He took her face in his hands. 'I've been wanting to do this all day.'

The whiskey on his tongue brought her back to the floor of the workshop. She opened her eyes and saw Helen standing in the doorway in her dressing gown – Helen's eyes piercing through hers.

'Are you OK?' Peter asked.

Niamh blinked. Helen wasn't there. Peter's eyes crinkled. She examined the lines on his forehead to steady herself.

'I'm being a lot,' he said, sitting back in the couch.

She reached for his arm. 'You're not.'
'Really?'
She shifted in her seat. 'Really.'
'You want to do this?'
His face was so open.
She smiled at him. 'Yeah.'

Part II

Chapter 10

God in the Windows

Helen

HELEN COULDN'T REMEMBER the last time she was alone in the house. The girls had gone to Belfast for Maria's hen party. The lads were in Carrick-on-Shannon for Kevin's stag. He'd headed off that morning with Aoife who was looking forward to having a sleepover with her other granny and granddad. Helen didn't know what to do with herself. This time last year, she would have headed off down the country, but her run-in in Donegal with the mad Elvis couple had put a stop to all of that. She was back hiding in her own home, having to endure Maria's attempts to sign her up to Zumba classes in the parish hall.

The long summer evenings were a help. She enjoyed spending time in the garden with Aoife. Maria liked it too. Helen had consulted Aoife on the new hanging baskets they'd gotten to brighten up the patio. Pink and purple fuchsias and red begonias flourished in their wicker cradles. That morning, they had spent hours on their hands and knees, planting parsnips and peas, and checking on the potatoes that would be ready to harvest in time for the wedding the following month. Maria had decided to get married on the first weekend in July, which happened to be Liam and Helen's anniversary. Helen had done her best to seem delighted by this.

As the sun set, she drew the curtains in the conservatory, scolding herself for feeling paranoid that there could be someone out in the darkness watching her. She felt a twinge in her lower back and considered running a bath before scrapping the idea altogether. She would put on a film, she decided. That's what she'd do.

A couple of hours later, she was lying on the couch watching Meryl Streep in *Kramer Vs Kramer* when the doorbell rang. She cursed herself for jumping. It was eleven o'clock at night. John's wife Nadine was the only one who bothered with the doorbell.

It was definitely Nadine looking for something, Helen decided, as she went to answer the door, but there was nobody on the doorstep. She craned her head just in time to catch a glimpse of the fluorescent yellow bar of a taxi sign gliding down her driveway and disappearing into the night. The dog was barking. She could hear footsteps and coughing around the side of the house. She grabbed a hurley that was leaning against the inside corner of the utility room and went outside in her dressing gown and slippers.

Someone was throwing up in her hydrangeas. The dog was still yapping away. Helen shushed him. The woman from the Elvis B&B was on her hands and knees retching into her flowerbeds. She didn't seem to notice when Helen held back her hair.

The dog calmed down and came over to lick Helen's face. She batted him away and took Judy Doherty by the arm.

'Come on now,' she said, leading her into the house.

It had been more than six months since she'd last seen her. Judy could barely keep her eyes open. Helen managed to slide her onto a chair at the kitchen table which she sprawled across, slack-jawed, her hair hiding most of her face.

She tried to think. It was eleven o'clock at night. She couldn't call anyone and she couldn't leave her in her kitchen for the fella who was covering the milking for John to come in at the crack of dawn and get the fright of his life. Once she got her breath back, she hoisted Judy under her arms and moved her to the sofa in the sitting room, where she'd left Meryl Streep on pause, crying in an elevator.

'You're all right,' she said, as Judy groaned into the cushions.

Helen went to get the sick bowl from the kitchen. She came back in time for another round of Judy spewing her guts up.

'Good woman,' she said, rubbing her back in circles. 'Get it all up.'

It didn't take long for her to pass out afterwards. Helen cleaned her up as best she could. She unlaced her boots and felt a pang of tenderness towards her as the soft shuck of her heel came away from the sole. Helen got a blanket and tucked her up on the couch, laying her on her side and brushing her hair away from her face.

The next morning, Judy was gone. The only evidence of the night before was the bowl that had been washed and left on the draining board and the blanket that was neatly folded on the couch. Helen looked around for a note – she didn't know why she expected to find one.

It was only when she stopped at the traffic lights on her way into town that she realised what she was doing. She didn't know why she was looking for a woman she barely knew, why it all seemed like such an emergency.

The church was the first place she went. Somehow, Helen knew that she'd find her there – the only other person in the chapel sitting down in a pew to the side of the altar, looking up at the stained-glass window of the Virgin Mary.

Judy started when Helen slid into the pew beside her. She recrossed her legs and looked down at her clasped hands. 'I'm sorry,' she whispered, eventually. 'I don't know what's wrong with me.'

'That makes two of us,' Helen said, staring at the window in front of them.

She was as surprised as Judy was when she asked her back to the house for a cup of tea. They didn't say anything on the way home. The dog came over to have a sniff when they were getting out of the car and Judy bent down and scratched behind his ears.

'Who's this?' she asked.

'That's Tayto,' Helen said. 'Well, Tayto III to give him his full title. He's had two predecessors. We tried to call them all by different names, but Tayto is the only one that stuck.'

The dog was making a show of her, rolling over for Judy to rub his belly.

Judy followed her into the kitchen and took a seat at the table.

'I won't stay long,' she said.

Helen filled the kettle and busied herself setting the table.

'Don't worry about it,' Helen said. 'I get unwanted visitors all of the time, and I can assure you that you're not one of them. We have an elderly neighbour called Timmy Rafferty who still calls in looking for Liam. I don't want to upset him so I pretend he's out in the yard – Liam was never here when he called anyway. I was always the one who was left to listen to him harp on about training Liam's underage team. Anyway, he never rings the doorbell. I walk into my own kitchen and he's sitting at this table like an apparition, waiting for the tea to be made. The last time he was here he fell asleep. I had to turn on the hoover to wake him.'

Judy smiled. 'I've a few of those myself. Dennis befriends other Elvises on Facebook and invites them to stay with us. We had a Mexican Elvis stay for a month last year and I thought I was going to lose my mind. All he wanted to do was stay up drinking Jameson and singing rebel songs.'

They descended into silence again, allowing it to thicken the air until the click of the kettle boiling gave some relief to the tension that had settled around them.

'Are you down visiting your sister?' Helen asked.

Judy thought for a while before answering. 'Not exactly, no. I haven't been home in years, but Annie mentioned a school reunion the last time we talked on the phone. I offered to go with her. It was last night. I thought you might have been there.'

It was Mary Ryan who had organised the reunion. Helen had gotten the invitation in the post. She tore the card to shreds before putting it in the bin, covering the pieces with a layer of kitchen roll just in case Maria spotted it and made a case for her to go. As far as Helen was concerned, Mary Ryan could take her invitation and shove it up her hole.

Maria had already invited Mary to the wedding, for Niamh's sake. Helen had thought Mary would have had the decency to make up an excuse, but she'd accepted, and Maria was tearing her hair out over where to put her on the table plan.

Helen imagined Mary swanning around the hotel function room handing out name badges and introducing herself to Judy.

'I didn't tell Annie that I'd met you,' Judy said. Helen could tell that she was nervous she might get upset with her. 'But I was disappointed when you weren't there. I was staying in the hotel and when everyone went home, I kept drinking and convinced myself that it would be a great idea to order a taxi to your house . . .'

'And here we are,' Helen said.

Judy grimaced.

'We all sit in the same part of the church,' Helen said. 'The girls who went to the convent. I noticed it a few years ago at mass. We sit in the part of the church where the confession booths used to be.'

Judy sat back in her chair and crossed her arms. 'I wonder if we're all psychologically chipped, like those birds who migrate back to the nests in the rafters after winter.'

'The birds behind the windows!' Helen said. 'I thought I imagined them as a kid.'

They were both quiet for a moment. Helen thought about the stained-glass window in the church. The image of the Virgin Mary and her baby boy, flanked by two saints, offering gifts.

'Do you make stained glass?' Helen asked.

Judy looked at her like she'd accused her of something criminal.

'I'm sorry,' Helen apologised. 'It's just that when I stayed with you last year, I noticed that your garden shed seemed like some kind of artist's studio.'

'I wouldn't go that far, now,' Judy said. 'It's an expensive hobby.'

'How did you get into it?'

'The short answer? I lost my mind. Took to the bed for years. The only thing that got me out of it was night classes. I've done them all, from salsa dancing to Chinese for Beginners.'

'You speak Chinese?'

'Oh God, no,' Judy said. 'I lasted a week. I didn't finish most of them. I did an eight-week course in stained glass. It was simple stuff but it stirred something in me. I always sketched bits and pieces and did a bit of painting. Working with glass is the only time I'm able to shut down the part of my brain that just wants to get into bed and hide. There are days I struggle to leave the house, but I always make it as far as the shed to tip away at it.'

'I saw some of your work,' Helen said.

Judy's eyes widened. 'You snuck into the shed?'

'I did.'

'It's always the quiet ones you have to watch.'

'Those pieces – they're like nothing I've ever seen before,' Helen said. 'They're stunning.'

'You haven't seen much stained glass then. There's a lot of crap out there but the good stuff is . . .' Judy took a sharp inhale of breath. 'Have you ever been to Lough Derg?'

'I have.'

'The one and only time I went was with my mother,' Judy said. 'I was eighteen and was waiting for my Leaving Cert results. We got the bus up to Donegal and the boat out to the island for three days of nothing but dry toast and black tea, cutting the feet off ourselves on the stones, doing the stations of the cross in the lashings of rain. I made a show of poor Mammy at mass in the evening because I couldn't stop staring at the windows. When the night vigil began, everyone huddled together shuffling around with their eyes on the ground mumbling prayers. Mammy kept tugging my arm to keep up with everyone else. It got to a point where I started ignoring her because the God I was looking for wasn't in the prayers – he was in those windows. Forty years later, I'm not sure I believe in a man in the clouds anymore, but I believe in whatever was in that glass.'

Judy pulled the sleeves of her cardigan over her hands. 'You must think I'm mad,' she said.

'Well now, wouldn't that be the pot calling the kettle black,' Helen said, quietly.

'All of the best people have a screw loose. It was the thing I admired most about Dennis when we first met. In those early days of putting on the wig and the jumpsuit, he was terrible, like, chronically bad. He didn't have a note in his head but he loved it. And he didn't care what people made of him.'

'I fell in love with Liam when I watched him play hurling,' Helen said. 'All of my friends were mad about him. I didn't understand why until I saw him on the pitch—'

'Beating the crap out of other men with sticks. You'd have to be certifiable to play a sport like that.'

'It wasn't a macho thing with Liam,' Helen insisted, feeling the need to defend him. 'I could tell that he wasn't in it for himself. He was a team player. He cared about his teammates. I saw a vulnerability in him that I hadn't seen before in other men.'

'What did you want to be when you were younger, Helen?' Judy asked.

'I think I always wanted to be a teacher.'

'You were a teacher before you married Liam?'

'And for a few years after,' Helen said. 'It was only when I had Bláithín that I decided to stay at home. I remember a nun who taught us for a year in the convent. Sister Imelda was her name. She was the one who made me want to be a teacher. She used to put on these classroom plays. She cast me as Dorothy in *The Wizard of Oz*, and I just loved it—'

'You're an actor, Helen,' Judy interrupted her, looking like she was fit to burst. 'I met Mary last night and I felt like I'd met her before – you had her down to a tee. Her tone of voice, her mannerisms, the way that she holds her mouth, even the way that she held herself in conversation – it was like I'd met her in Donegal.'

Judy had gone too far before she realised what she was doing to Helen.

'What you saw in Donegal was a woman in the middle of a nervous breakdown,' Helen murmured.

'Isn't that all art is?' Judy asked. 'People having breakdowns. How else are we supposed to get through to each other?'

Chapter 11

Home

Kate

THE NIGHT BEFORE MARIA'S HEN, Kate had gotten a text from Helen.

'What did she say?' Ellius asked, turning over in the bed.

Kate showed him the message on her phone: *Hope the weekend goes well. Love Mam x*

'That's nice?' he suggested.

'She never texts me anymore.'

Kate was the one who sent texts – mostly photos – of the Palm House in the Botanic Gardens or the view of the city from Cave Hill, hoping that Helen would take her up on the invitation to visit. She fantasised about walking around Ormeau Park on a crisp autumn day, admiring the parade of well-heeled dogs as they passed.

She hadn't had a proper conversation with her mother in over three years. They'd learned to tiptoe around each other whenever she came home. When Helen spoke to her, the interaction felt both heightened and meaningless – like they were extras on a film set having a pretend conversation for the benefit of a scene.

Kate wanted to show her mother that she'd changed. The only way she could do that was to act like nothing had ever happened. Nobody else at home noticed any difference in her – they all saw the same old Blue.

'Try not to overthink it,' Ellius said, rubbing her head the way he petted Dolores. The dachshund was curled up at Kate's feet – the weight of her was comforting, as were the little sighs she let out of her snout.

Kate's phone pinged with notifications from the group. Maria had taken the lead on organising the trip to Belfast, conferring with Kate on the best places to go and allowing Niamh to collect money from the girls. Bláith was in charge of decorations. Maria sent photos of them having an arts and crafts day, making a scrapbook of Harry Styles with the odd photo of Maria and Kevin thrown in.

Kate couldn't sleep the night before they arrived, worrying about how she was going to play host to a bunch of girls from home who thought she was an attention-seeking whore.

'You're not still stressing out about that?' Ellius asked when she told him how nervous she was. 'It was ages ago.'

It had happened when they were still at university in Edinburgh. Kate had been home for Christmas and had gone out with the camogie team. She'd gotten hammered and ended up passed out in a taxi home. When she woke up, Nuala Corbett's brother Darren had had his tongue in her mouth and his hand up her skirt.

She'd sobered up quickly after that, enough to get out of the taxi and pour her fury into a Facebook post saying she'd been sexually assaulted. She didn't use Darren's name, but people had seen them getting into the taxi together outside the chipper. Everyone had their own opinions about what she was wearing, how she was all over him, talking about her open relationship while poking a plastic fork around in his curry chips.

The fear had kicked in the following morning, and she'd deleted the post, but by then, the damage was done. Up until that moment, she'd always been the quiet one on the team: the youngest Foley who wasn't great at camogie but gave it a go because she enjoyed having the craic down the club with the rest of them.

That evening, the doorbell rang. Helen answered it and Nuala was standing outside with Darren. Kate came downstairs hungover in her dressing gown. Her stomach nearly fell out of her when she saw who it was. Helen made tea for them in the front room where they exchanged small talk until finally, Nuala gave Darren a nudge and he mumbled an apology. The whole thing was mortifying.

Maria was livid with her. 'Everyone saw how you were with him.'

'I was drunk,' Kate said.

'You were all over him.'

'I was drunk,' she repeated. 'And unconscious, actually, so I wasn't in a position to give consent.'

From that night on, Kate's relationship with the camogie girls had never been the same. She rejoined the team for the few months that Vincent was sick so that she could spend more time with Niamh. She remembered standing outside the dressing room, overhearing Nuala interrupt a bunch of the young ones who were talking about the drama between Kate and Darren.

'Don't be bitching about Kate,' she said. 'She's harmless, really.'

Harmless. Kate flinched at the word, but she knew she deserved it. In that moment, she loved Nuala more than ever. She loved all the girls.

'Have you ever been part of a team like that?' she asked Ellius.

'Yeah, like, when I was—'

'A child?' she asked, jumping in before he had a chance to judge her. 'And you grew out of it, I suppose?'

'Yeah.'

'Yeah,' she said. 'We never did.'

'What time are they arriving tomorrow?' Ellius asked.

'Not until the evening. I'm going to meet them off the train after work.'

'Gives you plenty of time to brush up on your Troubles trivia,' Ellius replied.

Kate frowned. 'It's a hen party, not a school tour.'

'We'll see how long they last before they ask for a history of their own country.'

'What are your plans for the weekend?' Kate asked, changing the subject.

'I'll probably do something with Annalise.'

Just when Kate thought that she'd come to terms with being in an open relationship, Ellius had introduced her to Annalise. She had met a few of his dalliances before – men he'd met on nights out or on dating apps. She'd gotten used to their different reactions to the situation. Most of them thought that she was delusional, that it was only a matter of time before Ellius chose them over her, but he never did. They had established boundaries. Ellius told Kate who he was seeing and let her know if he wasn't going to be home. She even enjoyed having the bed to herself on nights he spent away.

Ellius had met Annalise at a writers' group organised by Dervla O'Donohue, a playwright who taught at Queen's. Every month, the group took it in turns to host a dinner party and talk about their work.

'I really think you'd get on with everyone,' Ellius said when he invited her along to one. 'And you'd enjoy it as well. You're always saying that you want to write more.'

She tagged along to the next session in Dervla's house on Rugby Road. They were late because Kate couldn't decide on what kind of wine to buy in the shop. In the end, she spent twenty pounds on a bottle of red.

'Ellius couldn't remember what wine you drank,' Kate said apologetically, handing it over to Dervla on her doorstep.

'Oh, I'd drink cat piss as long as it's white,' Dervla replied. 'But it's always nice to have red in the house. Come on in.'

She ushered them into the kitchen. Annalise got up from the table to greet them. Kate took in the nose ring, a maxi skirt and lace bustier worn underneath a knitted cardigan, the sleeves of which she clutched in closed fists as she hugged her.

'It's lovely to meet you at last,' Annalise said.

Kate pulled away and looked back at Dervla who was watching their interaction. She knew what was happening,

Kate realised, and was excited to observe the dynamic between them. She looked around the faces of the four other people in the room. They all knew.

'Ellius tells me you're a ballerina?' Annalise asked across the table at dinner.

'I used to dance,' Kate replied. 'I stopped a while ago.'

'You started going to classes again, though,' Ellius said.

She went to one class in the Crescent Arts Centre and knew as soon as she saw herself in a leotard in the studio mirror that she couldn't go back again.

Ellius was talking about how Annalise was writing a novel based on the life of the Russian dancer, Maya Plisetskaya. Someone else joined in the conversation, complimenting Annalise on the last chapter she'd submitted to the group for feedback. Kate took up her fork and concentrated on eating the pumpkin ravioli that Dervla had made from scratch.

'I can't believe you did that to me,' she'd said, on their walk home.

'Did what?' Ellius asked.

'Everyone knew.'

'Knew *what?*'

'You put me in a room of complete strangers who *all* knew that I was meeting the woman you're fucking.'

'Woah.' Ellius tried to put his hand around her waist.

She slapped it away. 'Don't touch me.'

'What are you talking about? Nobody knew, Kate.'

'They all knew.' She kept walking, the wet leaves on the pavement sticking to her boots.

The next morning, he'd made pancakes and put classical music on the record player. After breakfast, Kate curled up on the couch with the dog and watched the cat sunning herself in the window.

'Do you want to do the crossword?' Ellius asked, handing her a fresh mug of tea.

She sighed and took the mug from him.

'If you want me to stop seeing Annalise, I will,' he said, handing her a pen.

'It isn't about Annalise.'

Kate never went back to the writers' group. She'd met Annalise a few times since and tried her best to be friendly. It had been six months since Ellius had first started seeing her, and her career was beginning to take off. There were newspaper headlines about the six-figure publishing deal that she'd gotten earlier in the year.

'Maria said that you're welcome to join us at some point over the weekend if you like?' Kate asked, after she had brushed her teeth and climbed back into bed beside him. 'Bring Annalise along, sure.'

Ellius laughed. 'You're all right, thanks. Gutted I didn't make the cut for Kevin's stag though.'

'Are you still OK to play music at the wedding?' Kate asked. 'It's only for a couple of hours.'

'Of course,' he said.

Ellius didn't usually do weddings, but Maria had seen the traditional music set he did at Electric Picnic last year, and she wanted something a bit different to entertain her guests. It was a business transaction. Ellius knew that Maria wasn't his biggest fan. She'd made up her mind about him after she'd heard about the first time he told Kate that he loved her. They were teenagers having sex in the box room they shared in Edinburgh when he came out with it.

'I love you, you cunt.'

He'd said it just after he'd cum. There was a wild panic in his eyes as he stared down at her before he rolled away and faced the wall. It wasn't the word itself that bothered Kate but the look on his face, like he'd just been pushed from a helicopter and was crash-landing into a place he didn't want to be. Kate stayed lying on her back, breathing heavily and staring up at the Rorschach test of mould spread across the ceiling.

She messaged Maria the next morning.

He said WHAT?

Kate tried explaining that given the right context, it was practically a term of endearment. Maria was having none of it:

Kate, when a boy tells you he loves you, you shouldn't be thinking about the way he uses the word cunt. Talk to him about it.

But she couldn't, not even years later when she could have brought it up as a joke. Kate knew that he'd be able to sniff out the truth – that it was a story she used to tell random women in smoking areas on nights out. The oversharing was like impulse buying or binge eating or a flare-up of IBS, needing to get it all out of her system and welcoming the shame that came afterwards like an old friend.

She still caught herself in the middle of a conversation hating everything she was saying. Even if she could afford therapy, she couldn't listen to the stuff that came out of her mouth. The only thing that helped was going to work and making coffee. She was at home behind the machine – unscrewing the handles and dumping cakes of coffee grounds into the tray like broken sandcastles, the whirr of the grinder making new ones to stamp and twist into place, pressing the button and grabbing the pitcher to foam milk.

Kate liked the early morning shift because she opened the café by herself. Simon said that he usually needed two people to cover the mornings but she was so good that he could trust her to fly solo for a couple of hours.

Kate got on with Simon – he'd given her the job six months ago when she was in the depths of misery. During the interview, he'd asked her why she had changed jobs so much in the past two years. She ended up telling him about Joe.

Joe was a stalwart of Café Nero on the Ormeau Road. On her first shift, he'd looked her up and down and informed her that she was new.

She laughed and said, 'I am.'

He asked her where her accent was from, and then he asked if she knew the Foleys.

'I am a Foley,' she said.

'Ach now,' he said, 'I'm sorry for your loss.'

Joe was on the Antrim minor team back in the day and had an encyclopaedic knowledge of every club and inter-county GAA match that had taken place over the last century. He used to stay at the till chatting, begrudgingly stepping aside to allow other customers to place their orders. As time went on, it only got worse, even after her manager, Micky, had an awkward word with him about allowing Kate to do her job.

'I've not gotten you into trouble with that wee fruit, have I?' Joe had asked as soon as he was out of earshot.

'Ah now, Joe, behave yourself,' Kate said.

Micky had told her that it was her responsibility to maintain professional boundaries with customers. Kate tried her best with Joe, but she couldn't ignore the man altogether. His face was so open and lonely that it hurt to look at him.

'All you need to do is tell him to fuck off,' Ellius had said, whenever she came home from work and started complaining about all the time she'd spent trying to manage her interactions with Joe.

'I can't,' she said. 'I've tried.'

'Have you though?'

'What do I say? "Can you stop talking to me"?'

'Yes!'

'It's not like he's being a creep though. I think he's just really lonely.'

'We're all lonely. I'm lonely, you're lonely – we don't go around harassing people. I just . . . I can't understand how you're quitting your job instead of telling him that you don't have time to give him your undivided attention while you're trying to work. It's as simple as that.'

Kate didn't tell Joe when she handed in her notice, but one of the girls from Nero let slip that she'd moved to a quieter café down the road, where they had more time to chat when he came in. He set up shop at the table closest to the counter and wore the ear off her until closing time. She lasted three weeks before she started applying to places again.

She was a month into the new job when Joe wandered in off the road and saw her. Simon seemed to know what was happening by the look on her face and the awkward reunion.

'How are you, sir?' he'd asked, taking over from Kate at the till. 'What can I get you?'

'That girl there knows my order.'

'Very good,' Simon said, walking over to Kate who was frothing milk. 'Stay at the coffee machine and try to ignore him,' he murmured into her ear.

Joe tried his best to talk to her over the noise of the grinder, leaning his forearm on the counter like he was in the Hogan stand of Croke Park. The hardest part was to pretend he wasn't there. He left within an hour. The last time she saw him, he was sitting in Café Nero staring into space.

*

'Any plans for the weekend?' Simon asked as they were closing up.

'It's my sister's hen,' Kate said.
'Oh aye? Where are youse headed?'
'Here!'
'A wee trip to Belfast to get blocked before the big day?'
'Yep.'
'How many of them are coming up?'
'About twenty of us. We're going to head into town tomorrow.'
'Happy days. Whereabouts are youse going?'
'The Cathedral Quarter? I think we're going to start off in the Dirty Onion and go from there.'
'I might see youse there!'

She wasn't expecting him to be sat on his own waiting for them.
'Who's that?' Maria muttered, as he walked towards her.
'It's my boss,' Kate said.
'You invited your boss to my hen?'
Simon came over to congratulate Maria and insisted on buying a round.
Kate pulled Maria to the side. 'I swear, I didn't invite him.'
'Then why is he here?' Maria said, through a forced smile.
'Maybe he's waiting for someone else? I think he's just trying to be nice.'
Kate already knew by looking at him that Simon was coked off his head. He was in his late forties and kept himself fit. Most of the regular customers fancied him but looking

at him handing out shots to the camogie team, he was just another man on a night out with a smell of want off him.

She watched him scan the group and take them all in. Maria had insisted that she didn't want any learner plates or willy straws, but they managed to get a sash on her, and Lynn and Ronnie were walking around with an inflatable penis they'd bought in Poundland and brought to brunch earlier.

Simon clocked Niamh standing next to Bláithín, laughing and dancing to the band, wearing a black crop top and jeans. Niamh had lost even more weight since Christmas. Maria had had to return the bridesmaid dress she had ordered for her last year and replace it with a smaller size. Everyone was talking about how great she looked – the girls slapped her arse and twirled her around.

Kate watched as Simon made his way over to Niamh at the bar. Bláithín was having absolutely none of him. She took Niamh by the hand, pulled her away and turned her back to him.

When he tried to approach them again, Bláith tapped him on the shoulder.

He bent down so she could shout into his ear, 'We don't want to talk to you.'

He patted her on the shoulder and tried to laugh her off, but she said it again, loud enough for everyone to hear.

'You're off?' Kate asked, when Simon came back over to her with his blazer in his hand.

'I think your friend sobered me up,' he said.

'That's my sister.'

'Your sister? She's great,' he said, looking over at Bláith who was giving him daggers.

'She's a pain in the arse, but we love her.'

'No, it's great to see . . . great to see her out and having a good time with friends, it's great,' he repeated. 'I don't know what's wrong with me. I found myself at a loose end and I remembered that you said you'd be out with your friends and . . . I don't know what's wrong with me. You just . . . you never come to work nights out, you know? And I was curious to see what you're like on a night out because you're great, but you're so –' he clenched his fists and brought them into his chest, '– closed off in work. It's like you're just there to do your job – and don't get me wrong, you do a great job – but there's more to you, I can tell.'

Kate could feel Maria watching their interaction.

He took her shoulders in his hands. 'You're great.'

'Thanks,' she said.

'Right, I'll see you on Monday, sure.'

'I'll see you on Monday.'

He kissed her on the cheek before he left.

'I don't want to talk about it,' she said to Maria, who had walked over to ask for an explanation of what had happened.

Kate went to the bar and ordered another round of shots while the girls cheered her on. They knocked the tequila back, biting into lime wedges and squirming.

There was a weird energy in the air when everyone started teasing Niamh about Peter. Kate knew that Peter had kissed some of the girls on the team when they were teenagers at GAA discos, and she could tell that some of them still carried a torch for him. When she was younger, there were times that a girl would be nice to her and Kate would think that she had made a friend until she realised that they were only trying to get closer to Peter.

The girls were talking about how Peter and Niamh had been spotted looking cosy in the corner snug of the pub at the weekend. Niamh was denying everything, batting them away. Kate forced a smile and tried not to think about the last time she had teased Niamh about Peter.

Instead, she concentrated on mentally checking off things on the list that she'd made for the weekend. After work on Friday, she had checked in to the apartment Maria had booked and had decorated it with photos and balloons before going to meet everyone at the station. Kate was in a toilet cubicle when their train got in. Maria was texting her asking where she was, but she ignored the messages. The last thing she needed was for the camogie team to know about the state of her bowels.

She'd met them outside the station and threw her arms around her sister. As she looked around the group, she could see her teenage years reflected in their eyes. Kate was never good at sport, but she didn't have a choice when it came to being a part of the team that Liam trained. She came on as a substitute in games that didn't matter as much. Liam taught her how to dive in order to win a free. At the time, she didn't know that he was teaching her how to cheat.

Niamh was at the back of the group and avoided making eye contact with her. The Airbnb was in the Holylands. The girls piled out of the taxi, laughing at the street names.

'There's a Jerusalem Street and a Palestine Street?' Maria said. 'This is gas.'

'Yeah, colonialism,' Kate replied. 'Gas altogether.'

It was the first time anyone from home had come to visit her. Kate caught sight of herself every so often, presenting the city to them like an estate agent showing off a property. She felt personally responsible when Maria's data roaming wouldn't work.

'You can use mine for the weekend,' she said, thrusting her phone into her sister's hands.

'Don't be stupid, it's fine. It's just mad that my phone is telling me I'm abroad in my own country,' Maria said.

They had decided to stay in and play games that first night. They were drinking cans at three o'clock in the morning when Maria started needling her.

'Come on now, Kate, we need to know what we can and can't say when we're out tomorrow night,' Maria had said, taking a handful of Doritos from a bowl. 'Would it be all right to bring up religion?'

'You'd be surprised at the amount of atheists around here,' Kate said. 'Especially in the places we're going – atheists and gays, mostly. Often both.'

'Do people talk about, you know, the Troubles?' Julie asked, her eyes widening.

'Does Ellius talk about it?' Maria asked.

'I used to ask him stupid questions—'

'See, what stupid questions?' Maria asked. 'These are the things we need to know.'

'I don't know, it's hard to explain.'

'Do you feel at home here?' Ruth asked.

'I don't know.'

'Classic Kate,' Maria interjected. 'Living up North. Having a gay boyfriend. She's always gone out of her way to make life difficult for herself, and then she wonders why she's stressed out.'

'Maria,' Niamh whispered, putting her hand on her knee.

Kate could tell by Maria's eyes that she'd taken a turn.

'And you're beautiful, we all know you're the beautiful one,' Maria said, pointing a finger at her and narrowing her eyes. 'But you do this thing where you flirt with men and then clutch your pearls when they flirt back. It's like you're baiting them, waiting for them to bite so you can turn on them.'

'Hold on now, Maria,' Lynn said. 'I think it's time for bed.'

'Look at her, she'll start crying now.' Maria nodded at Kate who felt the tears prick at her eyes.

'Look! Look! There we go!' Maria started clapping. 'I'm the bitch and everyone feels sorry for her.'

The next morning, Maria had crawled into the bed beside her. She groaned into the pillow.

'I'm so sorry, Blue. I didn't mean any of that.'

Kate turned over in the bed to face her. 'I've forgotten all about it. It's your hen weekend. You can do what you like.'

'I never want to drink again.'

'Listen, you got overexcited. We've all been there. We'll take it easy today.'

'I need to apologise to everyone.'

'Maria, it was two minutes – less. Nobody remembers.'

A team meeting was called before they left the apartment to go to brunch. Kate looked at her feet while Maria gave her speech and tried not to feel like she was the one in the wrong.

Seven hours of steady drinking later, they had arrived at the nightclub. Everywhere Kate looked, there were men lurking around women who were trying their best to pretend they weren't there.

'Kate!' Maria shouted at her, pulling her away from a teenager who was coming up and thrusting into them. 'For God's sake, just ignore him!'

She went to the bathroom and texted Ellius on the toilet.

There are creeps everywhere.

He was online and saw the message but didn't reply. Kate didn't need him to reply. She just needed him to know. Everything in her life felt more manageable when Ellius knew about it. She left the toilet cubicle and washed her hands, watching her reflection move around in the bathroom mirror.

She was on her way back to the dance floor when she saw a guy kissing a woman who was barely able to stand. He opened the door to the disabled toilet and tried to push her inside.

'Woah, no,' she said, taking the woman's hand. 'She's not sober enough to go in there.'

'Who are you, her ma?'

The guy was a good-looking posh boy with a baby face – he couldn't have been any more than twenty. Kate took the girl by the hand and led her away. She was almost completely passed out. Kate sat her down on a chair and put her head between her legs. She was looking around, wondering what to do when she saw the same guy grinding up against Niamh on the dance floor.

Kate ran over and shoved him away. 'Leave her alone!'

He swayed and leered at her, taking her by the hand and twirling her around. She untangled her fingers from his and slapped him across the face.

As she turned around, she felt him grab her by the ponytail and pull her back. There was a moment of relief – of vindication – when a black pain shot through her face.

*

In A&E, the triage nurse asked how many times he punched her.

'Twice?' she guessed, like a gameshow contestant. 'It could have been three times. It definitely wasn't more than four.'

The nurse tutted while she cleaned up the blood and bandaged the cut on her cheek.

She gave her an ice pack and painkillers and sent her back out to the waiting room.

The girls insisted on going to the hospital with her. All the seats were taken, so they sat on the floor and huddled together, falling asleep on each other's shoulders. Kate begged them to go home without her but Maria wouldn't hear of it.

It was Saturday night in A&E – a guy in a tracksuit was off his face, wandering in and out of the waiting room like he was still trying to get his head around the concept of gravity. A young girl was slumped semi-conscious in the corner in a short dress. Kate wanted to go over and pull the dress down for her, or at least throw a jacket around her to cover her arse cheeks that were on show.

Beside them, a father was trying his best to be there for his son – a gangly teenage boy with his head bowed, his long hair hiding his face. He was mortified when his dad arrived with camp chairs for them to sit on and a backpack filled with sweets and energy drinks.

'Remember your box breathing,' the man said, reaching over to squeeze his hand.

The son pulled his arm away. 'Do you want a box?'

Kate could see the blue veins popping out of arms that gripped the sides of the chair and the red welts on the inside of his wrists. She imagined him sitting beside his dad in those camp chairs at a festival in ten years' time drinking cans in the sun, a girlfriend and a boxer dog at home, tattoo sleeves on both arms to cover up the scars – he just had to make it that far.

*

Her dad had been the last person in her family to lose patience with her. Kate had always been a fussy eater. As a child, Sunday was her least favourite day of the week because her mother would make a roast dinner. When they were summoned to the table, Kate sat down beside Liam and waited for a meteorite of a potato to land on her plate. She could feel her mother's eyes bore into her as she peeled it.

Helen ordered her to have a bite. Kate already knew what it tasted like. It felt like biting into a bar of crumbly old soap.

'Come on now,' Liam said.

Kate felt tears well up in her eyes.

'For God's sake, Kate,' her mother said, wiping sweat away from her top lip with a napkin. 'One bite won't kill you.'

Her siblings were bored of her dramatics. Maria and Peter were talking with their mouths full, arguing over what colour Power Ranger was the best. Bláith was slurping gravy from a spoon like it was soup.

'Here,' Liam said, leaning over to her plate. He gestured to the milk jug in the centre of the table, the butter and salt. Kate lined them up in front of him and waited for the consecration to take place.

A river of milk rushed over the potato. Butter dribbled into the flood plain. By the time her dad had worked his magic, Kate was making her way through the field of fluffy yellow mash, taking precise forkfuls, furrow by careful furrow, into her mouth.

'Good girl,' Liam said.

'Don't be mollycoddling her Liam,' Helen scolded him. 'You'll have her ruined.'

By the time she was a teenager, every dinner time was a silent protest. She had fainted in the kitchen on a Sunday morning before mass. Her dad had bundled her into the car and drove to A&E where they waited hours for a doctor to assess her.

Liam had broken down in tears when the doctor sent them home.

'We can't cope,' he said.

'Mr Foley, Kate is already part of an outpatient programme,' the doctor said. 'The best place for her to be right now is at home.'

'I just don't understand why she's doing this to herself,' he said. 'I'll never understand it.'

It was only when Liam pulled into a Chinese takeaway on the way home that Kate realised he hadn't eaten all day. He called Helen to ask what everyone wanted before he went in to place an order, leaving her to sit in the car alone. She couldn't stop crying, couldn't stop apologising when he came back with the brown paper bags which he handed to her in the passenger seat, snaffling prawn crackers and keeping his eyes firmly on the road ahead.

'I can't do it anymore, Blue,' he said, his greasy fingers gripping the steering wheel as she tried not to gag at the smell of the food in her lap. 'I just can't do it.'

Kate was eleven years old when Helen brought the bockety old scales down to the kitchen to weigh Liam's suitcase for a golfing holiday. It was his idea to start guessing how much everyone weighed.

Helen was the only one who refused to do it – the rest of them placed their bets and lined up in order of age: Liam, Vincent, John, Maria, Bláith, Peter, Niamh and Kate. It was like being at the Grand National. Everyone shouted out numbers and slapped their hands on the table to do a drumroll before the weight was announced. Peter was lying belly-down on the floor, making sure the scales were properly aligned.

Kate knew that she was the smallest, but she didn't know how small she was until she stepped onto the dirty cream platform and watched the red pointer make the leap from zero to –

'Five stone, eight pounds!' Peter shouted.

'Not even six stone!' Liam exclaimed.

'Sure, there's not a pick on her,' Vincent said. 'You could put her in your pocket.'

That was when the weighing started. Years later, when a therapist asked what her ideal body looked like, she couldn't tell her, but she always knew what weight she wanted to be. Anything under six stone was safe.

*

After about an hour waiting in A&E, an Elvis impersonator walked through the doors with a pile of pizza boxes and shouted, 'Are there any Foleys in here?'

The girls waved him over.

'Your mother sent me,' he announced, setting the pizza boxes down in front of them.

'Helen ordered a stripper?' Lynn whispered.

'Sorry, how do you know our mam?' Maria asked.

'I don't. I was doing a gig in the city centre tonight when my wife rang me. She said to go to the Royal Victoria A&E with pizza and ask for the Foleys.'

Elvis handed out the pizza boxes. He offered a slice to the teenage boy and his dad in the camp chairs.

'A pizza delivery from the King himself,' the man said, nudging his son who sank further into his chair. 'Do you've a song for us?'

'Dad,' the boy moaned.

Elvis put down his slice of pizza, stood up in front of the entire waiting room and in his best drawl said, 'I hope y'all aren't too shook up out there, and y'all are seen to shortly. I don't have my guitar with me, so I'm gonna do an acapella number. Feel free to join in if y'all know the words.'

The mood shifted as soon as he sang the first line of 'Can't Help Falling in Love'. He was good. The tension that was in the air at the prospect of witnessing a man embarrass himself in public left the room. People started to record him on their phones.

At the very end, he did a verse in Irish. There was a split second of silence before the whooping and clapping started. He bowed and sat back down, tucking back into his pizza.

'Why don't you perform as yourself?' Kate asked. 'You're good enough to go out on your own.'

The man shrugged. 'I love Elvis.'

'You know that he met Priscilla when she was fourteen?'

'Oh, here we go,' Maria said. 'Can you see how she got the broken nose?'

It was another hour before Kate was seen by a doctor who gave her the all-clear.

'Don't be worrying about taxis,' Elvis said. 'I have the van outside as long as you don't mind piling into the back of it.'

Kate sat in the front with an ice pack pressed to her nose. The rest of the team organised themselves in the back of the Ford transit among the amps and equipment. The car radio came on – the Spice Girls were singing 'Wannabe'. Elvis turned up the volume so that they could sing along.

She wound down the passenger side window and felt the wind and rain on her face. The headlights of cars lit up the tyre tracks in the water. Kate closed her eyes and leaned back against the headrest.

The doctor had asked her if she'd broken her nose before. Kate surprised herself when she answered, 'I think so.'

They'd found an ice rink down the Scribbeen when they were kids: Maria, Bláith, Peter and Niamh, who walked beside Kate, both of them in their dads' old wellies stuffed with socks and old newspaper. They got excited when they saw the sheet of ice that covered the grass, thick enough to hold up under the weight of their boots.

It was early in the evening, but the sun had already gone down. Flashes of silver cut through the dark. The sky was clear and star-speckled. Kate was looking up, trying to find to find the Plough when she tripped over a loop of barbed wire and fell face down on the ice.

Maria came over to shush her. 'You're all right,' she said.

Kate's nose was blocked. She could taste blood. She also knew that Maria wasn't asking a question but giving an order, wrestling her back into a version of reality where she had to act like nothing had happened to her.

Now, Kate looked at her sister in the rear-view mirror as she struggled into Elvis' tricolour jumpsuit in the back of a moving transit van, making the most out of the hen weekend she would later blame Kate for ruining. She wondered if Maria could see a change in Niamh, who was helping her into the jumpsuit, turning her around to zip up the back. There was no way that Kate would dream of telling Maria, but it didn't mean that it wasn't there anyway, in the effort that Niamh was making, the act she was putting on for the sake of everyone else. Maria put her arm around Niamh's shoulders in the back of the van as though leaning on her to create a happy memory. Kate caught Niamh's eye in the mirror and they both looked away, back to Maria's version of reality where nothing had happened and everything was OK.

Chapter 12

Birds

Helen

THE NIGHT BEFORE THE WEDDING, Maria thrust the Child of Prague statue into Helen's hands like she was giving her an Academy Award.

'It's supposed to be the matriarch of the family who does the honours,' she said.

'Surely that's Nan,' Peter argued.

'It's grand, I'll do it,' Helen replied, happy to step up to the plate rather than entertain Nan for the evening.

Maria looked doubtful. 'No, Peter's right. I'll go over and get Nan. We don't want to tempt fate,' she said, as though she was running the risk of divine retribution and not just a bit of rain on her big day.

The statue gave Helen a smug grin. Earlier that week, she'd brought her own Child of Prague out of retirement for Maria's inspection.

'It's a bit small,' Maria had said, tilting her head in contemplation. 'And it's supposed to be luckier if it doesn't have a head.'

'Will we bring him to the guillotine?' Helen joked.

'No, it doesn't work when you do it on purpose. It's supposed to fall off by itself.'

Maria ended up going to Nan, who called in a favour from one of the women at bingo to give her a lend of a headless one. Helen's Child of Prague was relegated back to his place on the table of tat next to the washing machine, his cherubic face turned to the wall.

Within ten minutes, Nan had appeared in her kitchen with a bag full of rollers that she handed to her.

'I was beginning to think you'd forgotten,' Nan grumbled, shuffling her way towards her seat at the head of the table.

Helen took the rollers from her mother-in-law. There was no point in arguing with the woman. Helen hated styling Nan's hair with every fibre of her being. There was a time when she had tried her best not to mess it up before realising that the more she tried, the worse it turned out. It was yet another genius move by Nan to showcase her shortcomings. She could already imagine Nan at the wedding, asking people what they thought of her hair, telling them that she wasn't sure about it, but that Helen was very good to offer to do it and she didn't want to upset her by going to someone else.

'What's for dinner?' Nan asked.

Maria sent Peter out to the microwave in the utility room to heat up the leftover roast dinner from the day before.

Nan looked offended. 'You've eaten without me?'

Helen was searching her handbag for a hairbrush. 'No, Nan. We went out for dinner with Kevin's parents today. You were invited, remember? You said that you had bingo.'

'I said no such thing. I would have cancelled bingo if I had known.'

'Nan,' Maria said, sitting down at the table beside her grandmother. 'I was wondering if you'd be up for putting the Child of Prague out in the garden.'

Nan blinked at her.

'You know,' Maria continued. 'It's supposed to be better luck if it's the matriarch of the family who puts the Child of Prague out the night before the wedding.'

'The matri-what?'

Maria delved into a clumsy explanation while Nan frowned and shifted in her chair. 'And here's me thinking you'd give me a proper job.'

Maria's face fell. 'I didn't think you'd want . . . I mean, it's not too late. What would you like to do?'

'Well,' Nan said, clasping her hands together, 'I was thinking that you'd need someone to give a speech – from the Foley side of the family.'

'Do you think you would be up to doing that?' Maria asked.

'I'm old, not dead,' Nan said, picking up her knife and fork and tucking into the dinner Peter had set down in front of her.

Hours later, Nan was still at the kitchen table in a hairnet of pink foam rollers, chain-smoking cigarettes and using Helen's favourite mug as an ashtray. It was only when Maria had asked her to put out the Child of Prague for the third time that she finally did the honours, making a dig at the health of the hydrangea bush while she was at it.

'Right,' Nan said, steadying herself on her walking stick. 'I suppose I should go work on this speech. Where is John?'

'He's feeding the calves, Nan. Do you know what we'll do? John's Nadine has a real way with words,' Helen said. 'I'll send her over to you with the laptop and you can work on your speech together.'

Helen didn't feel bad about throwing Nadine under the bus if it meant getting Nan out of her kitchen. She sent Peter over to Nadine to deliver the bad news and spent the rest of the evening listening to the *Best of Mary Black* album that Liam had given her for Christmas one year. She could hear the kids downstairs in the front room having a few drinks. Kevin had gone to stay with his parents. The way that Maria had acted outside the chapel when they said goodbye, you'd swear he was going off to war. Helen was mortified standing next to Father Angelo watching them maul the face off each other.

It was after ten o'clock when she got the text from Judy. *I've just arrived. Take your time.*

Helen thought about popping her head in the door to say goodnight to Maria. She made it as far as the hall where she could see Peter sitting beside Niamh on the couch. He'd glued fake eyelashes onto his eyelids and she was fixing them with tweezers, telling him to hold still. Helen watched as waves of happiness broke across her son's face. Ever since they were kids, she had hoped this moment would come. She felt an ugly tug in her gut. She pulled her eyes away from them and walked down the corridor and out the back door.

*

It was hard to believe that only a month had passed since Helen had found Judy throwing up in her hydrangea bushes. Judy was sitting at her kitchen table having a cup of tea when Helen had gotten the call from Maria in Belfast. She had heard the panic in Maria's voice and immediately thought the worst. It was only a matter of time before Kate told everyone about what had happened. Helen had been waiting for the moment to come ever since the day they found Liam.

Kate had broken her nose, Maria said. Some guy in a nightclub punched her in the face. The flash of a memory crossed her mind – Helen slapping Kate when she tried to tell her about Liam and Niamh.

But it was OK. Kate hadn't told anyone.

She burst into tears, out of relief more than anything. She wanted the ground to swallow her, especially when Judy tried her best to comfort her.

'It's just a broken nose,' Judy said, patting her on the back. 'It'll heal in a couple of weeks.'

Helen didn't know what Maria was saying at first when she rang her again the morning after Kate's accident, banging on about an Elvis who had delivered pizza to them in A&E, but then the penny dropped.

'Judy must have sent him,' Helen said.

'Who's Judy?' Maria asked.

'His wife. She called in for a cup of tea last night and she heard about what happened.'

Helen was driving back from dropping Judy at her sister's house. They had stayed up the night before chatting, and Judy had ended up staying in the spare room. Helen made breakfast in the morning, which was interrupted by John's boys who came in after hurling training still in their football boots with clumps of grass matted into the studs. The children stopped in their tracks when they saw the strange woman sitting at the kitchen table.

'Hello,' Judy said, turning around and leaning her elbow on the back of her chair.

'Who are you?' Arwin asked.

'I'm Judy. I'm a friend of your granny's.'

'Granny doesn't have any friends,' Elmo had said, climbing up on the seat furthest away from Judy.

Helen laughed into the awkward silence. 'The boys are in for their hot chocolate after training.'

'And big marshmallows this time, Granny,' Arwin said. 'Not the small ones.'

Judy had put her number into Helen's phone as she was leaving.

'You won't come in?' she asked, when they pulled into her sister's estate.

'No, I'll keep going.'

'Let me know if you need anything,' Judy said, giving her a look that could have meant any number of things.

Helen didn't know if she'd ever hear from her again. The next day, her heart leapt in her chest at a notification on her phone. Judy had found her on Facebook and invited her to join a stained glass group. She started sending her photos of churches that she'd been to and invited her on her next trip to see an Evie Hone window in Dublin.

Helen was getting ready for mass when she decided to send Judy a link to a website that advertised staying overnight in old churches.

Fancy a sleepover in St Brigid's?

It had taken Judy a while to respond. Helen felt her phone vibrate in her coat pocket during the Our Father and couldn't wait until the prayer ended to look at the reply.

Give me a date and time and I'm there.

Helen thought she was joking. It was only when Judy started sending her photos of sleeping bags and a flask that she'd bought for their 'camping trip' that she realised that she was serious about it. She broke into a smile so big that little Aoife asked what was wrong with her.

'Nothing, pet,' Helen said, pulling her into a hug. 'I'm just happy. I'm excited for the wedding. Are you excited?'

*

Helen pulled up outside the chapel and saw Judy taking two suitcases out of the boot of her car.

'Are you planning on moving in?' she asked.

'This is nothing,' Judy replied. 'Wait until I whip out the camp chairs and the air mattress.'

Helen carried a suitcase up to the doors of the church and fished around in her coat pocket for the spare set of keys Father Angelo had given Maria for nativity rehearsals. She panicked when it didn't fit.

'The bastards changed the locks,' she said.

'Hang on.' Judy took over, turning the key upside down. It slid in and the door opened.

Everything was amplified once they were inside. Their footsteps on the tiles echoed around them as they wheeled the suitcases up the middle aisle. It had only been a few hours since Helen had been in the church, and it smelled different in the dark. She hadn't noticed the stale incense that hung in the air after Mrs O'Donovan's funeral.

Mrs O'Donovan was a quiet woman in her late seventies who couldn't stop smiling. Helen couldn't quite tell if she could help it, or if the smile disappeared when she was alone. She sat in the pew opposite Helen at mass, smiling with such force that even to look at her was exhausting. Everyone watched her at mass every Sunday, passing around the collection basket. Her husband had gone to school with Nan and had died in his sixties. Nan had tried to get her claws into her, inviting her to play bingo and bridge with her crew, but Mrs O'Donovan kept to herself. It was only when she died that Helen realised that she didn't know the woman's first name. She looked it up on RIP.ie: Mairéad O'Donovan (née Kelly.)

During the offertory collection at the funeral, Helen imagined taking the wicker basket from papery, blue-veined hands, looking into the woman's eyes and whispering, 'Thanks Máiread.'

They set up camp underneath the stained-glass window, its power lying dormant in the darkness. Helen trundled the electric heater out of the sacristy. Judy wasn't joking about the air mattress. Every time she went back out to the car, she brought something else back in – bedsheets and pillows, flasks of hot water and chocolate biscuits.

'Ah Jesus,' Helen whispered, when she came in with a bottle of Sauvignon Blanc and wine glasses.

'I've been radicalised after Lough Derg,' Judy said. 'If I'm spending the night in a church again, I'm going to make myself comfortable.'

There was something ceremonial about the way she placed the wine glasses down on the tiles of the floor. The stations of the cross looked down on them as Helen steadied the stems of the glasses and Judy poured.

They settled into camp chairs with blankets across their knees and clinked their glasses together. Their voices grew from whispers to low murmurs.

'What's he like? The fella she's marrying?' Judy asked.

'He's a clown.'

'That's what my family thought when I brought Dennis home.'

'Well, I've lived with this lad for the last few years, and my instincts were right.'

'Maybe he'll surprise you.'

'Did your family change their mind about Dennis?' Helen asked.

'Oh yeah. Big time. They're mad about him. They could take or leave me, but Dennis has a way of winning people over.'

'You make a beautiful couple,' Helen said.

Judy looked at her. 'You know Dennis is gay, don't you?' She gave Helen a wry smile as she watched her face drop. 'Don't worry, I didn't realise either. I was head over heels for him. I still love the bones of him. He's my best friend.'

'*What?*'

'I know.'

'I have so many questions,' Helen said. Her head was dizzy with them.

'Fire away, I'd love to answer them. It's rare I get to talk about it with anyone. I haven't even told my sisters.'

'They don't know?' Helen asked.

'Of course they don't. I wouldn't give them the satisfaction. They're mad jealous of my marriage. They can't understand how I don't have the same problems with Dennis as they do with their husbands. What they don't know is that we haven't slept in the same bed since 1981.'

Later, they changed into pyjamas like schoolgirls at a sleepover. After a few minutes of Helen insisting that she was fine to sleep in the camp chair, Judy coaxed her onto the air mattress which was just about big enough for the both of them. Listening to the creak of the old wooden pews in the dark, it was like the church was breathing with them.

'Can I ask you a question?' Judy whispered, just as they were drifting off to sleep.

'Of course.'

'What happened between you and Mary?'

Helen sighed. 'A whole lot of nothing.'

It was the silence that followed that shifted something between them. Helen grazed Judy's hand underneath the covers. Judy took her fingers and pressed them to her lips. She kissed her hand again and again, sending the small, smacking noises up to the high ceiling.

It was Helen who pulled her towards her – their foreheads banged together.

'Christ,' she whispered.

They both nearly fell off the mattress laughing.

'Are you OK?' Judy asked, reaching out to find her again.

Her hands cupped Helen's face and she moved slowly towards her. By the time their lips touched, they were both crying. Judy wiped the tears away from her face and stroked her hair. They began to move together, touching each other with such care. Helen didn't realise that she was holding her breath until she began to make choking noises – Judy kept going until a moan rose up from her body into the night like a prayer.

The birds woke them in the morning. Helen opened her eyes and smiled at the sound of their fluttering wings. Judy's arm was wrapped around her waist. They both stirred politely, not wanting to break the spell of sleep.

A triptych of windows towered above them – the Virgin Mary in the middle holding her newborn with angels crowning her in gold. Two saints flanked her on either side: St Catherine in red, kneeling with a sword and St Elizabeth in green, offering bread and wine. They had been looking down on generations of congregations long before Helen was born. The older she got, the more tired the women seemed.

The birds chirped as the first rays of sun came through the windows. Shafts of light showered the colours onto their makeshift bed. They lay there, basking in the glow of the saints who looked down on them – tired women resting in the broken light of dawn.

Chapter 13

The Story

Kate

THE NIGHT BEFORE THE WEDDING, Kate decided to make a playlist for the morning of Maria's big day. She had opened Ellius' laptop when she noticed an email in his inbox from Annalise. It was feedback for a short story. Kate bristled. She had always been his first reader, but Ellius hadn't even told her that he was writing again. She clicked into the Word document and began to read.

He was late home from work. Kate was sitting cross-legged on the bed giving Dolores ear scratches when he came into the bedroom, bitching about the new guy his boss had hired.

'You just have to look at the head on him to know he hasn't set foot behind a bar before. Here, I'll probably have to head off early on Sunday morning after the wedding. I have to practice the set I'm doing for the gig in the Limelight.' He clapped his hands and bowed his head. 'I haven't eaten dinner yet. Do you want to order something?'

'I've read your story,' Kate said.

'What?'

She kept her eyes on Dolores, running the tips of her fingers over the dog's belly.

'The story you sent Annalise,' she said.

He frowned. 'That's private.'

'Yeah, it is private.'

Dolores' eyes were closed and she was beginning to doze off, like a middle-aged woman getting a massage.

'It's a story, Kate. Fiction.'

'Fiction about my family.'

He sighed and sat down on the bed beside her. Dolores rolled out of her zen state and hopped onto Kate's lap. 'It might have been inspired by—'

'*Inspired by*? Are you for real?'

'Yes,' he insisted. 'Inspired by things that happened—'

'Things that happened to *me*.'

'It's an important story, Blue.'

'Don't call me that.'

'Why not?'

Dolores peered up at her to check if she was OK. Kate rubbed the dog's ears and stared at the collage of postcards on the wall in front of them, the trans and pride flags draped on either side like stage curtains. A noticeboard of pins – Repeal the Eighth badges, a Palestinian watermelon stuck to the front cover of *An Béal Bocht,* the book that Ellius had given her all those years ago in the Gaeltacht when they were just kids.

'I'm in a better position to write about it,' Ellius said. 'You're too close to the source material –'

'– The source material is my dead fucking father!'

'Exactly!' he said. 'And I've tried my best to translate the story into fiction, where these difficult questions can be explored in a safe space.'

Kate stared at him. 'You are scum.'

'This is why I was waiting until I had it in better shape before I showed it to you. If you feel this strongly about it, I won't share it with anyone.'

'You've already sent it to Annalise,' she said, getting off the bed. Dolores followed her towards the door.

'Is this about Annalise again? Where are you going?'

'Home.'

He ran his hands through his hair. 'Give me five minutes here.'

'You're not coming.'

'To the wedding? Wait, what? Kate, calm down.'

'I am calm,' she said.

'What about the gig?' he asked.

'I'm sure we'll survive without you.'

She'd already packed up everything she needed in the boot of her car. She left her set of house keys by the bedside table.

'So, this is it?' Ellius asked. 'We're not going to even talk about it?'

Kate paused in the hallway to catch her breath and steady herself. 'We don't need to talk about anything.'

She scooped Dolores up in her arms.

'You're not taking her with you, are you?'

She turned to look back at him. 'She's the only reason I've stayed for this long.'

Dolores sat upright in the passenger seat looking out of the window on the drive home. They passed the tree on the motorway – the field had been harvested, stripped of the rapeseed that had turned it golden in the spring.

Kate remembered the look on her dad's face the last time she had made the trip down home on her own, when she had tried to make him reach for words that didn't exist, words that would make everything OK again.

She had found him in the office of the workshop with his reading glasses on, his phone in one hand and a tumbler of whiskey in the other. She'd built herself up to ask the question on the drive home, saying the words out loud again and again so that she wouldn't choke on them when she faced the reality of him in front of her.

'Kate,' he said, looking over the rim of his glasses and standing up from his chair. 'Shouldn't you be back across the border?'

He was drunk. She could see it in his eyes, in the clumsy way he beckoned her towards him for a hug. She stayed where she was on the other side of the workshop.

'Are you all right, Blue?'

She couldn't trust herself not to cry, not to allow him to comfort her. She stared down at the wood shavings on the floor.

'Did you have sex with Niamh?'

She looked up at him. He was staring into the distance like she hadn't said anything at all.

'Well, did you?'

He sat back down in the chair slowly, as though he couldn't trust it to still be there. Then, he picked up a hurley and a spokeshave, and started shaving bits of wood away from the stick.

'Dad?'

Kate tried to hand him her phone, but he wouldn't take it. She put it down on the table. 'I saw the messages.'

He hesitated before putting the hurley down and picking up the phone. Before Niamh had wrestled her phone back, Kate had taken screenshots of the messages and sent them to her own phone. She watched as Liam frowned at the screen. It looked so small in his hands. She'd spent hours one Christmas trying to teach him how to text on an iPhone. He was like a toddler, sticking his tongue out in concentration, trying his best to get his giant thumb to land on the letter he wanted. Now, he took off his glasses and closed his eyes, pinching the bridge of his nose.

'This is Niamh we're talking about,' Kate said. '*Niamh?*'

He sighed.

'If you slept with her, Dad, it wasn't consensual.'

'No,' he said firmly, shaking his head. 'You've got the wrong end of the stick, Kate. It's not like that.'

'What's it like then, Dad?'

He put his head in his hands.

'Does Mam know? Will we tell her?'

Kate went to leave, but she heard the scrape of his chair on the floor. He scrambled across the workshop, grabbing her by the shoulders and pinning her up against the wall.

They both looked down at his hands on her. He loosened his grip. 'Blue – please don't do this.'

Helen was in the front room watching television.

'Dad has something to tell you,' Kate announced, standing in front of the television.

'What?' Helen snapped, annoyed by the interruption.

'It's nothing, Helen,' Liam said. 'Kate's got the wrong end of the stick.'

Helen had already shooed her out of the way with one hand, craning her neck to see the characters on screen. Kate unplugged the television from the wall and turned around to face the silent room.

'What is this about?' Helen asked in a tired voice, getting up from the couch.

'Dad had sex with Niamh,' Kate said, looking over at Liam whose eyes were on the floor. 'And it wasn't consensual. He raped her.'

Kate felt the sting of her mother's hand across her face.

'Apologise to your father,' Helen said.

'You want *me* to apologise to *him?*'

Helen was looking at her as though she was a spoiled child. 'He told you that you got the wrong end of the stick, which you obviously have.'

Kate left the room and ran upstairs to her bedroom. She closed the door and lay face down on the bed. Her heartbeat felt like it was coming from the walls.

She recognised his footsteps coming up the stairs. Liam knocked on the door before he came in.

'It's not what you think, Blue,' he said, sitting down on the bed beside her. 'Have you talked to Niamh about it?'

Kate turned onto her back and looked up at the glow-in-the-dark stars that were still stuck to the ceiling of her childhood bedroom. There used to be bunk beds squeezed into the other side of the room. Niamh always slept on the top bunk whenever she stayed over.

'Do you know what Niamh told me on the drive up to Belfast today?' Kate asked, staring at a piece of Blu Tack that had been up there for decades, long after its plastic star had fallen. 'She loves Peter. She has always loved Peter. They've been together for the past few months. They didn't want anyone knowing yet because it's all so new. I was worried about Niamh, though. She didn't seem like herself. But then, I thought, of course she's not herself. I can't imagine what it must be like to lose your dad. And then, I see these messages on her phone from a delusional old man. I don't know the man who sent those messages, Dad.'

Liam let out a shaky breath before the convulsions started. The only other time Kate had seen him cry was when Vincent died. The entire bed was shaking beneath them. Kate went to give him a hug before she realised what she was doing.

'No,' she said, standing up. 'You don't get to be the one who is comforted in all of this.'

He clasped his hands together. 'I promise you, Kate, we both wanted it. We were both drunk – I know it's no excuse but—'

'You raped her! It was rape!'

Liam stood up from the bed. Kate turned her back to him and listened to the sound of his footsteps disappear down the stairs.

Chapter 14

Better

Kate

IT WAS LATE by the time Kate arrived home, the night before Maria's wedding. She presumed that everyone had gone to bed until she saw the light on in the kitchen. Peter and Niamh were sitting at the table trying to console Maria who turned around when she heard Dolores' claws on the kitchen tiles.

'You brought the dog?' Maria asked.

'Yeah, it's a long story,' Kate said. 'What's wrong?'

'We can't find Mam,' Peter replied in a tone of voice that warned against further questions.

Niamh was holding a mirror up for Maria to try to salvage her fake eyelashes – the ones that hadn't fallen out were clumped together. She was trying to tell her that the makeup artist would fix them, but Maria was intent on trying to separate what was left, pausing every so often to let the tears out.

Kate sat down at the table and waited to be asked to do something – anything – to help. Her index fingernail began tracing the spirals that were carved into the edges of the wooden table. The spirals in front of her own chair were deeper than the others, from years of picking away at them at dinner time. The scraping noise always annoyed Maria who looked at her pointedly now. 'Kate, please.'

'Sorry,' she said, drawing her finger into a closed fist. She was already in Maria's bad books for not making it down in time for the church rehearsal. Ellius had been working a late shift so they had originally planned on driving down in the morning.

'Where's Ellius?' Maria asked

'He's not coming,' Kate said. 'We broke up.'

'Really?'

They were all looking at her now.

Kate avoided Niamh's eyes. 'Yeah.'

'What about the reception music?' Maria asked.

'I've rung the hotel and asked them to provide a replacement. They have a pianist—'

'A pianist? I wanted a trad musician.'

'You've got a pianist.'

Maria sniffed and went back to brushing her eyelashes. 'And who's going to mind the dog?'

'I don't know yet.'

'You're not bringing her.'

'I know,' Kate said. 'I'll figure something out.'

They convinced Maria to get a few hours' sleep before the hairdresser and makeup artist arrived. Kate sneaked Dolores upstairs to bed with her and woke up before her alarm went off to bring her outside to go to the bathroom. Niamh was already cleaning the sitting room, arranging family photos and flowers so that it would be ready for the photographer.

Kate was about to start cooking the fry for breakfast when Helen appeared in the doorway in her pyjamas, her cheeks flushed.

'Hi Mam,' Kate said.

Helen gave her a sheepish smile.

Niamh rushed into the kitchen with a bin bag full of empty cans and crisp packets from the night before. 'Helen,' she said. 'Hi.'

'Is that Mammy?' Maria shouted from upstairs. She rushed down to the kitchen. 'Where were you?'

'I was with a friend,' Helen said.

'A friend?'

Helen shrugged. 'Yeah.'

'Why?'

'Why do you need to know?'

Maria's jaw clenched. She took a deep breath before answering. 'It's my wedding day, Mam. I bawled my eyes out because I was worried you wouldn't be here to walk me down the aisle.'

Kate rubbed Maria's back in circles. 'It's OK. She's here now.'

A car was coming up the drive. The makeup artist had arrived.

Maria sent Kate upstairs to get Bláithín out of bed. The light from the landing spread into the darkness of Bláith's bedroom which had been redecorated since Kate had last been home. The Harry Styles and One Direction posters had been replaced with family photos hung on a string, clipped on with tiny wooden pegs like a clothesline of memories.

'Bláith,' she whispered.

Bláith pulled the blanket over her head. 'Is that you, Blue?'

'Yeah.'

'Do I have to get up?'

'Your glam squad awaits.'

'Is Ellius downstairs?'

'No,' Kate said, sitting down on the bed. 'Ellius isn't here. We broke up.'

Bláithín poked her head out from under the duvet. 'What?'

'I've broken up with Ellius.'

Bláithín frowned. 'No, he's coming today. You said he was coming.'

'That was before we broke up.'

She sat up in the bed. 'But he needs to see me in my new dress.'

'Not today, Bláith.'

'He has to.'

Bláith's eyes were filling up. Kate went to hug her and was surprised by the force with which Bláithín pushed her away.

'I'm sorry, Bláith,' she said, but Bláithín had already pulled the covers over her head and was sobbing now.

Kate backed out of the room and paced the landing as she tried to figure out what to do. Maria called up the stairs, asking which one of them would like to be first to get their hair done.

'Just give us a minute!' Kate said.

'All OK?' Maria asked.

'Yeah!'

Bláith's crying was losing momentum when Niamh climbed the stairs.

'Ellius?' she guessed.

Kate sighed. 'Yeah.'

'You go down and get your hair done,' Niamh said. 'I'll talk to her.'

The hairdresser made the mistake of doting over Dolores while Kate was upstairs. Maria had asked if she would be willing to pet sit for the day and the woman had agreed. Kate felt both relieved and guilty in equal measure that Maria had taken care of another problem she'd brought into her life on her wedding day.

By the time the hairdresser had curled Kate's hair, Bláith was twirling around the front room, showing off the spray tan that she'd gotten the day before.

Maria looked at Kate in a panic. 'You said you were going to do your own tan.'

Kate looked down at her pasty arms.

'You could put on some instant tan?' Niamh suggested. 'I have some with me.'

*

The last time Kate had put on tan, she was sixteen. She had auditioned for a production of *Swan Lake* in Dublin and had gotten into the corps de ballet. The weeks of rehearsals were made more intense by her mother complaining about having to drive her back and forth to Dublin. The night before the opening show, Maria had helped her put on fake tan. The next morning, her body was a disaster zone.

'Did you fall into the slurry pit?' Peter asked when she came down for breakfast.

'Don't worry,' Maria said. 'It will wash off in the shower.'

'I've already had a shower.'

'Have another one.'

Kate ended up trying to scrub it off in the bath. She found a pumice stone in a gift set that she'd gotten for Christmas and pressed it into her skin. It was beginning to work when Helen began to bang on the bathroom door telling her to hurry up – they needed to leave before the traffic hit. She scrubbed harder and faster. It was only when she got out of the bath that she realised how much she was bleeding.

Kate cried the whole way to the hospital as blood poured out of her, insisting that she was fine, even while the nurses were bandaging her up.

'No,' she said, when the doctor told her that she wouldn't be able to dance. 'We're already late. I have to make the show.'

She was still in tears as Helen linked her arm and walked her out towards the car park.

'I'm so embarrassed,' she said.

'Who's going to tell anyone?' Helen asked. 'There's nothing you can do about it. As far as everyone at home is concerned, we're on our way to Dublin. The show is going to go brilliantly. We'll stay the night in a hotel.'

Kate sniffed. 'What about Dad?'

'What about him? You cover up those arms and legs when we come home tomorrow. Nobody needs to know.'

*

Kate squirted the brown mousse onto a foam mitt and rubbed it into her skin. Niamh did her back in silence while she shivered half-naked in the bathroom. They presented her to the bride for inspection. She turned around underneath the light of the sitting room feeling like a rotisserie chicken.

'It's better than nothing,' Maria concluded.

The hairdresser and makeup artist gushed that she looked much better and everyone calmed down again. It was hard to know if Maria had relaxed or was pretending to for the benefit of everyone else. The photographer and videographer had arrived and the atmosphere had changed. It felt like they were on the set of a reality television show.

Kate sat down on a high stool and closed her eyes while the makeup artist went to town on her face. Her nose had mostly healed since the break. Kate wasn't sure if the bump had always been there until Maria pointed it out to the entire room.

'Was your nose always a bit wonky, Blue?'

'No,' Helen said. 'It was perfect before.'

'It's probably only swelling,' Maria said, realising that she hadn't explained what had happened to the rest of the room. 'Kate had a bit of an accident last month.'

'A bit of contouring will take care of that,' the makeup artist assured her. 'Don't you worry about it.'

After an hour of struggling to make small talk, the woman held up a mirror to show Kate the face of a drag queen in a local pantomime.

'Thank you,' Kate said. 'I love it.'

'AUNTIE BLUE!'

Aoife was running towards her.

'My mammy and daddy are getting married today!' she shouted, jumping into her arms.

'How exciting is that?' Kate twirled her around, landing her little feet back on the carpet. 'Are you going to be the best flower girl ever?'

'Yep,' Aoife said, putting her hands on her hips. 'You wanna see my wheelbarrow?'

'Of course I do.'

'Auntie Ni-Ni got it for me,' she said with pride, taking her by the hand and giving her a guided tour of the stickers on her sparkly pink wheelbarrow.

'Wow,' Kate said.

'We need to check on the potatoes.'

'No digging up potatoes,' Maria called after them. 'Do you hear me? Kate, make sure she doesn't get dirty.'

Aoife's ponytail swung from side to side as she drove her wheelbarrow down the garden.

'Where are the potatoes?' Kate asked.

'They're in their lazy beds,' Aoife answered.

The vegetable patch was in the field closest to the house, at the bottom of the small hill where the fairy tree stood looking down on them. Aoife gave her the lowdown on the different crops – the carrots, beetroots and radishes that she'd planted with her Granny Helen.

Before Kate knew it, she was standing in the same spot where she'd found Liam that morning. She had still been angry on her way out to the workshop: angry that she was the one who felt guilty when she hadn't done anything; angry that she felt a responsibility to fix what she hadn't broken; angry that he wasn't where she thought he would be, in the shed or in the milking parlour; angry that he was making her more and more angry, before she caught sight of what her anger had done to him.

'The peas are ready! Look at them!' Aoife shouted, splitting a pod open with her fingernail. 'Look how *cute* they are!' She stamped her feet excitedly. At the sight of the potato plants, she gasped, forgetting about the peas that spilled from her hand. 'Flowers!'
    White petals peeped out of the green stalks. Aoife plucked a blossom and presented it to her aunt in a cupped palm.
    'What's wrong, Auntie Blue?' she asked, putting a hand on her hip. 'Did a nettle sting you?'
    Kate sniffed, taking out a tissue to dab underneath her eyes.
    Aoife crouched down and picked a dock leaf. 'Where does it hurt?'

Kate sat down on the grass beside her. 'Just there,' she said, pointing to a random spot on the outside of her ankle.

Her niece stuck out her tongue in concentration as she rubbed the leaf into her skin, wiping away a patch of fake tan. Kate looked up at the sky and the hedges and the tree that towered over them.

'Right,' Aoife said, putting on her best grown-up voice. 'No more tears, Auntie Blue. You're all better now.'

Chapter 15

The Wedding

Niamh

THE FLORIST DELIVERED the wrong bridal bouquet to the house. It didn't matter how much they tried to convince Maria that no one would know the difference, she wouldn't budge.

'I need the orchids,' she said. 'They're for Dad – so I feel like he's there when I walk down the aisle.'

The florist sped back to the shop to correct the mistake. The hairdresser was packing up her things, talking about how she always bought herself a bunch of flowers in her weekly shop in honour of her late sister who loved pink carnations.

Helen took a long sip of prosecco. She was wearing a cornflower-blue lace jumpsuit, her hair beautifully coiffed. There was something different about her that Niamh couldn't put her finger on. She was there on the couch beside Kate and Bláith but seemed a million miles away.

Aoife wanted to change out of her flower girl dress.

'It itches,' she said, scrunching up her face.

'No, it doesn't, pet,' Maria said. 'Remember we tried on all those dresses to find one that doesn't itch?'

Niamh knelt down beside her. 'Can I see your potato flowers?'

Aoife's face lit up. 'Me and Auntie Blue were in the garden and Mammy said we weren't allowed to pick potatoes, but we picked potato flowers and we put them in here.' She handed over the crisp packet that she had refused to be parted with while changing into her dress.

Niamh marvelled at the crushed, sweaty petals covered in the silt of the cheese and onion flavouring. 'They're beautiful.'

'I know.' Aoife sighed. 'I miss my potatoes.'

Niamh went upstairs to fix her makeup. The bridesmaid's dress was black satin and clung to her body. She practiced walking down the aisle in front of the full-length mirror and imagined Peter looking at her. She looked good, she thought, but she felt outside of herself, the way she did when they had started having sex again. It all felt like it was happening to someone else.

'Jesus!'

Bláithín was standing at the top of the landing, watching her.

'Sorry Bláith,' she said, putting a hand to her chest. 'I didn't see you there.'

Niamh had already put in a shift with Bláithín that morning, trying to convince her that Ellius wasn't the right man for her. The right man would show up for her, she told her. It was the least she deserved.

Bláith beckoned her into her bedroom. 'Do you want to see something?'

Niamh followed her into the room and watched her take a shoebox out from the bottom of her wardrobe.

'Promise you won't tell Maria?' Bláith asked.

'I promise.'

She opened the box. Inside was a babygrow, a soother, a tiny pair of socks and a polaroid photo of Bláith and Liam at a One Direction concert.

'If I have a baby, I'm going to call him Liam, after my daddy.'

'That's gorgeous, Bláith,' Niamh said.

'Will you be his godmother?'

'Yeah, of course I will.'

She watched as Bláith put the lid back on the box and stowed it away in the back of the wardrobe again.

Aoife was crying for her wheelbarrow when the florist arrived back with the bouquet. The cries turned into screeches when they tried to distract her with the basket of rose petals that she was supposed to scatter down the aisle.

'Just bring it!' Maria shouted, climbing into the back of the vintage car she'd hired for the day.

John had offered to drive the bridesmaids down to the church in his car. Kate got into the front while Niamh squeezed into the back, between Bláith, Aoife and the upside-down wheelbarrow. She got a packet of baby wipes and tried her best to clean the muck of the farm off the pink sparkly plastic that Aoife was holding onto for dear life, her legs swinging from her booster seat.

Aoife ended up bringing the wheelbarrow down the aisle, stopping halfway to scatter petals. The congregation watched as she stuck her hand into the crumpled Tayto foil and pulled out a handful of crushed petals with the flourish of a magician.

She spotted Kevin at the top of the altar and abandoned the wheelbarrow to run up to him. He twirled his daughter around and put her on his hip. Kate, who was walking behind her niece, bent down to pick up the handles of the wheelbarrow and wheeled it the rest of the way.

On her walk down the aisle, Niamh saw her mother sitting in a pew by herself, her mouth pursed and hands clasped together. She tried to catch her eye but Mary looked straight ahead. She didn't want to be there, but she didn't want to give the Foleys the satisfaction of not going either.

Niamh didn't realise that Peter and John were groomsmen until the rehearsal, even though neither one of them were particularly close to Kevin. His best man was a childhood friend who was so painfully shy that Niamh felt bad for making eye contact with him.

The harp instrumental to 'Over the Rainbow' began, and everyone turned around to see Maria in her dress – an expensive ball gown with puff sleeves that she'd had second thoughts about ever since she'd bought it.

Maria was nervous and emotional, but it was Helen who stole the show, transforming into a proud mother walking her daughter down the aisle. She beamed at people on her way to the altar. Her eyes glazed over with tears as she gave Kevin a hug and went to sit next to Nan in the front row.

After the mass was over, Peter linked her arm and they walked down the aisle. The camogie team had lined up outside the church to make an arch with their hurleys for them to walk through, clapping the wood together.

'Come on,' Peter said, handing her a hurley.

A long queue of well-wishers had formed to congratulate the happy couple. Niamh put down her bouquet next to the wall and started to puck around with Peter. The camogie team joined in, and soon, they had a huge circle of people passing a ball around the church grounds. A drone flew above them, capturing footage for the wedding video.

Niamh broke away from the group when she saw her mother coming out of the church.

'Mam!' she called.

Mary turned around. She was wearing the same lilac trouser suit she'd worn to her boss' daughter's wedding the year before.

'You look lovely,' Niamh said.

'She was an hour and a half late.'

'It wasn't that long, Mammy.'

'Don't tell me how long it was, sure wasn't I there waiting for you?'

'There was a mix-up with the flowers,' Niamh said.

'Imagine leaving people to sit there for an hour and a half?'

'Are you heading straight to the reception?' Niamh asked.

'Well, I presume they're going to feed us after all that.'

'I've to stick around to get some photos taken, but I'll see you over there?'

'Great,' Mary said. 'More waiting around.'

The photographer was taking family photos outside the church. Kevin's parents stood on either side of the bride and groom. Then, it was the Foleys' turn. Helen, John, Bláithín, Peter and Kate assembled around their sister and new brother-in-law.

'Now, partners and kids?' the photographer asked, looking around at the crowd.

'Ellius!' Kevin shouted. 'Where's Ellius, Kate?'

Maria tugged his arm and murmured in his ear. Kate was fixing her dress, trying her best to ignore the flurry of whispers that spread around the churchyard. Nadine and the two kids stepped forward.

'Niamh?'

Peter was looking at her.

'What?' she asked.

'Get in here!'

A round of applause broke out among onlookers as she walked over to Peter. There was something about the way that he put his hand on the small of her back. It felt like it was Liam standing beside her.

Her mother was drunk by the time they got to the hotel.

'An hour and a half,' she was saying to the pianist who was hired to play at the drinks' reception at the last minute.

'I'd understand if it was fifteen or twenty minutes, but an hour and a *half?*'

Niamh gave the man an apologetic smile as she steered Mary towards the table with finger food.

'Will you have some coffee and a scone, Mam?' she asked.

'A scone? No, I'd like my dinner.'

'Well, will we check the table plan and see where you're sitting?'

Mary narrowed her eyes. 'Do you think I need a babysitter? Is that it?'

'Right, I give up.'

'Yeah, go back to your real family,' Mary said. 'It's a big day for you all.'

Peter was driving Aoife through the hotel corridors in the wheelbarrow, followed by the videographer and John's boys who were chasing after them. Nan was sitting down with a cup of tea and saucer in her lap, surrounded by the Foley side of the family.

Niamh passed by groups of people who were all looking at her differently.

'Look at you!' Liam's cousin, Annette, took her by the hand and spun her around.

'Nan was telling me who you were and I couldn't believe it. I remember you running around the back garden with a hurley in your hand. You were a little barrel of a thing. My young lads were afraid of you! Let me tell you, they'd be afraid of you now for very different reasons,' she said, winking at her. 'But a little birdie told me you've only gone and nabbed our Peter.'

Niamh let out a nervous laugh.

'Now listen to me,' the woman said, grabbing her by the wrist. 'People are going to say what they like. Sure, weren't they raised in the same house like siblings, they'll say. That sort of thing. Don't you listen to a word of it. They're only jealous.'

Niamh went to the bathroom to escape. She walked in to find Kate washing her hands at the sink. Her eyes were bloodshot.

'Are you OK?' Niamh asked.

Kate tried to wave the tears away before giving up and rushing back into a stall.

A toilet flushed and a woman came out of a cubicle to wash her hands. Niamh went into the stall next to Kate and typed out a message on her phone: *Is it Ellius?*

She heard the vibration of Kate's phone and waited for the reply that came within seconds: *It's everything.*

Maria had decided to do the speeches before the meal. Niamh saw her mother's face drop when the microphone came out. Mary was sitting at a table in the far corner of the room next to Nan's posse of friends from bingo and bridge, a group of elderly women who were fiercely loyal to the Foleys and didn't have the patience to be civil towards her.

The best man mumbled his way through an introduction and handed the mic over to Kevin who acted like he was doing a slot at an open-mic comedy night.

'For ages, Maria was just a girl I was shifting,' he said, putting his hand on the shoulder of his new wife who looked fit to murder him. 'I knew that she was a teacher,' Kevin continued, oblivious to the faux pas he had made. 'And that she played camogie. I impressed her with my credentials of my misspent youth on the Junior B club team where I played left-back – on the bench!' He raised his eyebrows, waiting for the punchline to land with the audience. 'Anyway, I think it was our third or fourth date when I took her out for a Sunday roast, a carvery dinner in my local. There was a hurling match on the telly. It was half-time and the pundits were in the studio, commentating on the first half of the game. I nodded at Farmer Foley on the screen and said, "I love that man." Maria smiled a funny little smile to herself, so I asked, "What? The man's a legend. How could you not love him?" She took a long sup of her pint before she said, "No, I do. I ought to love him, anyway. He's my dad." From that moment on, ladies and gentlemen, Maria was no longer just a girl I was shifting. I didn't want to be on the wrong side of the Farmer. The first time I met the man, he nearly broke my knuckles with a handshake. And then, sure, when Maria became pregnant, it was time to step up to the mark. Aoife came into our lives, and we've never looked back. Maria is one of the most remarkable people I have ever met. She has this magical ability to bring people together. She is always putting other people over herself. So, for today, and all the days to come, I promise to put you, Maria, at the centre of my life. If everyone could join me in raising a glass to my extraordinary wife.'

Niamh breathed a sigh of relief that Kevin had managed to finish strong. The microphone was passed to the father of the groom, who surprised everyone by keeping his speech short, thanking everyone for coming and wishing the happy couple the best in their married life.

Nan stood up before the best man had finished struggling through his own speech. She got a standing ovation before she'd even made it to the top table, where she sat down in the best man's seat. When he gestured for her to hold the microphone, she shook her head and pointed at him as though offering him the role of her human microphone stand was an act of charity for which he should be grateful. Niamh smiled. Nan was legend. The woman knew how to work a room.

'Thank you for your patience with an auld one like me,' Nan said, smiling up at her new assistant. 'Huge congratulations to Maria and Kevin on what has been a wonderful day so far. I know that I am not the only person here who misses Liam. Maria, love, he would be exceptionally proud of the person you have become. The thought occurred to me during the week that a member of the Foley family should welcome Kevin into the fold, on Liam's behalf. Helen wouldn't be one for the limelight, and so that duty has fallen to me.'

At the far end of the table, Helen had an imperceptible smile on her face. Nan was known for shooting from the hip, and Helen was often caught in the crossfire. Niamh could never quite tell if it annoyed Helen or amused her.

Nan cleared her throat, pausing her speech to take a handkerchief from her pocket to wipe spittle away from her mouth. 'Excuse me,' she said, passing the used tissue to the best man. 'So anyway, I thought that instead of you listening to me harp on, we could all take a trip down memory lane.'

A photo of a young Liam holding baby Maria in his arms was projected onto the white wall behind them. Niamh knew that this was coming. The night before, Peter was getting messages from John and Nadine panicking because Nan had bullied them into making a photo montage. It was Peter's job to sneak old family photo albums out of the front room and send pictures on to John for the slideshow, all without Maria noticing.

Peter had done a great job – there were photos of Maria's christening, her communion and her confirmation. It didn't take much for Maria to start crying – she was wiping her eyes with the corner of her napkin as she watched the years of her childhood unfold: Liam standing beside her in her school uniform, the two of them at a match together in their club jerseys.

Then, a photo flashed up on screen that hit Niamh in the chest – Liam with a little girl on his knee. She was about eight years old with a head of curls and a gap-toothed grin, clutching her favourite hurley. It wasn't Maria. Some people had clocked the mistake. Niamh tried her best to ignore them looking over at her. She glanced over at Kate who was trying her best to hold it together too. They locked eyes for a split second – holding each other's gaze – and then, they were back in the room again.

The slideshow came to an end and Nan asked everyone to raise their glass to absent friends. Everyone stood up from their seats for the toast and clinked glasses. The best man passed the microphone to Father Angelo who said grace.

The bowls of soup were served. Niamh passed the breadbasket around and stirred her soup without taking a sip, concentrating instead on the goblet of gin and tonic in front of her which she drained. The ice cubes had melted, leaving a swamp of wilted mint leaves and a slimy strip of cucumber.

By the time the main course arrived, Niamh was on her third glass of white wine. She picked at the salmon. The vegetables were boiled to within an inch of their lives and tasted of tepid water.

After dessert, she went over to check on her mother. Mary was sitting alone, rolling a profiterole around the plate with a fork. The rest of her table had gone to sit in the lobby. Niamh could tell by her eyes that her mother had sobered up.

'How are things, Mam?'

'The meat was dry.'

'I got the salmon,' Niamh said.

Her heels were pinching her feet. She had blisters on both her baby toes, but it was too early to change into one of the pairs of flip-flops that Maria had in baskets in the bathroom.

Niamh looked up and saw Helen walking towards them. It had been years – decades – since the women had been in the same room. Niamh glanced at her mother to see how she'd navigate the moment Helen walked past the table, if they would make eye contact, say hello or if they'd ignore each other completely.

Helen sat down in the chair next to them.

'How are you, Mary?' she asked.

'I'm grand Helen, and yourself?'

'I'm good, thanks. How was your meal?'

'Lovely. The whole day has been just beautiful,' Mary gushed.

'Thank you so much for coming.'

'Thanks for having me. I enjoyed Nan's speech,' Mary said, folding her napkin on her lap.

Helen smiled. 'I would have said a few words myself, but there is no talking to Nan once she gets an idea in her head.'

'You should have,' Mary said. 'We need more speeches from the mothers of the bride.'

Helen raised her eyebrows and glanced over at Niamh. 'Well, you never know. It might be your turn next.'

'Ha! I don't know about that now,' Mary replied. 'Not with this one. I'll have to knit a man for her.'

Helen looked over at Niamh. 'I'll leave you both to enjoy your dessert. Thanks for coming, Mary,' she said, standing up and placing a hand on her shoulder. 'It means a lot that you're here.'

'Not at all. I wouldn't miss it.'

They watched as Helen walked away.

'She always loved the sound of her own voice, that one,' Mary said. 'If she was an ice cream, she'd eat herself.'

Niamh stayed with her mam until it was almost time for the first dance. Tables were cleared away and the band started to set up. The sight of Elvis walking into the function room put a smile on her face.

'He played at Maria's hen party in Belfast,' Niamh said, pointing him out in the crowd.

Mary perked up. She loved Elvis.

'We must go to an Elvis tribute night together some time,' Niamh said.

'That would be nice.'

Elvis invited everyone to the floor for the first dance. Niamh saw Kate searching for her and got up to join the bridal party.

'Are you coming?' she asked.

'I will,' Mary replied, sprucing up her hair as she got up from her seat.

'I have to go dance with one of the groomsmen but I'll come find you after?'

'All right.'

She left her mother in the circle of onlookers to go over to Peter who'd already lost his tie and a couple of buttons off his shirt.

'Where were you?' he asked.

'With Mam,' she said.

He slipped his arm around her waist. Elvis began to sing 'Can't Help Falling in Love' and everyone watched Maria and Kevin shuffle together self-consciously for the first few bars until they signalled for them to join in.

Peter led her out onto the floor and began to slow dance. Bláithín and John banded together, and Kate tried her best with the best man, who was reluctant to take her hand or go anywhere near her. They ended up acting out the lyrics like it was a game of charades. Niamh could sense her mother watching her with Peter. She tried to break away and join in on the charades, but he pulled her in for a kiss and the crowd started to cheer. By the time she opened her eyes and adjusted to the room, her mother was gone.

After the dance was over, Niamh went to find her but she was too late. The girl at reception told her that she'd already taken a taxi home. Peter followed her into the lobby.

'Can we go to the room?' she asked.

'Hell yeah.'

'Not like that. We need to talk.'

'Are you thick with me?' he asked as they got into the elevator.

'I'm confused,' she said, pressing the button. 'You never asked me.'

'Asked you what?'

'To be your girlfriend,' she said.

'Well, what did you think we were?'

'I don't know.'

'What do you mean you don't know?'

The elevator doors binged open and Niamh searched her handbag for the keycard to the room. 'I just don't know why you've decided to make whatever this is official, on today of all days.'

'Niamh, what are you talking about?'

The keycard wouldn't work. She waved it back and forth over the sensor and the light flashed red. Peter took the card from her and went down to reception. She sat down on the carpet and closed her eyes, feeling the cold plaster of the wall against her back.

A few moments later, the elevator doors opened again. Peter was walking up the corridor towards her. She watched him open the door in silence and followed him into the room.

Inside, he started to walk around while she sat on the bed to take off her shoes.

'I'm sorry,' she said. 'It's just that Mam didn't know about us. I hadn't told her, and she's after leaving without saying goodbye.'

'Is that what this is about?' Peter asked. 'Niamh, your mother is a wagon. Everyone knows this – *you* know this. I don't know why you'd be expecting her to give us her blessing.'

'She's my mother.'

'Yeah, and we're going to have to deal with her.'

'*Deal* with her?'

'You know what I mean.'

'Because the Foleys are perfect.'

'Far from it, but Jesus Christ, Niamh, you already know this – your mam was never there for you. It's only now that she's bitter and lonely that she wants you all to herself. Think about it. She despises Mam for being more of a mother to you than she was. She hated Dad for the same reason – he always wanted the best for you.'

Niamh looked at Peter and saw the face of the boy who believed in Santa Claus. It was that look on his face that would come to her months later, whenever she struggled to remember the way his eyebrows creased together when he was trying to understand her, the blood blister on his bottom lip as she kissed him.

'Are we OK?' he asked, pulling away and searching her face for a sign that the fight was over.

'Yeah,' she said.

'Are you sure?'

'Well, if you want me to think about it more . . .'

'No, no,' he said, rubbing her shoulders. 'Don't be at that craic. Thinking is overrated.'

'Let's go back downstairs,' she said.

'Only if you're sure you're OK.'

'Yeah, I am.'

'I'm sorry for talking about your mam like that,' he said, as they walked down the corridor. 'I know she's family. I'll get better at that kind of stuff – I promise.'

They got into the elevator and pressed the button for reception. The doors closed and Niamh watched her reflection as she leaned her head on Peter's shoulder.

Down in the lobby, they saw Helen talking to the Elvis impersonator and a woman wearing a check shirt and jeans. Niamh wasn't used to seeing Helen tipsy. There was a giddiness in her eyes when she saw them and beckoned them over.

'This is my son, Peter and this . . .' Helen hesitated, stumbling over a potentially new way of introducing her. 'This is his partner, Niamh.'

The woman made intense eye contact with Niamh as she shook her hand. 'It's lovely to meet you. I'm Judy. You've already met my husband in Belfast, so I hear?'

Elvis reintroduced himself as Dennis. It turned out that Maria had only booked him to do the first dance song. He'd thrown in a few extra tunes before the wedding band took over.

Peter was happy to make small talk with the couple until the band started to play AC/DC's 'Thunderstruck'. He excused himself from the conversation to head to the dance floor to join the rest of the lads.

Helen took Judy by the arm and led her towards the ballroom. 'Wait until you see this,' she said.

Niamh and Dennis followed behind the two women who were giggling together like schoolgirls. Peter had joined the rest of the hurlers. They all rolled up their trousers to just below their knees, and then their shirts came off, exposing abs and beer bellies. Every time St Brigid's won a championship, 'Thunderstruck' was blasted out of speakers in the dressing room after the match and continued to play in the pub, nightclubs and house parties into the wee hours of the morning, where only the most hardcore drinkers would be still standing.

Niamh stood back and watched as the lads egged each other on, encouraging onlookers to get involved in the craic. She kept coming back to Helen and Judy, arm in arm, pink with happiness.

When Judy and Dennis eventually said their goodbyes, Niamh was left standing in the lobby with Helen, who gestured towards the couches.

'I need to sit down. My feet are killing me,' she said, collapsing back into the plush cushions and kicking off her shoes. One of her heels grazed Niamh's shin as it fell onto the carpet.

'Oh Niamh, I'm so sorry!'

Helen had been drinking red wine. Niamh couldn't stop looking at the stain around her lips as she spoke.

'You know, Niamh, I'm sorry I haven't been there for you.'

'Not at all, Helen—'

'No, no. I haven't been myself. I haven't been myself for a long time. I think,' Helen leaned over and clasped her hand. 'We can look back and choose to remember the good times.'

Niamh looked at the woman who taught her how to love. She glanced down at the hands she knew so well, hands that had brushed her hair, taught her how to make brown bread, hands that had spun Sister Imelda's globe on sick days and rubbed her small hands to warm them up when she came in from a long winter's night milking cows. Helen still wore her wedding ring.

'I didn't choose what happened to me, Helen,' Niamh said, pulling her fingers away. 'Liam did.'

She managed to look her in the eye before she walked away.

Niamh spent the rest of the night on the dance floor. Peter and Kate managed to drag Bláithín up for a Harry Styles medley that the wedding band had put together at Maria's request. John and Nadine joined them once the jiving started, and Peter spun Niamh around for the craic. They escaped outside to have a smoke and a kiss whenever they were in danger of being poisoned by Guinness farts. Later on in the night, the DJ played 'Lose Yourself', and they shouted the words at each other like they were kids again.

When the music finished up, the St Brigid's lads put Maria and Kevin on their shoulders and started to chant, 'There's only one Farmer Foley.' Niamh looked around the room at the young lads videoing the chaos with tears in their eyes.

Peter put his hand around her shoulders and stood there stoically, watching as the procession passed by. The sing-song started in the residents' bar and Peter stood up to sing 'Raglan Road'. It was Liam's party piece. Niamh could tell that he had practiced it – the words were coming easily until the last verse, when he stumbled on the line about old ghosts. She joined in, helping him pick up the thread of memory. He looked at her with relief and smiled with nothing but love in his eyes.

Chapter 16

The Morning After

Niamh

PETER WOKE AND REACHED OUT for her in bed. He realised that she wasn't there and raised his head from the pillow, frowning when he saw her already dressed and sitting on a chair behind the table on the other side of the room.

'Did I miss breakfast?' he croaked.

'No,' Niamh said. 'It's early.'

'What are you doing over there?'

'Thinking.'

'Don't be at that.' He opened the duvet out to her. 'Come on.'

'I can't.'

'What's wrong with you?' he asked.

She had realised the night before that she'd never be able to tell him about what happened with Liam. No matter how hard she tried, she couldn't fit inside the idea he had of her.

They were the last ones to leave the residents' bar at five in the morning. Peter had collapsed into bed as soon as they'd gotten back to the room. She had taken off his shoes and stayed up listening to the waves of his snores.

A few hours later, she got out of bed to the sound of birds outside the window and showered, feeling the water crash down on the plastic of the shower cap. The orange and lemongrass body wash cleansed her of the day before. Afterwards, she wiped the steam away from the mirror with a towel and watched herself putting on makeup. She knew that she was as ready as she would ever be, but now that Peter was looking at her, all she wanted to do was crawl back into the bed beside him.

'I can't do this,' she said, concentrating on the diamond pattern in the carpet.

Peter flopped down on the mattress. 'Can we have this argument when we aren't hungover?'

Niamh stood up and went to get a bottle of water from the fridge. She sat it down on the bedside table and opened the curtains on her way back to her seat. Sunlight came streaming in through the window, clean and bright, shocking the room into life. 'No,' she said. 'I can't do another day of this.'

Peter was in the middle of downing the bottle of water. He stopped and swallowed hard. 'Another day of what? Niamh, it's taken us ages to become a couple, why can't we just—'

'It didn't take me ages,' she corrected him. 'It took you ages.'

'What?' His eyes widened, the way they used to when he caught her cheating during Monopoly, stealing an extra hundred pounds when she passed Go to speed up the game. 'That's not fair,' he said, his voice husky from the hangover. 'You're acting like I rejected you when I'd no idea. Even when we first got together, I still couldn't get a read on you. And then you didn't come with me to Australia so I thought, OK, I'll be able to get over you over there, but I couldn't. I had to come home.'

She looked back down at the carpet. 'I've just realised that there are . . .' She paused. 'There are things that I can't tell you.'

'Who the fuck are you? James Bond?'

'I knew you'd do this,' she said.

'Do you want to know what I think?' he asked, sitting up in the bed and pulling his legs into his chest. 'I think the problem is that we've always been competitive with each other. Both of us want to feel like we're winning – like we're the ones with the power. It's the way we were as kids – I've spent my childhood always wanting to get one up on you. I think that's why it took us so long to get together. We're still getting used to this.'

'It's more than that,' she said.

'It's not.'

He was annoying her now.

'How are you so sure?' she asked.

'I just know.'

'Well, you're wrong.'

'Go on then – tell me why I'm wrong,' he insisted.

'I can't.'

He let out a sigh. It felt like they were back in the Foleys' kitchen studying for the Leaving Cert. Helen had asked her to help Peter with his French homework even though he was a year ahead of her in school. Peter had acted like the entire French language was irrelevant because he didn't have the patience for it.

'So, like, are you breaking up with me?' he asked. There was an arrogance in his voice, like he couldn't believe that she would go through with it.

'Yes,' she said.

'Why?'

'I can't tell you.'

'Niamh!' He pronounced her name the same way that Liam did, with two syllables – *nee-av*. 'I've just told you that I can't imagine my life without you. What more do you want from me? Do you need more of a declaration of how I'm useless without you? I can't even get through breakfast without thinking about you. I once saw you eating blueberries in porridge and thought, oh, that looks nice, and now I can't have porridge without blueberries. You can probably have porridge without blueberries, but I can't anymore.'

'What am I supposed to say to that?' she asked.

'Something that makes sense! Jesus Christ, we have a chance to be together! To be happy! And you're trying to fuck it up? For what?'

'There is a reason, I just—'

'What? You just what?'

'—I just want to f-f-f-forget about it.' Every time she stuttered, she felt ten years old again. 'I wanted to f-f-forget about it. It would have been f-fine if everyone f-f-forgot about it.'

'I've no idea what you're talking about.'

A flash of anger brought her voice back to her. 'You know what the most fucked-up thing is? We wouldn't be here if I hadn't lost weight – none of this would have happened. I starved myself for years waiting for you to see me. You never fancied me before Dad got sick. It was only when I stopped eating . . .'

He got out of bed and crossed the room towards her. She wished she had a hurley in her hand – something to defend herself – and then she felt his arms around her.

'No,' she said, pushing him away. 'This is what I mean – *this*. I can't let you touch me. I can't do this.'

'OK.' He breathed out and sat down on the end of the bed in his boxers, rubbing the stubble on his chin. 'We don't have to do anything you don't want to, Niamh. But I love you. You don't have a choice in that.'

'That's the thing,' she said, her eyes filling with tears. 'I do.'

He was taking her seriously now. He was looking down at the carpet too. She could see him scanning the diamond pattern, searching for the right words. 'Do you want to know something that scares the shit out of me?' he asked, finally. 'I see the way you are with Aoife and I imagine our kids. I imagine making hurleys for them. Bringing them down to the pitch for a puck around. Seeing you in a white dress walking down the aisle in St Brigid's church. Standing in front of everyone we know and telling them how much I love you. I imagine our dads looking down on us, how proud they would be that we've managed to make a life for ourselves together.' His voice broke and he took a moment to recover. 'It's absolutely mental that you think I'm some gobshite who wants you to be skinny when I want our life together to be big.' He opened out his hands. 'Full, like. I want to grow old and fat together.'

'I'm not mental,' Niamh said, quietly.

'What?'

'You called me mental.'

'No! I was describing this conversation – it's mental! I'm trying to tell you how much I want to be with you and you're throwing it back in my face. Why are you being like this? Have you slept with someone else? Is that it?'

Her heart was hammering inside her chest. She walked over to her suitcase, pulled up the handle and moved towards the door.

'Tell me, Niamh. Please, I want to know.'

'I can't.' She turned to look back at him and hesitated, looking down at the carpet. 'Ask your mam what happened. She knows.'

The door closed between them and she wheeled her suitcase down the corridor.

Chapter 17

Coffee

Niamh

николая ARRIVED EARLY to the coffee shop. She had already moved seats three times in the few minutes it took the barista to make her latte. The armchairs were too awkward, the long bench too communal. She settled for a table by the window. Her phone vibrated and she looked down at the screen. It was a message from Kate: *Let me know how it goes. Sending lots of love x*

Kate was the only member of the Foley family who Niamh still spoke to. A year ago, she'd arrived home from the hotel after Maria's wedding and booked a one-way ticket to Barcelona. A week later, she was drunk in the toilet cubicle of a hostel when she rang Kate's number and cried down the phone.

After that, they messaged every day. It was Kate who suggested going back to therapy, and kept gently nudging her until Niamh found Brenda, a psychotherapist based in Dublin.

Brenda cursed a lot for a therapist. 'Fuck!' she'd exclaimed within seconds of welcoming her to their first online session.

'Sorry, Niamh, I've just spilled coffee on myself like an eejit. Hang on there and I'll clean myself up.'

Niamh began to relax after that. Towards the end of the session, Niamh began to choke up when she tried to talk about Helen. Brenda did a breathing exercise with her, and the way that she spoke – the way that she was looking at her – it was like she knew already, like Niamh didn't even have to tell her.

The first sip of coffee burned the roof of her mouth. Niamh ran her tongue over the rawness and looked out the window, scanning cars as they passed. Brenda had said in their last session to imagine that she was there, on the other side of the café if Niamh needed her.

'And I'll have my phone on too,' she'd said. 'You can ring me, but you won't need to. You're ready for this. I'll be thinking of you.'

Helen walked through the door of the café. She paused to hold the door open for a mother pushing a buggy who was coming in behind her. The woman thanked her as she manoeuvred the buggy into the queue. Helen glanced around and their eyes met across the room.

Niamh smiled as Helen made her way over. She didn't know whether to stand up – if Helen would go for a hug. She stayed seated. Helen put her handbag on the chair opposite her.

'It's great to see you, Niamh,' she said, taking off her coat and hanging it on the back of the chair. 'I'm going to get a cup of tea. Do you want anything?'

'No, I'm grand. Thanks.'

She watched as Helen joined the queue behind the woman with the buggy. Helen had always been beautiful, but there was a lightness in the way that she moved which was new. She arrived back to the table with a tray and put down the teapot, a jug of milk and a cup and saucer.

'Two seconds,' she said, going back to the counter to return the tray.

'Now,' Helen said, sitting down and opening the teapot to stir the teabag around with her spoon. 'How are you? How's the new school?'

'Good.'

Niamh had taken a position as vice-principal in a small country school. The staff room was friendly and the kids were great. Most of all, she didn't have to worry about teaching the children of people from home.

'And the new gig?' Helen's eyes shone.

'Yeah!' She nodded. 'It's great too!'

Niamh had opened her laptop one evening after school to find an email from a television producer at RTÉ, asking her to appear on a panel for the Sunday Game. She had surprised herself by agreeing to it. Before she knew it, she was in the studio and the host was introducing her, reeling off a list of her achievements.

'And as well as all of that,' he'd continued, 'you basically grew up on Farmer Foley's farm. You must have some stories.'

'I suppose I do,' Niamh said. 'Not all of them are fit for television.'

That got a laugh. Niamh imagined the Foleys at home, watching a close-up of her face on the television.

'I think you're brilliant on it,' Helen was saying.

Niamh took a sip of her coffee. When she looked up at Helen, it was right there again, between them.

Helen took a breath and steadied her voice. 'I thought I was doing the right thing – by not talking about it . . .' Her eyes were filling up. She took a tissue from her sleeve. 'But then, well, there's only so much that you can blame on grief.'

'I used to call that Helen's trick,' Niamh said, showing her the tissue that was peeking out of her own sleeve. 'I remember you showing me how to hide a Kleenex up the sleeve of my school jumper. I still do it. The amount of tissues that accidentally end up in bits in the washing machine, stuck to all of my clothes.'

'It's a nightmare, isn't it?' Helen smiled, wiping her nose.

'How are you, Helen?' Niamh asked. 'In general, I mean.'

'Mostly happy, actually. Believe it or not.' Helen sniffed and rolled her eyes at her tear-stained face. 'How's your mam keeping?'

'She's good,' Niamh said. 'We've actually been getting on better, now that I've moved out of home. She visits me a lot. We're going for lunch tomorrow.'

'That's great. I've been up to Belfast to visit Kate. It's nice to spend time together.'

They were back on solid ground. The next time Niamh looked at her phone, two hours had passed. She told Helen that she needed to go.

'Where have you parked?' Helen asked. 'I have something small to give you. It's in the car.'

They walked out to the car park. Helen opened the boot of the Volkswagen Golf, took out a hurley and handed it to her. Niamh smoothed her fingers down the handle – the grain was straight all the way down until the bottom, where it curved. There was a note taped to the bas. Peter's handwriting hadn't changed. It was the same scrawl it had always been since they were kids:

If you ever want a puck around, I'll be there x

Chapter 18

The Leaves of the Tree

Helen

THE NIGHT BEFORE Liam's fifth anniversary, Helen was in the kitchen making sandwiches for after the mass. Maria was busy slicing white cabbage for the coleslaw. Kate sat beside her, spreading mayonnaise on slices of brown bread and peeling slimy strips of smoked salmon away from gold foil.

'Guess who I ran into in Supervalu?' Maria asked, looking around the table.

Helen was glad that Maria and Kevin's planning permission had finally gone through, if only because it meant enduring less local gossip in future.

'Who?' she asked.

'Niamh Ryan.' Maria pursed her lips together.

'She must be visiting her mother,' Helen said.

'She had the cheek to ask after Peter,' Maria told them.

'It's not a sin to break up with someone, Maria,' Kate said.

'It's not the break-up that I have a problem with. It's the way she went about things. It's like she's forgotten us altogether. She doesn't talk to me anymore. I don't even know where she lives.'

'She's renting an apartment on the far side of town,' Kate said.

'How do you know?'

'We keep in touch.'

Maria threw her hands in the air. 'How is she answering your messages and not mine?'

'Maria, you're the best in the world, but we both know the first thing you'll do is try and get her down to training.'

'Because she should be down at training! She's happy enough to be on the telly talking about camogie, but where is she when her club team needs her?'

The back door squeaked open and Peter walked into the kitchen.

'What's happening?' he asked.

'We're in the trenches here,' Maria said, slicing into a fresh head of cabbage. 'How was your day?'

'Good, yeah.' Peter drummed his fingers on the kitchen countertop. 'What can I do?'

'You can run across to John's to get bags for the sack race tomorrow?' Maria suggested.

Peter saluted and backed out the door, leaving the women to their work.

Maria waited until he had gone before she spoke again. 'He'll never get over her.'

'You'd be surprised,' Helen said. 'The kind of things people get over.'

'Why are you both sticking up for her?' Maria asked.

'I'll never say a bad word against Niamh,' Kate said.

Maria gave Helen an accusatory look.

All she could do was shrug and say, 'Me neither.'

Helen could still hear Peter banging on her hotel room door the morning after Maria's wedding, asking if she knew what had happened to Niamh. She tried her best to explain, but Peter wasn't having any of it. He wouldn't talk to her for weeks. It took a lot of coaxing to get him into a room with Kate. He wanted everyone to know. He even threatened to tell Maria himself. Kate was the one who talked him down.

'What would happen then?' she'd asked. 'Would Maria even believe it? Would she stop talking to Niamh? Cut herself off from all of us? And if Maria and John deserve to know, what about Bláith?'

That was the clincher. Peter agreed that Bláith didn't deserve to be put through any of it. He promised to keep it to himself, but he was angry. He didn't want to attend the anniversary mass, but Kate had worked her magic again.

'Dad couldn't forgive himself, Peter,' Kate said. 'That's why he's not here. Do you want to go through life with that same energy? Or do you want to look after the ones he has left behind?'

Maria handed Helen a bag of carrots. 'Do you mind peeling these, Mam?'

Kate put a hand on her shoulder and asked if she wanted a cup of tea.

'Yes please, pet.'

'Make a pot, Blue,' Maria said. 'I'll have one too.'

Kate had come down from Belfast that afternoon with Bláithín, who had been up to visit her. The pair of them had become a lot closer since Kate had broken up with Ellius. Bláith had had such a great time at Maria's hen that she'd wanted to go back to Belfast. Helen was nervous dropping her off at the station to get the train up all by herself. Kate had calmed Helen down, assuring her that she would be at Grand Central Station to welcome Bláith to the city. Helen was relieved to see the happy heads of the pair of them when they arrived back home after a successful few days up North, with Dolores the dog in tow. Helen was warming to the little dog who was curled up on Kate's lap in the kitchen.

Helen still worried about Kate. She was living in a house-share off Botanic Avenue and had gotten a job in the university library that seemed to suit her. Helen had been up to visit over the summer. Judy came with her under the pretence of wanting to see some stained glass.

They stayed in the Europa Hotel for the weekend. On the Saturday morning, Kate met them outside the hotel with the dog and brought them to St George's market. Helen had the same tired argument with Judy over being too touchy-feely as they wandered the stalls, waiting for Kate to come back from the bathroom.

'All I want to do is link your arm,' Judy said, tugging Dolores' lead in the other hand to keep her away from the food stalls. 'I don't know what's wrong with that.'

'Kate will know,' Helen whispered.

'Kate already knows.'

'She has her suspicions. That's not the same as knowing. She can guess all she wants,' Helen said, feigning an interest in a stall that sold framed prints of the north coast.

'I don't think she'd tell anyone,' Judy said.

Helen peered at a photo of the Mussenden Temple and knew that Judy was right. Kate wouldn't tell a soul.

Helen knew before introducing Judy and Dennis to the rest of the family that if anyone could suss what was going on, it would be her youngest daughter. A few weeks after Maria's wedding, Judy had come to stay with them while she worked on a stained glass commission. Helen had introduced her to Father Angelo who was looking for a window design for the new parish hall. She had cleaned out Liam's old workshop so that Judy could set it up as her studio.

There was no reason for Judy to stay with Helen when she could do the work in Donegal, but she stuck around for a few more months. It helped that every one of the Foleys warmed to Judy in their own way.

'I think we should go to Pride this year,' Judy had said one night as they were lying in bed together.

Helen turned on the bedside lamp and got out of bed.

'Not as a couple or anything,' Judy said, sitting up and watching as Helen searched for pyjamas that were caught up in the folds of the duvet. 'You don't even have to be gay to go to Pride.'

Helen ignored her.

'I'm not trying to get you to come out.'

'Of where?' Helen asked, pulling on her pyjama bottoms. 'I'm not gay.'

Judy looked at her like she was stupid. 'What have we been doing in the middle of the night, then?'

'We're friends,' Helen said.

'And you do this with all your friends, do you? You have sex with all of them?'

Helen laughed. 'You think we're having sex?'

'Wow,' Judy said. 'OK. I think it's time for me to go home then.'

Helen sniffed. 'Yes, I think that's probably for the best.'

It took a while for Maria to recognise Dennis out of uniform when he arrived at the farm to collect his wife. He kept his sideburns in his pocket and took them out when she gave up trying to guess who he was.

She squealed and hugged him. 'I can't believe it's you! Your wife is an absolute hero, by the way. She's working wonders around here. We all adore her.'

John, Nadine and the boys came over to say their goodbyes to Judy before she went back to Donegal. Aoife jumped into her arms and made her pinky promise to come back to see the cabbages that they had planted together.

Helen had planned on giving her a stiff hug goodbye, but she couldn't help breathing in the smell of her hair at the nape of her neck before they pulled away. Judy left the house without looking back at her.

'They're such a lovely couple,' Maria said, waving to them as they got into the van.

Kate had come down home for a visit the following day and gave her mother a longer hug than usual. She asked if she wanted to go for a walk. They didn't talk about anything – Kate didn't even ask about Judy – but it was enough to know that Kate might know how she was feeling. It was a relief.

She couldn't stand not seeing her. After a few months of not speaking, Helen sent a text asking Judy to come to Belfast with her. They met in the hotel room. Judy arrived at The Europa before her and sent a message to say that she'd checked in. Helen's heart was fit to burst as she made her way down the corridor and knocked on the door to their room. They were both so overwhelmed in the end that they ended up talking for hours before they could do anything else.

The following morning, after St George's Market, Kate took them to the peace wall and told them about the burning of Bombay Street and the Falls Curfew. Bobby Sands smiled down at them from his mural. That evening, they had gone to a production of Swan Lake in the Grand Opera House. Helen squeezed Kate's hand as they watched the chorus of dancers bend to the will of the conductor and made a silent vow to have more moments like this together.

On the Sunday, Judy took them to see a stained-glass window in a church on the Malone Road.

'I've seen it before,' Judy said, gesturing for Kate to hand her the dog leash. 'You two go on. I'll stay outside with her ladyship.'

A crowd was spilling out of the chapel after the service. A sacristan met Helen and Kate inside the door.

'Can I help you?' she asked.

'We're looking to see the Wilhelmina Geddes window,' Helen said.

The woman's face brightened. 'Of course.'

She transformed into a gallery owner, leading them up the aisle and reciting the history of the church. Helen could tell that she'd studied for this moment. Her heart ached for her.

'It was commissioned as a war memorial,' the woman said. 'For a William Wheeler. The line that Geddes chose to illustrate is from the Book of Revelations: "The leaves of the trees were for the healing of the nations."'

When she got to the end of her spiel, she apologised for her lack of knowledge. 'I'm embarrassed about how little I know, really.'

'This is my favourite bit,' Helen said, pointing to the group of women in bright pink and blue robes with blazing gold hair, walking and talking in a forest of trees. 'You'd love to know what they're talking about. They all look so serious.'

'Yeah, you'd think they'd be a bit happier to be in paradise. Who's this fella?' Kate asked, pointing to a monk in a habit with a halo around his head, a chalice in one hand and a stick in the other.

'That's St Brendan,' the woman said.

Kate tilted her head to the side. 'It looks like he's carrying a hurley.'

*

Helen was glad when Judy told her that herself and Dennis would make it down for Liam's anniversary. When people came back to the house after the mass, Aoife gave guided tours of the garden. Peter had taken over Foley Hurleys, and had rented a bigger workspace on the other side of the town.

Helen had decided to renovate the old workshop, transforming it into a greenhouse. People stopped to look at the stained-glass panels installed on either side. The first was a glass tapestry of Liam holding a hurley, surrounded by fields. The second was a portrait of a woman who, on closer inspection, was made up of hundreds of other women's faces. The longer Helen spent looking at her, the more faces she saw. It was days before she saw the twinkle in her left eye – the sun shining through a stained-glass window onto two figures embracing in a bed on the chapel floor.

It was stupid how nervous Helen had been to introduce Judy to Nan Foley. Up until Liam's fifth anniversary, she'd managed to choreograph things so that the two women were never in the same room, but that evening, Nan finally nabbed Judy and Dennis out on the patio. Helen saw it happening, but it was too late to do anything about it. She decided it would be better if she didn't join the conversation. Nan might be better behaved if she wasn't around.

Maria was in the kitchen slicing oranges and putting them into lunchboxes to bring down to the Scribbeen. The charity hurling match was a new addition to the sports day's schedule of events. John had invited county and club players to compete for the Liam Foley Cup.

'This should be plenty. What do you think?' she asked.

'You've enough there to cure scurvy,' Helen said. 'What's the score?'

'I think Peter's team are winning.'

Judy rushed into the kitchen and grabbed Helen by the hand, leading her towards the utility room.

'What are you doing?' Helen asked.

'She's a weapon,' Judy said, pacing back and forth in the cramped space between the washing machine and freezer.

'Who, Nan?'

'I didn't realise how bad she was,' Judy said. 'Do you know what she's just told us?'

'That I drove my husband to suicide?'

'Yes!'

'Well, that's no surprise.'

'But it was the way she did it. If I didn't know you, I'd have believed her. She is out there bitching to whoever will listen, blaming everything on you.'

'And?' Helen asked.

'And you're just going to let her?'

'What am I supposed to do, go out there and tackle an eighty-five-year-old to the ground?'

Judy started biting her thumbnail. 'She's not that old, is she?'

'She looks well for her age,' Helen said. 'She was out in the milking parlour this morning at the crack of dawn.'

'Yeah, she told us,' Judy said, rolling her eyes. 'I don't care what age she is – you can't let her talk about you like that in your own home.'

'Well, technically, the farm is in her name.'

'It took all my strength not to say something.'

'Judy, if you so much as say boo to that woman, I will never talk to you again.'

Judy looked her in the eye. 'You're being serious.'

'Deadly,' Helen said, opening up the freezer to search for the ice lollies for the grandchildren.

'You think she's right, don't you?' Judy asked. 'You blame yourself for what happened.'

The packet of ice lollies was stuck down the back of the bottom shelf – Helen had to tear them away from a sheet of ice. She'd have to defrost it soon.

She turned around to face Judy. 'As far as I'm concerned, Nan has earned her right to say anything she likes about me. She gave me Liam and I loved the bones of that man. He gave me my children and grandchildren. That old woman out there is the reason we're stood here arguing, because if I hadn't had my life with Liam, I wouldn't have found my way to you. We really should be thanking her. Now, if you'll excuse me.'

Judy stepped aside and let her go back outside.

Helen gave the ice lollies to Elmo to distribute to the rest of the kids. Then she joined Bláith who was sitting with

Nan and the rest of the Foleys on the patio. Judy emerged a few minutes later. She sat down on the other side of Helen and handed her a cup of tea – a peace offering.

Aoife came trundling up the garden path with her wheelbarrow, parking it next to Bláith and hopping up on her auntie's lap.

'Were you down watching the match?' Bláith asked.

Aoife took a long drink of water and smacked her lips together. 'No, I was with Auntie Blue.'

Kate had taken to spending most of her time at home in the garden. Aoife was both her sidekick and teacher as they figured out the plan for the year. Bláith listened as Aoife gave a progress report – they had picked radishes and peas and weeded the cabbage patch.

The sun shimmered gold down on the fields. Helen could just about make out Kate's silhouette poking out of the base of the oak. From a distance, it seemed like her legs were the roots of the old fairy tree.

Bláith had to wave a hand in front of her face to bring her back to the conversation. Nan was asking Helen if she could remember the first time she had watched Liam play a hurling match.

'Yes,' she said. 'He was brilliant.'

'He was, wasn't he?' Nan said. 'It was such a pity he was so young when he stopped playing.'

Everyone murmured in agreement. Liam was thirty-nine when he finally retired from inter-county hurling, after years of Helen begging him to give it up. He played with St Brigid's well into his forties. John had even gotten to play alongside him for a few years on the senior team before Liam hung up his boots. Even after his playing days, Liam's time was taken up with managing teams, making hurleys, attending charity gala dinners and going on trips away to training camps with Vincent and the lads, all the while expecting her to stay at home and raise his kids, to wash other women out of his clothes and keep the show on the road.

Helen looked around the table and allowed herself to imagine what would happen if she were to lean over and kiss Judy full on the mouth in front of them all. She pictured Nan's face – Aoife's, Maria's, Bláith's, Father Angelo's. She hadn't been to confession in years.

'We're blessed with the weather,' Nan was saying for the hundredth time that day.

'Steeped,' Helen agreed, excusing herself from the table.

She walked the path towards the field, feeling the September sun on her face. Kate was sitting with her back to the trunk, her legs pulled in towards her chest. Helen crouched down beside her, running her fingers through the grass.

A breeze moved through the leaves. They stayed there for what seemed like a long time, listening to the sounds of the hurling match in the distance, the final whistle, the celebrations. They didn't speak, not even when they could hear everyone's voices shrink and disappear.

The sun was beginning to set when the starlings appeared, a black cloud of them bending and twisting against a golden sky. A murmuration – that was the name Liam had put on them. There was a time when he'd call the whole family outside to have a look at the flock of birds making shapes in the sky. Now, the sight of them caught in her chest. They flew towards the tree, a torrent of wings whipping around them before they broke away, dipping, diving, retreating back towards the heavens. Then they were gone. It was quiet again. An owl hooted in the distance. They looked around at the last of the world that Liam had seen – the steady pulse of their silence beating into every beautiful thing.

Acknowledgements

Thanks to my agent Marianne Gunn O'Connor for continuing to dwell in possibility, and to Norah Finn for her kindness, wisdom and warmth. Thank you to Anne-Marie Kelly, Linda Galbraith and everyone I met during the One Dublin One Book campaign in 2024. It was such a privilege to meet and work with such a special group of people.

The first chapter of this book was written while on a residency in the Literarisches Colloquium in Berlin. Huge thanks to Sinéad MacAodha and Literature Ireland for affording me the opportunity to write there.

Thanks to everyone at Manilla Press and Bonnier Books and the team at Harper Collins for their work in getting the book onto shelves and into the hands of readers. I am indebted to literary translators for bringing my novels to life in different parts of the world.

Special thanks to William L. Rukeyser and the estate of Muriel Rukeyser. I am also grateful to Pinkie Maclure for answering my questions about the art of stained glass.

The following thanks and gratitude to people who have given insights and feedback on the novel: Laura Sheary, Niamh McCann, Sadie Sheary McCann, Andrew Cunning and Mícheál McCann. Thanks to the members of COFO for their company in the trenches, and to Liv and Sheila for the dandelion lamp and everything before and since. Go raibh míle to Rebecca O'Keeffe for voice notes and walks along the canal. All my love and thanks to Ciara and Rado. Welcome to the world baby Nora – your parents are magic. Thanks to Mary Nagle, Rivkah, Chris, Theo and Sara for great nights, and to Anna for my leaba in Dublin.

A shoutout to Kieran Sands and the team at 5A for keeping me caffeinated during the writing of this novel, and to my improv friends for keeping me unhinged. I never thought I'd be a thirty-four-year-old snail training for a marathon but here we are, trying our best™.

Grma to Padraig O'Meiscill for his support and encouragement throughout, and for sourcing Elvis tribute acts for research purposes.

One of the greatest joys I've had in life was to grow up as part of a camogie team in rural Kildare. I am a proud Cappagh woman. I highly recommend *The Grass Ceiling* by Eimear Ryan to any reader looking to learn more about the GAA.

Thanks, as ever, to my family: my parents, Tommy and Hilda and my siblings and their partners – Michael, Stephanie, Sarah, Paul, Catherine and Cathal. A special mention to my nieces and nephews – Sophie, Lucy, Teidí, Hayley and Cáit. Looking forward to meeting the new addition to the gang soon.